PRIMAL Redemption
Book 3 in the Redemption Trilogy

JACK SILKSTONE

Text copyright © 2016 Jack Silkstone
All rights reserved.

Published by Jack Silkstone

www.primalunleashed.com

ISBN-13: 978-1533617637
ISBN-10: 1533617635

BOOKS BY JACK SILKSTONE

PRIMAL Inception
PRIMAL Mirza
PRIMAL Origin
PRIMAL Unleashed
PRIMAL Vengeance
PRIMAL Fury
PRIMAL Reckoning
PRIMAL Nemesis
PRIMAL Redemption
PRIMAL Compendium
PRIMAL Renegade
SEAL of Approval

PRIMAL Redemption is dedicated to my mother Lynne, who allowed a small boy's mind to run free in a world of adventure and excitement. She is the reason that PRIMAL can exist.

PROLOGUE

KUNAR PROVINCE, AFGHANISTAN, 2012

The four Blackhawk helicopters thundered through the night sky. Skilled pilots held the aircraft in formation as they weaved through the valley, beating their way toward an unsuspecting target. The birds had launched from Jalalabad forty minutes earlier as part of a larger force. The other aircraft, having already peeled off, headed to their separate landing zones or circled above waiting to dive down and provide close air support.

In the cabin of the lead airframe Staff Sergeant Shaun Clem glanced at the Suunto watch strapped to his heavily tattooed forearm. He whispered a prayer and looked up at the loadmaster in anticipation. The helmeted aviator manning the side machine gun turned inward and raised two gloved fingers.

"Two minutes!" Clem bellowed grasping the shoulder of the man next to him.

The call rippled through the helicopter and the soldiers conducted final checks on their equipment.

Clem increased the illumination on the red-dot sight mounted to his M4 carbine. He was feeling confident; his squad of nine men had performed similar missions countless times. They were Rangers and they were ready to lead the way.

"Thirty seconds!" yelled the loadmaster.

The squad leader felt the nose of the helicopter lift as the pilot flared to slow their descent. He adjusted one of the night vision tubes that hung from his helmet and gripped his carbine. Glancing around the cabin, he gave the boys a broad grin and unclipped his retention lanyard from the floor. "Here we go, Ranger buddies."

They touched down with a thud. Clem leapt through the open door into the maelstrom of dust thrown up by the rotor wash. They were now in the bad lands. Jogging toward their

RV he glanced over his shoulder to check that the two fire teams were following. He scanned the terrain to his front as the birds roared into the sky. The thud of rotors faded into the distance.

"Alpha Two-Zero, this is Alpha Two-One, we are in position," he reported as they approached the shallow wadi to the south of their objective. His squad fanned out providing all round security while he checked his map. The choppers had put them down only a few hundred yards from their target compound. He scanned the terrain around them. Through his night vision he could see the steep valley walls glowing green. They were the reason the helicopters had been forced to land so close to the objective. He was surprised that shots still hadn't been fired. Surely Terry Taliban hadn't slept through the racket of a helo assault.

He eyeballed the cluster of mud-brick walled buildings to their front. The intel guys had identified it as a key Taliban facilitation node. They had reports that weapons and IED components were being brought in from Pakistan for distribution. That's if the intel was correct. So often it wasn't. This could well be another dry hole.

"Alpha Two-One, this is Two-Zero, support by fire is in position. Commence infil," transmitted the platoon sergeant.

Clem acknowledged the call and shook the squad out into an assault line. With a wave of his hand they surged forward. His pulse quickened and he flicked his M4's safety off. Senses heightened, his finger was poised on the trigger. They were halfway to the high mud-brick wall when an AK barked, its muzzle flash bright through his goggles. The squad returned fire as they hit the deck. A gunner blasted the compound with a burst from his SAW machine gun.

"Bound forward!" bellowed Clem over the noise.

One team kept firing as the other four Rangers scrambled to a closer position. Like a well-oiled machine they leap-frogged until both teams reached the compound wall.

"Everyone good?" he asked when they were behind cover.

They checked in. No one had been hit.

Around them the valley echoed with gunfire as the other elements of the assault force made contact with the enemy. The radio was alive with call signs coordinating fire support. Clem glanced up as an Apache gunship sent its rockets streaking into the darkness. A moment later an explosion flashed on a hillside.

"OK, let's do this."

Clem's men stacked, one behind the other, on the doorway into the walled compound. It was open and most likely covered by an AK-wielding Talib. He waited as one of his Rangers lobbed a 9-bang through the entrance. It detonated with a chain of sharp blasts and he charged inside.

He spotted a silhouette on the roof of the building to the rear and engaged, his finger pumping the trigger. The target fell. Behind him the rest of the squad swarmed inside the compound.

More gunfire broke out from the building and he felt the sting of rounds hitting the wall behind him. His machine gunner replied with a long burst. An AK barked again before the thump of a 40mm grenade silenced it. Clem rushed across the dust and smoke-filled courtyard weaving between piles of firewood, bundles of straw, and a tethered goat. The rest of the team followed.

He aimed his weapon through one of the windows and activated the IR flashlight. Invisible to the naked eye, the room was illuminated through his goggles. There were sleeping mats and blankets strewn on the dirt floor. He spotted an AK leaning against the wall. As he turned back toward the entrance he saw Rangers making entry. Gunshots rang out as he followed them in.

There were three bodies in the first room. One had taken the full force of the 40mm grenade. He was literally blown in half, his entrails smeared across the floor. The other two were bloodied corpses riddled with bullets.

"Good job," he grunted as he scanned the living area. The building was single-story with one adjoining room; the bedroom he had already cleared through the window.

"Holy shit," said his Alpha team leader, inspecting a stack of crates on the back wall. "We're fucking lucky, man. If that guy hadn't taken the forty mike-mike to the chest it might have set this shit off. This right here is a crap load of one-twenty-two mill rockets."

Clem flipped his night vision goggles up and inspected the boxes using a light attached to his body armor. They were marked with Chinese characters. The team leader helped him lift one of them down and he prised off the lid with his multi-tool. Inside were two pristine olive-green rockets.

"Two-Zero this is Two-One, Objective Batman secure," Clem transmitted. "We've uncovered a major cache of rockets."

"Two-Zero, copy. Two-Two is taking fire from Objective Robin. Get a SAW gunner up on the roof, ASAP."

"Copy." He turned to his second-in-command. "Rig this to blow." Then he led the gunner out to the courtyard and up mud-brick stairs to the rooftop. His other fire team was already hunkered down pulling security. He glanced at the Taliban fighter he had shot, before positioning the gunner at the edge of the roof.

"Hey Clem, you might want to get back down here," transmitted his second-in-command over the radio.

He trotted down the steps and back inside.

The Ranger was standing over a hole in the floor. A heavy rug and a wooden cover had been hauled aside. "Chops found it."

Clem frowned. "Where's he at?"

"Down there."

He knelt by the hole and peered in. The beam from his flashlight revealed steps carved into the rock. They led down into a basement no bigger than a broom cupboard. He could see Chops standing looking at something.

"What have you got, Ranger buddy?"

"There's a guy down here."

"Taliban?"

"Nah bro, he's whiter than a bleached asshole and he's pretty fucked up."

***

LANDSTUHL REGIONAL MEDICAL CENTRE, GERMANY

Landstuhl Regional Medical Centre was the largest US military hospital outside the United States. The three hundred and ten bed facility was constructed in 1953 and had been providing surgical treatment to American servicemen ever since. In the 1990s it had been expanded and with the commencement of operations in Afghanistan and Iraq it became the closest advanced surgical facility for critically wounded personnel.

Colonel Kevin Baker had been posted to the hospital for over a year. In that time the doctor had seen hundreds of mangled bodies come through the facility's operating theaters. Most were the victims of IEDs; home-made explosives that tore limbs from bodies, incinerated flesh, and caused horrific damage that he and his team would try, often in vain, to repair.

He yawned as he did his rounds. The previous night had been exhausting with four new patients. He'd performed emergency surgery on three Marines who'd been blown up in Helmand province. Their Humvee had hit a stack of anti-tank mines. One of them had succumbed during surgery. The other two were clinging to life. If they made it through the next twenty-four hours he gave them a fifty-fifty chance of survival.

The fourth patient, a solidly built blonde-haired Caucasian, was an anomaly. Baker stopped at his bed and picked up the chart. Discovered in a Taliban stronghold during a raid, he had been imprisoned underground. His wounds were horrendous; he'd lost a leg below the knee. His right arm was mangled almost beyond repair and was infected with gangrene. Thick scar tissue covered his torso and one side of his square jaw was badly burned.

Baker shook his head. He had seen worse wounds but never this old. In his opinion the injuries had been inflicted well over a month ago and it was a miracle he'd survived with only the barest of field medicine provided by the Taliban. He was a hard man; the damage to his body was evidence of that.

Footsteps rang on the polished floor and Baker turned to greet one of the nurses. She flashed him a bright smile as she checked the IV bag hanging above the wounded man's bed.

"God knows how he survived," she said checking his dressings.

"Big guy's got the constitution of an ox."

She studied the patient's face. "He's handsome too, such a waste."

Baker turned his attention back to the chart he was holding. "His vitals are good. If we can get him out of the coma he should be OK. Have we had any luck identifying him?"

She shook her head. "No sir, we sent back a full set of prints. Heard nothing yet."

"Might take them a while. Did he come in with any personal effects?"

"No, nothing."

"It's strange. No one's mentioned any missing coalition soldiers."

"He might be a contractor or a journalist."

"True. So we've also sent photos through to ISAF headquarters?"

"Yes sir, they haven't got back to us either."

"Our first John Doe?"

"Looks that way." The nurse gave the unconscious man's mouth a dab with a cold compress then moved on to the next patient.

Baker spent a few more seconds checking the chart before hanging it on the end of the bed. He sighed. "Hang in there, buddy. You'll be alright."

***

Baker was sitting at his desk staring at the charts for John Blonde, as the nurses now called the mysterious casualty. In the seven days he had been at Landstuhl his vitals had improved dramatically. They now had the infection under control and his wounds had started to close over. However, he still hadn't come out of the coma.

He picked up the MRI report and read it again. The brain surgeon had identified significant bruising but that had begun to subside. He was baffled as to why the hulk of a man hadn't regained consciousness. He dropped the report and leant back in his chair. What's more they still had no idea who he was. Everyone they had sent his fingerprints and photos to had come back with zero hits. It was as if the guy never existed.

"Dr. Baker."

The urgency of the nurse's tone told him something was wrong. She stuck her head into his office. "Sir, there's a bunch of men here and they're trying to take John Blonde."

He frowned, left his chair, and strode out of his office. He stormed past the duty desk and into the recovery ward.

There were four men in civilian clothing standing around the patient. His head nurse was glaring at them with hands on her hips. "What's going on here?" he asked as he arrived.

The men all turned toward him revealing their scruffy beards. He noticed that one of them was wearing a pistol on his hip.

"You do realize this is a hospital and weapons are not allowed."

"Hey bro, we're just here to collect the stiff," said one of the men as he chewed gum.

Baker clenched his jaw. "I'm not your, 'bro'. I'm a Colonel. Show me your identification." He thrust out his hand.

The man shrugged as he displayed his ID.

Baker checked it. It was as he suspected, they were CIA. "So, Mr. Weddell, do you have paperwork for the transfer?"

"Course I do." He reached into the pocket of his cargo pants, pulled out a piece of paper, and handed it over as he chewed.

Baker inspected the transfer document. It was correctly signed. There was nothing he could do.

"Are any of you by chance a doctor? I can only release this patient into the custody of a qualified medical professional."

The guy chewing dipped his head in the direction of one of his team. "Miller here is a medtech, that should cover it. OK boys, let's get the retard loaded up and get on the road."

Baker held up his hand. "I don't think you heard me. The receiving officer needs to be a doctor. It's standard operating procedure."

The team leader stared at him for a few seconds. "Look pal, I don't think you get what's happening here. The CIA is taking custody of a goddamn terrorist. You can bitch and moan about needing a doctor as much as you want but it ain't gonna change a thing. This asshole is coming with us."

Baker made eye contact with the head nurse. She shrugged. "Fine. But I want you to know that I will be lodging a formal complaint regarding this."

Weddell gestured for his men to grab the patient. "No problem. If I was you I wouldn't waste the time but if that's what you want to do, knock your socks off."

Baker watched as the men moved the unconscious patient onto the steel gurney.

The medic transferred the IV bags to the gurney. He took the paperwork from the end of the bed, folded it half, and stuffed it in his pocket. "We're ready."

The leader flashed Baker a broad smile. "Thanks, doc, been good doing business with you."

They wheeled the casualty into the corridor. Baker followed at a distance wracking his brain for a way to stop the transfer. Something told him if the patient left the hospital he was going into a far worse situation.

***

CAMP X-RAY, GUANTANAMO BAY

Secluded in the furthest corner of Camp X-Ray was a cluster of buildings off limits to all but a select few. A closely guarded secret, the facility was known as the Bin by the men who worked in it, and the Extreme Rendition Site by a select number of senior CIA officials. Even the President and his closest advisors had no idea it existed. What's more, they wouldn't want to know what was going on behind its blacked-out fences.

The Bin was small; only a single interrogation room, an office, and holding cells for half a dozen prisoners. However, it wasn't the size of the facility rather the techniques employed within that made it unique. Unlike Camp X-Ray where interrogation was tightly controlled and monitored, there were no rules in the Bin. All video footage was wiped on a regular basis. When a prisoner was sent there they literally had two options; talk or die.

For Detainee 3459 the journey to the Bin had started with three weeks in the Guantanamo Bay medical facility. Five days after arriving he had come out of his coma thanks to an experimental drug that stimulated brain activity. The doctors had granted him an additional two weeks to recover before allowing him to be interrogated. Despite having no recollection of who he was or where he had come from, the CIA had moved him to the darkest corner of the camp. It was there that he met the Company's most experienced and innovative interrogator, Aaron Small.

A qualified medical practitioner specializing in the study of pain, Small had been contracting to the CIA since the late nineties. Initially he was a consultant for the Directorate of Science and Technology, however, after 9/11 he'd been brought onto the books full-time.

The Company's psychologists had labeled him a sadist; a sociopath who took great pleasure in dealing out pain, both physical and psychological. Small saw himself as a professional with a set of skills that some senior CIA directors felt were necessary in the Global War on Terror.

With slick black hair receding to a widow's peak, dark

brown eyes that looked almost black, and a narrow pasty-white face, Small resembled Bram Stoker's Dracula. It was an image he frequently enhanced with dark eyeliner. The subjects were usually terrified by his appearance, sometimes breaking before he had the chance to employ any coercive techniques. Detainee 3459, however, seemed totally unfazed by Small, much to the veteran interrogator's frustration.

He'd been working on 3459 for three days and failed to get anything out of him. The horrendously scarred invalid simply did not seem to remember anything, even when juiced up on a cocktail of psychoactive drugs. Small shook his head and leaned forward on his desk scrutinizing a video screen. The detainee was sound asleep in a room filled with white noise and flashing strobe lights.

He glanced down at 3459's file and flicked through the pages again. James Castle had an impressive record, both with the Marine Corps and the CIA. However, it was the intelligence report contained in the file that was most intriguing. After allegedly faking his death in 2004 Castle had disappeared. The rogue operative had remained off the grid until a month ago when he was found half-dead in Afghanistan.

That was reason enough for the CIA to be concerned. They needed to know exactly what Castle had been doing over that period of time. They also wanted to establish whether his partner, Vance Durant, was alive. The report assessed it was likely the two of them had conspired to assassinate a very influential member of the UAE government. That was another mystery that needed to be solved and Small was yet to produce any answers.

He was actually beginning to think that Castle had truly lost his memory. It was not inconceivable considering the significant traumatic brain injury the man had received. He'd never worked on a detainee that had suffered such severe blast injuries. The cripple had maintained the amnesia story through multiple sessions of water boarding, electric shock treatment, and even blunt force trauma.

Small had only ever had one other detainee who'd

maintained his innocence right till the end. In that case the man's heart had given out and he died. Castle on the other hand was a hard man. His body had endured and Small had no doubt he could take the interrogation even further.

He rose from his desk, walked down the corridor, and turned into what he called his 'lab'. It had been built to his exact specifications. In the center of the room was an adjustable chair not unlike a dentist's, except it had nylon straps on the arms, legs, and headrest. The chair could manipulate a prisoner's body as he saw fit. He could lay them flat, tip them head down for water boarding, or sit them up so they could see exactly what he was doing to their body. It was an effective contraption in which he took great pride.

He sat on one of the stainless steel cabinets containing his tools and studied the chair as he planned his next session with Castle. A knock at the door broke his concentration and one of the guards stuck his head in. "Sir, we've got trouble."

"What? More detainees?"

"Ah not exactly, sir."

Small followed the guard down the hallway, through a security door, and into the front office. On a screen displaying the camera feed from the front gate, Small could see the problem. The Commandant of Camp X-Ray was there with Small's boss from Langley, Thomas Larkin. "Have all the drives been cleared?" he asked the guard.

"Yes, sir, half an hour ago as scheduled."

"OK, let them in."

Small waited in the reception area for Larkin to appear.

The barracuda-jawed CIA officer stormed in with the Army Colonel in tow. He thrust a document into Small's hand. "This facility is now officially closed, Aaron." He locked eyes with the interrogator. "All prisoners will be transferred into the custody of the good Colonel here and into Camp X-Ray."

Small glanced at the paper. "As you wish, sir."

He stepped aside as a squad of Military Police and medical staff streamed in. It only took them half an hour to remove the two prisoners and search for evidence of torture. When it was over Small sat on a bench outside the fence and smoked a cigarette. His boss joined him and they stared out over the blue water of the Caribbean Sea.

"What now?" asked Small.

Larkin turned to him. "I've got something developing and I'll need someone with your expertise."

"When?"

"Can't say right now. I've got you a contract back at S&T to cover the gap."

"Thanks." Small knocked the ash from his cigarette.

"How do you feel about the cold?" asked Larkin.

Small shrugged. "Makes no difference to me."

"Good, I'll call you when everything is ready."

"What's going to happen to the cripple?"

"James Castle? He'll stay here at Gitmo till he decides to talk."

"If he ever actually remembers anything."

"Do you really think he's lost his memory?"

Small stubbed out his cigarette and shrugged. "Everyone cracks eventually but he hasn't."

"Well he's got nothing but time here."

"Hey, what shut us down this time?"

"Whistleblower. I'm still getting to the bottom of it. Don't worry; I've got it covered. The next one will be even further from the prying eyes of Washington. I'll call you."

Small watched the CIA contracting officer stand and walk down the hill to Camp X-Ray. He had known Larkin since he started consulting to the Agency. The man always got the job done. Results were all that mattered to him and if something went wrong he was like Teflon. Nothing stuck to him, the closure of the Bin was evidence enough of that. Whatever Larkin had planned was definitely going to be worth his while.

CHAPTER 1

KRUGER NATIONAL PARK, SOUTH AFRICA, 2015

The stripped-out Land Rover Defender slid down a steep embankment and hit the river with a splash. The driver kept the revs up and it scrambled over the submerged rocks before launching up the opposite bank. It left muddy wheel ruts on the sandy track before plowing through a thicket of scrubby trees and punching out to the wide-open savannah.

Dominic Marks eased off the accelerator as he spotted movement in the grass. The former New Zealand Army soldier was an outdoorsman; solid with a square jaw and a head of salt and pepper hair. The sleeves of his khaki shirt were rolled up revealing thick muscled arms deeply tanned from long days in the sun.

Dom had fallen in love with the African bush on a holiday five years earlier. Selling everything he had, he established an anti-poaching foundation and began to train park rangers. However, today he was acting as a tour guide for his girlfriend Christina and two of her friends. "Look, can you see over there where the grass is moving? That'll be the pride, it's a favorite spot of theirs."

In the back of the safari truck, on a raised platform, Bishop and Saneh sat side by side with binoculars glued to their eyes. They scanned the grass, searching for what Dom's keen eye had spotted.

An attractive couple, Afsaneh Ebadi was by far the more striking of the two. Her exotic looks were a tribute to her Persian heritage. With angular features, dark almond-shaped eyes, long glossy brown hair, and a body toned by hours of training, she resembled a movie star.

Aden Bishop, her lover, was not what people called classically handsome. He was good looking but not to the point

17

where he stood out in a crowd. Average height with an athletic build, the Australian wore a permanent half smile that gave the impression he was up to no good. His nose, broken on a number of occasions, was evidence he often was.

The PRIMAL operatives were on holiday and loving every moment of their time in Kruger National Park. It was a trip both had been looking forward to and Bishop hoped it would cement their sometimes-tumultuous relationship.

The Land Rover's brakes squealed as Dom brought it to a halt. "There's a small pride that usually hangs out here; a big female and a few juveniles. If we get lucky we might even see some of the cubs."

"What about the males?" asked Saneh.

"Too hot for the big guys. They'll be lounging under a tree somewhere."

"That would be right." Saneh laughed.

Bishop lowered his binoculars. "Hey, when you're out hunting all night a man needs to get some rest. Not everyone can stay home with the cubs all day."

"Actually the females do most of the hunting in the pride," said Dom. "The male is fixated on defending his territory and breeding."

"Typical." Saneh gave Bishop a nudge.

"I see them," said Christina Munoz from where she stood on the passenger seat. The petite journalist was bracing herself against the roll cage with her telephoto lens aimed at the grass. Since leaving New York she'd dyed her hair a vibrant red and tied it back in a scarf. Now she looked every bit the slightly off-kilter wildlife photographer. Turning to Dom, she smiled, and their loving gaze lingered.

"Get a room," said Bishop.

"Leave them alone," said Saneh as she elbowed him again. "I still can't see the cats."

The grass a hundred yards in front parted and a lioness slid out with the grace of a dancer. She stopped and fixed them with a pair of golden eyes, her black-tipped tail swaying slowly from side to side.

"She's beautiful," murmured Bishop.

Another smaller cat with darker facial features, a juvenile, joined the lioness.

"Oh, my god," whispered Saneh as a pair of cubs tumbled out between the legs of the lioness. The cubs wrestled for a moment before spotting the Land Rover. All four animals froze, silently staring at them.

"Now that's not something you see every day," said Dom.

As they watched, the lioness turned and disappeared into the grass. The younger cat followed but the cubs lingered, enthralled by the vehicle. After a moment the cubs realized their mother had departed and scampered after her. Saneh clutched Bishop's hand. "Thank you for bringing me here."

He leant across and kissed her on the cheek. "Thank you for coming."

She turned her head and pressed her lips against his.

Dom coughed from the front of the truck as Christina snapped a photo of the lovers. "About that room."

They all laughed, Dom revved the engine, and they took off along the narrow track.

"So what else is on the cards for today?" asked Saneh as they skirted the savannah and followed the river.

"I thought we might go back to the camp for lunch before heading up north to see if we can find a few rhinos," said Dom.

Saneh's eyes lit up. "I've never seen one in real life."

"My favorite animal," added Bishop.

Dom eased the truck through a gap in the bushes and onto a well-worn dirt road. "Soon you might not be able to see them at all. At the rate that the poachers are killing them the population here at Kruger is going to be wiped-out within five years."

"That's terrible," said Saneh. "Is there anything that can be done?"

"We're trying, but there are only so many rangers and it's a big park."

"You need to get a few drones in the air," said Bishop.

"We're working on it but they're expensive and the best technology is restricted to the military. Makes it bloody hard to get an aircraft with decent range and endurance."

The conversation on the challenges of countering poaching continued until they reached the semi-permanent tents where Saneh and Bishop were staying. Dom's cabin was on the other side of the resort.

"I've got to refuel the truck. We'll join you at the kitchens at 1330, OK?" said Dom as his guests jumped out.

"No worries," said Bishop.

Christina waved cheerfully from the passenger seat as the Land Rover drove off in a cloud of dust.

The PRIMAL pair walked up the wooden stairs to their canvas-sided accommodation. Bishop had initially been apprehensive about staying in a tent. However, the accommodation was superb; air-conditioned, and immaculately furnished with a luxurious bathroom complete with a huge brass tub that overlooked the savannah. It was rustic, romantic, and despite there being over thirty separate abodes, relatively private.

Saneh flopped backward onto the king-sized bed and stretched her arms over her head. "I could get used to this."

Bishop dumped his backpack on a chair in the corner. "How about we extend our sabbatical and help Dom out for a bit?"

She sat up, her eyes bright. "I was thinking exactly the same thing."

"Yeah, I'd love to help Dom with the rhinos. I could talk to Mitch about the UAV piece."

"That sounds fantastic. I can help Christina with her photography." She glanced across at the clock on the side table. "How long do we have till lunch?"

"About twenty minutes."

"Perfect." She sat up and pulled him down on top of her. Kissing him passionately she unclasped the latch on his belt and slipped her hand into his pants. "Just enough time," she whispered in his ear.

"For what?"

She tugged his pants down. "For you to make love to me twice."

***

BOSTON

Terrance Howard smiled to himself as he sipped a skinny caramel latte. He was sitting in a Starbucks in a residential suburb of Boston, people watching. Only a block from his apartment and always filled with an eclectic mix of characters, the café was a favorite haunt. None of the customers paid attention to the overweight intelligence analyst dressed in chinos and a rumpled golf shirt. To them he resembled another wage slave, just another cog in the machine. He smirked over his coffee. They would be shocked to know the truth.

Howard's phone vibrated in his pocket and he fished it out. A broad grin split his flabby features. The message was from Mistress Axera, the dominatrix he'd met in Las Vegas. It confirmed their weekend appointment. The petite Asian was flying in and he'd booked a suite at the Boston Harbor Hotel. He felt a flutter of excitement in his stomach as he contemplated the sordid weekend they would have. Overwhelmed with anticipation he downed his coffee, left the café, and hurried home.

He burst through the front door of his three-bedroom luxury apartment and ducked into the office. Dropping onto a chair he opened a web browser and was about to dive into his favorite BDSM porn site. As an afterthought he opened the black Redemption Network laptop that sat on a stand to the side of his desk. Placing a finger on the biometric scanner it unlocked and he saw a flashing icon on the screen. Forgetting his carnal urge he clicked on it.

The application that opened was a facial recognition platform still in beta-build. The NSA was developing the system in collaboration with the Israeli SIGINT National Unit.

It used cutting edge algorithms to search for faces across all the major social media networks. The Agency had standing agreements with many of the big firms such including Facebook, Twitter, and Google. Companies that refused to collaborate had been placed under intense pressure. Most had folded and allowed access. Those that didn't soon found out what it was like to be on the wrong side of the world's most powerful signals intelligence organization.

In accordance with NSA legislation it was illegal for Howard to use the software to target American citizens. He gave exactly zero fucks when it came to following that particular policy. He worked for the Operational Support Program, an innocuous name for a CIA off-the-books team of intelligence professionals. It gave him access to the Redemption Network, a system that put him above all the red tape. In his mind he was an intelligence assassin, a patriot who could target anyone who posed a threat to US interests.

He clicked on the alerts menu and an image appeared on screen. An Asian couple, he guessed Korean, had taken a selfie with their grinning faces center of screen. In the background the software had detected another person. A woman whose elfin features and petite frame he knew oh so well. It was Christina Munoz, an American journalist and suspected collaborator with the Major League Network.

Codenamed by Howard, Major League was a terrorist organization that had destroyed infrastructure, kidnapped US citizens, and stolen almost a billion dollars from an American private equity fund. Christina had collaborated with the terrorists to publish a sensationalist news story that had gone viral, ruining the fund's reputation and a number of associated businesses. Her biased article had omitted any mention of the terrorists' crimes and it incriminated government agencies including the CIA.

He checked the metadata associated with the photo. The corner of his mouth turned up in a smirk; smart phones made intelligence collection so much easier. The couple had left the location services on the device active and a set of coordinates was imbedded in the shot. Entering them into a mapping program he watched as the screen zoomed from a global perspective down to Africa, South Africa, and finally Kruger National Park. "Boom!" He pumped his fist in the air.

Fingers flashed on the keyboard as he accessed the target package he was building on Christina, code name Objective Blue Jay. The file included previous reporting, photographs, and known associates. He updated the location data then accessed the tasking tool. The backbone of the Redemption Network, the contracting website allowed him to outsource the operational side of his work. It gave him the ability to reach across the globe and destroy America's enemies.

Today he would reach out to Christina Munoz. He selected the geographical region of the operation, chose the task 'Rendition', and typed in the target objective name. Finally he filled out a risk profile template and submitted it for tender. Carefully vetted professionals would receive a message that a new job was on offer. They would bid for the contract and he would select the winner. Then they would receive access to the Objective Blue Jay target pack and it would be only a matter of time before Christina was captured. He leaned back in his chair and smiled; this was real intel work.

***

GES FACILITY, VIRGINIA

The Ground Effects Services estate in Virginia was the hub of the private security organization. The five thousand hectares contained training facilities, operational staging areas, a secure intelligence center, accommodation, and administrative offices. A month ago GES had managed contracts in fifteen countries employing nearly two hundred special operations veterans. Now, a series of setbacks had changed everything. Charles King, the CEO, had been forced to dramatically downsize the company. He had let go nearly all of his training staff and operational personnel.

The team he had recalled to Virginia consisted of twenty operators. Each had been carefully vetted to ensure their suitability for a new style of operations.

Today, King had invited them to his residence on the estate. A modern take on a southern plantation mansion, it was an informal setting for a barbeque, beers, and a chat. Once everyone had eaten, he stood on the back step of the house and called for silence.

The men immediately stopped talking and turned to face the tall former Special Forces officer.

"So a lot of you are wondering what the hell has been going on over the last month."

They all nodded.

"I'll try to keep it simple, guys. We were targeted by a terrorist organization and as a result we lost ten good men and all our Agency contracts."

A few side conversations broke out before one of the men spoke up, "What the fuck, boss? Terrorists? You expect us to believe that shit?"

"Yes. Look, I can't give you much more than that. However, I can tell you that whoever fucked with us is currently a priority CIA target." King spotted the two operators who'd survived the massacre and gave them a nod. Matt's jaw was still black from where he'd been punched, while his buddy, Chris, had one side of his head shaved where they had repaired a fracture in his skull. They were the lucky ones.

"I know a lot of you are upset. You've lost friends and we've had to let a lot of good guys go. But this isn't the end of GES. In fact this is the beginning of a new opportunity; an opportunity to hit back at the bastards who killed Shrek, Jimmy, Pershing, and the others. It's an opportunity to serve our country and earn some damn good money doing it."

A murmur rippled through the group.

"Hey, I know some of our contracts have been driven more by financial return rather than service. But that time's over. We're going to be leaner, more agile, and ready to take on the toughest national security tasks the CIA has to offer."

His comments prompted more discussion.

"I thought we lost all our contracts," said Hammer, one of the most accomplished team leaders. Tall and lean, the former Green Beret was sharp as a whip.

"You're right, we have lost our long term contracts. But we've been given the opportunity to join a new program and bid for the CIA's priority short-notice tasks. They pay better but the risk is significantly greater."

"How much better?" asked Hammer.

"As much as a hundred grand per man for a job, depending on the risk profile and duration."

Hammer gave a low whistle and nodded.

"The work will be more sensitive and compartmented than what we've already been doing. You'll be read on to each job on a need-to-know basis, and you can expect complete deniability from Langley. I don't expect this to be a fit for everyone. If it's not what you want to do you can walk away right now."

The men stared at him intently.

"So that's it, boys. You'll all be held on a retainer here at the facility. You'll be allocated teams, train hard, and when the jobs come up you'll take names and kick doors. Anyone got questions at this stage?" He scanned the crowd.

"Yeah, I've got one." It was Matt, the operative with the bruised jaw. "When do we get to take down the guys who killed Shrek and the rest of the boys?"

***

FORT YUKON RESEARCH STATION, ALASKA

"Sir, the cabin door is open," the stewardess announced.

Thomas Larkin nodded and continued working on his Redemption laptop. He had the master mission list open and scanned over the recent tasking that Howard had added. Good, the fat analyst was making headway. Closing the laptop he made a mental note to call him in the next day or two for an update.

The barracuda-jawed CIA officer left the chair and smoothed the creases out of his grey woolen suit. He threw on a down jacket before walking to the front of the private jet and down the stairs into the hangar. "Good lord!" he hissed through clenched teeth as the frosty air hit him.

The man at the bottom of the stairs laughed. "It's even colder outside." Aaron Small took a drag from a cigarette and extended his hand to the Operational Support Program director. "Sir, welcome to Dead Land."

"Charming name, you come up with that yourself?" He frowned at the smoke that lingered in the air.

"No, it's what the locals call the area." Small took the hint and crushed the cigarette against the concrete floor with his boot.

Larkin glanced around the hangar. He noted the presence of a civilian registered C-27J transporter. "I trust our old friend has been made comfortable."

"Yes, a moving reunion." The pale-skinned interrogator smirked. "Although I'm not sure why you sent him here. The invalid doesn't know anything. I established that when I worked on him at Gitmo."

"He's not here because of what he knows, Aaron. He's here because of who he knows. Now are you going to show me around before I freeze to death?"

"Of course, let's head across to the operations room."

Larkin had flown up from Langley in the early hours of the morning to inspect his latest OSP facility. Situated in the barren wastelands of Alaska, the former USAF research station had been abandoned for over fifteen years. A cold-war relic, it was isolated, forgotten, and in one of the harshest environments on earth. That made it the perfect site for a rendition and interrogation facility as well as the primary server farm for the Redemption Network.

Larkin followed Small out of the hangar and through an enclosed walkway into another building. "How many men do you have now?" he asked as they walked down a long corridor lined with accommodation.

"Eight."

"Including you?"

"Yes. Five guards and two IT technicians. You said keep it light."

They passed a dining hall and reached metal stairs at the end of the corridor. Their heels rang as they walked up to the next level.

Larkin noticed the fresh paint on the walls. "The place looks in good order."

"You haven't seen anything yet."

At the top of the stairs Small punched in a code and the door unlocked. Pushing it open they entered the base operations room. Larkin glanced around the state-of-the-art setup. A large flat panel screen surrounded by smaller monitors dominated the far wall. In front of it sat one of the base personnel. He was monitoring a curved bank of touch screens that reminded Larkin of something from a sci-fi movie.

"We've worked through a few bugs but overall the systems are green across the board."

"Good, give me a run-down of what you've got."

Small gestured for his man to vacate the command chair. He sat and his fingers danced across a touch screen. The image on the main monitor changed from a snowscape to a map of the facility. "I'll start from the outside in. If you check the top right monitor you can see the feed from one of our surveillance drones."

Larkin glanced up; it showed a feed from an airborne camera, not dissimilar to the Predator feeds in the command center at Langley.

"The drones are battery powered quadcopters. Heavy-duty versions of the toys kids use. They've got an endurance of over an hour and can patrol up to fifteen miles out from our perimeter."

"Are they armed?"

Small shook his head. "No, but the Talons are." He gestured to another screen that showed the feed from an unmanned ground vehicle. "They're an enlarged version of the Army bomb-disposal robots. Got a machine gun, grenade launchers, and a patrol range of about five miles. We've had a little trouble with them freezing up but only in extreme conditions."

"Isn't all the weather out here extreme?"

"You haven't seen extreme. When a storm comes we batten the hatches and wait it out. The drones only form our outer security layer. When they can't fly we've still got the fence with movement sensors, cameras, and six remote weapon towers. Like the Talons, the towers can be fully automated or controlled from in here."

He nodded. "What about the detention facility?"

Small's fingers tapped a screen and the central image changed to a map of a rectangular underground complex. It consisted of a central corridor with a number of rooms on either side. Larkin counted ten small squares, the cells, and three larger rooms closer to the entrance.

"Do you want to take a look?"

"Does that require me to go outside in the cold?"

"Yes, it's separate from this building."

"The map will suffice."

"No problem. The complex used to be an underground testing facility, perfect for us. We can handle nine detainees at any one time. There's a gas incinerator next door to take care of any disposal requirements."

"And my server racks?"

"We converted one of the cells to hold them."

Larkin pointed up at the screen. "Can you show me our guest?"

"Sure." Small tapped a touch panel and the central image switched to a high definition shot from the corner of a tiny concrete room. Lying on a bed that appeared too small was a bearded figure with a heavy mop of blonde hair. The giant was

28

dressed in dark green prison fatigues. He was missing the lower part of his right arm and most of his right leg below the knee.

"The mighty Iceman," murmured Larkin.

Small stared at the image. "You said he's here because of who he knows."

"Yes, I'll have my people send you the latest intel. One of my analysts has linked him to the Major League Network."

"Major League?"

"A terrorist group that recruits highly trained operatives. They're responsible for a recent attack against a US mining operation in Mexico. We think our friend here was one of the founding members."

"Well, that is an interesting development. I've got some new techniques I'm eager to test." Small rubbed his hands together. "I'll wring the truth out of Mr. Castle."

Larkin shook his head. "No, he's not to be touched. It is imperative he remains alive."

Small scowled. "As you wish."

"Be patient. I have a number of rendition operations underway. Soon you'll have additional detainees to work on. Now, I've got to be back at Langley. I'll show myself out." With that Larkin left the operations room. As he walked down the corridor back toward the hangar he shuddered involuntarily. He couldn't even begin to imagine what 'new techniques' the little creep had in mind.

CHAPTER 2

GES FACILITY, VIRGINIA

King placed a coffee mug on his desk and pulled out the leather office chair. He ran a hand over his shaved head as he sat, turned, and gazed out the window of the study. Sleep had eluded him for weeks. Ever since Larkin bailed him out of prison he'd felt like he was being watched; that at any moment the CIA would demand something he wasn't willing to give. Not that he had a choice; Larkin now owned him and GES. His contracts would be exclusively through OSP. The master would whistle and he would come running, like a well-trained dog.

He took a sip from his coffee and logged into the desktop computer. His email account overflowed with internal company correspondence; the administration associated with downsizing and refocusing the company. He opened an email from Larkin to find the logon details and link to the new contract-bidding tool he was supposed to use. The site, called Redemption, loaded and he typed in his handle and the password. His IP address and personal details had already been registered during the vetting process for contract managers.

The site was reasonably intuitive. A sidebar displayed the active jobs. There were currently only three; a collection operation in South East Asia, a rendition in South Africa, and an interrogation job, also in South Africa. He clicked on the rendition. His heart skipped a beat when he read the target codename, Objective Blue Jay.

King didn't know who Blue Jay was but he guessed they were part of the Major League Network. That's if Larkin's people hadn't changed the naming convention. Why would they? No, it made sense that this new objective was an associate of the terrorist known as Aden, or Objective Yankee.

The icon to bid for the mission was inactive and the status read PENDING. "Son of a bitch."

He shoved the mouse away in frustration and glared at the screen. Aden and his associates had killed some of his best men, two teams of highly trained professionals who had been the backbone of his organization. These 'terrorists', whoever the hell they really were, had also single-handedly bankrupted the private equity fund where King had been a director. To say he wanted revenge was an understatement. As he watched, the status of the mission changed from PENDING to UNDERWAY. King slapped the desk. "That's bullshit." He grabbed his phone, activated the Redemption communication app and dialed Larkin's number.

The Director of OSP picked up after three rings. A shrill tone announced that the call was secure. "Charles, what can I do for you?"

"The Africa job. I want it."

"This is a simple rendition on the other side of the world. The asset that has been allocated is more suitable for the task."

"What about the interrogation? No one has a better understanding of everything that has transpired. I should be there."

"Again we have assets that are closer and suitable. Charles, I need you to focus on GES and preparing capable teams for short notice deployment."

"With respect, Thomas, I already have that capability."

"Good, then you can bid as the work is made available."

He gritted his teeth. "I have assets that could be helping track down the Major League Network."

"I'm aware of that. When a mission is posted bid for it. If your capability is suitable it may be allocated to you. That's the way the system works. Now I'm very busy, so goodbye." Larkin terminated the call.

King slowly placed the phone on his desk and continued to stare at the computer screen. The call had confirmed something he already knew, that his company, which had once been one of the most respected high-end security contractors, was now merely a pawn for Larkin to move as he saw fit.

***

KRUGER NATIONAL PARK, SOUTH AFRICA

Robert Hunter was unremarkable-looking; five foot ten with light brown hair and a lean build. A former South African Special Task Force operator, he was one of the few African-based contractors vetted and briefed into a new online contracting program. He had bid for and won the latest rendition task shortly after it was posted. Hiring a Pajero four-wheel drive under an alias, it had taken most of the day to drive from Johannesburg to Kruger National Park.

Hunter parked his four-wheel drive at the far end of the resort's dusty parking lot. He stretched his legs as he gave the rustic property a once over. Well-appointed canvas tents were clustered around a dining hall, kitchen, pool, and bar. He'd booked for three days but doubted he would need the entire time. If his target was still at the resort he would find her quickly and abduct her at the earliest opportunity.

He walked toward the reception area, waving away an eager porter. Once checked in, he was heading back outside to grab his bag when the clatter of a diesel engine caught his attention. A cut-down Land Rover pulled up in front of him in a cloud of red dust. Taking out a handkerchief he held it over his mouth until it cleared. When it did he found himself staring at, Christina Munoz, the woman he'd been tasked to capture.

He dropped his gaze, walked across to his vehicle, and unloaded his backpack. There were two men and another woman with the target. The men looked fit and capable. Avoiding eye contact with the group he followed the path that led past the central entertaining area and up to his room. He unlocked the door, entered, and dropped his bag next to the bed. Pulling back the canvas flaps covering the window, he watched as the newly arrived group made their way to the bar. The target held hands with the larger of the two men. The other pair also seemed to be a couple.

The resort's bar was nestled under the branches of an Umbrella Thorn tree. The high leafy canopy offered natural protection from the sun. Picturesque and cool, it was the perfect place to enjoy a drink after a long day in the park on safari.

Hunter opened a laptop on the folding camp table in his room. Using his phone for a connection he logged into a website and updated the mission status. Regular communication was encouraged and improved his contracting profile. Update complete, he packed the device away and pulled a novel from his bag. Relaxing in a canvas chair on the tent's porch, he found his page. An occasional glance was all it took to keep tabs on his target as he read.

At the bar Bishop collected four gin and tonics and took them to where Saneh, Dom, and Christina were sitting. "Can't go on a safari without gin."

"Sorry we didn't find any rhinos, bro," said Dom in his New Zealand accent.

"The giraffes and cheetahs more than made up for it." Bishop distributed the drinks and took a seat.

"We'll have more luck tomorrow."

"A toast," offered Bishop. "To rhinos and the rangers."

"Rhinos and the rangers," echoed the others as they raised their glasses.

Dom took a sip. "Thanks guys, it's going to be a long battle."

"Saneh and I were wondering if we could hang around and help."

Dom broke into a broad smile. "That would be fantastic. Although I'm still not sure what either of you do."

"I told you," said Christina. "Aden works for the UN and Saneh is a project manager for an IT company."

"Skills that will be very useful. Now, let's celebrate with a boozy dinner."

"Our treat," said Saneh. "It's the least we can do considering the time you've taken off to show us around."

"It's been my pleasure. Like I said, tomorrow we should have better luck with the rhinos."

***

Bishop staggered up the stairs after Saneh. She tripped on the top step and almost fell through the canvas door of their tent. "You OK?" he asked.

She turned and gave him a sultry smile. "I will be when you're inside and I get your pants off."

He laughed. "Well let me get the door."

Saneh stumbled inside, shed her clothes, and reclined naked on the bed.

He took a moment to take in her curves. His eyes lingered on hers. "God, you're beautiful."

"And you're drunk."

"You'll find I am significantly more sober than you, my dear." Bishop peeled off his T-shirt.

"Are you saying I can't hold my liquor?"

"That's exactly what I'm saying." He sat on the bed and made to remove his shoes.

A faint scream penetrated the walls of the tent and he froze. "Did you hear that?"

Saneh sat bolt upright. "Yes, it sounded like Christina."

Throwing on his shirt Bishop dashed out the door and down the stairs. Christina and Dom's hut was on the far side of the resort. He sprinted the distance, past the pool and bar area, along a path, and almost tripped over Dom's prostrate body.

Fearing the worst he checked for a pulse. It was strong and he was still breathing. Another scream came from the direction of the parking lot.

Bishop grabbed the car keys from Dom's pockets then sprinted toward the sound. He rounded the reception building in time to see taillights disappearing in a cloud of dust.

He jumped into the Land Rover and turned over the turbo diesel. As he dropped it into gear Saneh appeared out of the darkness and climbed into the passenger seat.

"Is Dom alive?" she asked.

"Yes." Bishop stomped the accelerator to the floor as he spun the steering wheel. "I remember seeing that car earlier. The white Pajero." He flicked on the truck's powerful spotlights.

"Do you think it's GES?" Saneh clung to the roll cage as Bishop sent the truck careening around a corner.

"Who else?"

CHAPTER 3

KRUGER NATIONAL PARK, SOUTH AFRICA

Bishop fixed the white Pajero in the powerful spotlights of the Land Rover as he crunched through the gears. His safari truck had a slight disadvantage in power but he accelerated as fast as possible, crashing through the gears like a rally driver. The absence of a windshield didn't distract him as bugs smacked into his face, attracted to the lights.

He was familiar with the road and knew that on a number of bends the dirt surface was compacted with corrugations. As they approached a rough corner he eased on the brakes. Ahead, the Pajero hit the curve at pace and skipped sideways into the sandy shoulder of the road, shedding speed. Bishop closed the gap to a few feet. Squinting in the dust he dropped a gear and rammed the four-wheel drive, pushing it sideways.

The Pajero shot across to the opposite side of the road. Bishop came alongside and nudged the truck's steel sidebars against it. The kidnapper was forced onto a narrow sandy track that led away from the main road and into the park.

"Well done!" yelled Saneh over the roar of the engine and wind.

He glanced sideways. Her hair streamed out and her face was covered in bug splatter and grime. Ahead of them the Pajero bounced along the track in a cloud of dust. The Land Rover was in its element now. The knobby tires gripped the sandy track and the powerful diesel engine didn't miss a beat as they sped across the savannah.

"The river crossing!" yelled Saneh as the track descended.

He downshifted as they neared a fording point. The spotlights illuminated the white Mitsubishi as it ploughed into the river throwing up a bow wave. The driver nearly stalled but managed to keep the revs up, the road tires scrabbling for grip on the rocky river bed. By the time it reached the other side it had almost come to a halt. It struggled up the far bank, tires spinning in the wheel ruts cut by hundreds of safari tours.

Bishop slowed as they hit the river, gunned the big diesel, and aimed for the far side. The Land Rover roared like an angry beast as it shoved the water aside and bounced over the rocks. It caught the Pajero half way up the bank. Bishop shunted it forward with the bull bar and spun the wheel.

The Mitsubishi's mud-clogged road tires offered little traction and it skidded, spinning a full ninety degrees to the track.

With the four-wheel drive pinned sideways across the bull bar the spotlights directly illuminated the face of the kidnapper who calmly raised a pistol and aimed it through the side window.

Shots rang out. Bishop ducked behind the dash and stomped on the accelerator. The engine revved and they T-boned the Pajero flipping it onto its side. They gathered speed as the smooth side of the Mitsubishi offered little resistance. Bishop braked bringing both vehicles to a halt a dozen yards down the track. He jumped over the dash onto the hood and wrenched a pickaxe handle from the mounts. Leaping onto the side of the Pajero he drove the shaft through the bullet-holed window into the face of the attacker. Two solid blows stopped the man's attempt to exit the vehicle and another knocked him unconscious.

In that time Saneh had jumped out and run to the back of the Mitsubishi. She peered through the glass and saw Christina bound and gagged in the trunk. "Aden, she's here. I need your help."

Bishop grunted as he lifted the heavy swing door, spare tire and all, allowing Saneh to drag Christina's limp body out. She gently removed the tape from her mouth. "She's breathing." Saneh flicked open a blade, cut the tape from the unconscious journalist's hands, and checked her for injuries. "She's been sedated but nothing appears to be broken."

A flash of headlights announced the arrival of another Land Rover. Dom jumped out armed with a pump-action shotgun. "Do you have Christina?"

Bishop picked Christina up and carried her to Dom's vehicle. "She's here and I think she's OK." He gently placed her on the back seat. "She's been sedated. You need to take her back to the camp and get a doctor to check her over. You might want to get that head of yours looked at as well."

"Yes, of course, and I'll call the police."

"No, I want to have a chat with him first." He nodded toward the overturned vehicle.

Dom shot him a questioning glance. Bishop's steely gaze let him know it wasn't negotiable.

"OK, do you need any help?" he asked.

"No, get Christina back to the camp. We'll take care of this." Bishop turned his attention to the Pajero. He wanted answers and knew exactly how he was going to get them. "Saneh, can you give me a hand with our friend, please."

***

Hunter opened his eyes and immediately regretted it. Dazzling spotlights shone into his face adding to the pain splitting his head. He tried to stand before realizing that his legs were zip-tied to a camp chair. His hands were secured firmly behind his back. Panic assailed him as the events of the last few hours came flooding back.

"Welcome back to the land of the living." The voice came from beyond the lights.

Hunter squinted, trying to identify its owner.

"You've got a bit of a situation on your hands, Mr. Archie Bernard."

He recognized the name from the fake driver's license in his wallet.

"That's probably not your real name so I'm just going to call you Snack." There was a pause. "I know what you're thinking," continued the voice. "But it's a very appropriate name because if you don't talk that's exactly what you're going to be, a snack for the hyenas."

"What do you want?"

"We can start with who you work for. What's your association with GES?"

"GES? I don't know any GES. I work for myself, I'm a contractor."

"You going to be a smart ass, Snack? If you don't want to talk I'll put a bullet in each of your legs and leave you out here for the night. The hyenas will have you cleaned up in no time. By morning you'll be a handful of blood-soaked rags and a few hours after that you'll be a steaming pile of shit."

Hunter considered the words. This was supposed to be a low-risk job; grab the chick, make the delivery, and pocket fifty grand. There had been no mention of a protection detail and it was clear these people were serious operators.

"OK, OK. I'll tell you what you need to know. But, in return you let me go. I know how this shit works. I'll disappear and we never met."

There was no reply.

He fought the urge to fill the silence. A moment later he folded. "I took the contract from a website. They post jobs online, you bid for them, and if you're successful they give you detailed instructions."

"Go on."

"It was a simple grab and go. I won the contract and they sent me a bunch of instructions: target pack, location, handover, all the usual stuff."

"I don't believe you. Who's the contact? Who gave you the job?"

"You don't understand. You can check my laptop, it's all there."

Bishop was standing to one side of the Land Rover. He had the spotlights angled down at the South African's face. With Saneh's help they'd already stripped the kidnapper's vehicle of his belongings. There wasn't much. His bag contained a change of clothes, toiletries, spare magazines for his pistol, a phone, a roll of cloth tape, cable ties, and a battered laptop.

Saneh opened the laptop and placed it on the hood of the truck next to Bishop. She checked that the phone had a signal and plugged it in.

"What's the password?" asked Bishop.

He told them and Saneh wrote it down. She typed it in and the laptop unlocked to reveal a web browser.

"If you go to my favorites there is a tab called work stuff."

Bishop watched as Saneh followed his instructions. Sure enough a website appeared, simply labeled 'Online Contracting Portal'. A popup window asked for a logon and password. The kidnapper provided the details and they waited for the site to load.

"Holy shit," whispered Bishop as the contracting interface appeared. It was simple, intuitive, and exactly as described. In the corner of the screen Saneh found a tab called current tasks. There was only one displayed. She clicked on it and the details of the kidnapping operation appeared along with the operative's real name.

"Well, Mr. Hunter, it seems you're telling the truth."

"I don't have any reason to lie to you. Look, whoever gave me this job has landed me in the shit so I've got no loyalty to them."

"Then tell me who they are. Who recruited you?"

"I swear, I've never met anyone. A few months ago I was recruited online, put through a series of tests, and briefed into the program. I was paid up front for my first job, in bitcoin." Hunter had visibly relaxed. "The guys running the site, whoever they are, are real tight. I couldn't even give you a phone contact. They've got my number but they rarely call."

"So let me get this right. You take illegal privately contracted missions from some online entity that you know fuck all about?"

Hunter looked sideways. "It pays well."

"OK, let's assume I believe you. Who were you going to deliver Christina Munoz to?"

"Some guy called Derick. The handover's suppose to go down tomorrow, the details are all on there."

Bishop looked at Saneh who nodded. He took the roll of tape from Hunter's bag and walked in a wide arc approaching him from behind. He taped the man's eyes. "Mr. Hunter, you are now finished with online contracting. We know who you are now. If you talk to anyone about this you're a dead man."

"Understood."

"We're going to take your computer. If you try to log on from anywhere else we will know and we will find you." Bishop cut the cable ties securing Hunter's legs to the camp chair. With the pistol pressed into the small of his back, he walked him to the rear of the rolled Pajero.

"You'll be safe here till someone finds you in the morning." He pushed the man into the trunk, slammed the door shut, and locked it. With the internal safety cage he was trapped.

Bishop walked back to the Land Rover where Saneh had already packed away the laptop and equipment. "You take down all those passwords?" he asked.

"Yes, I've got screenshots as well. Even if we get locked out we still know the procedures he was supposed to follow."

"Cool. In the meantime we need to get Christina and Dom somewhere safe. Then we need to contact the Bunker and get Flash hooked into the website." Bishop executed a three-point turn and they drove back toward the river.

"If we move fast we might be able to take down the interrogation team. Find out whoever's behind all this."

"True, it could lead us to the next link in the chain." He paused as he downshifted and ploughed into the river. As they reached the far bank he slammed the steering wheel. "Damn, I should've shot that mercenary asshole. If he talks…"

Saneh shook her head. "He won't be talking any time soon. Besides, if we killed him, that would make us as bad as them."

"Yeah and right now we don't even know who them is."

***

POLOKWANE, SOUTH AFRICA

The Blue Horizons apartments were on the outskirts of the South African town of Polokwane, approximately three hours drive from Kruger National Park. Saneh had found them online and booked one of the self-contained units under a fake identity. Christina was already lying low with Dom, staying with one of his friends in Pretoria. Bishop was confident she would be safe there; the intelligence report included in the contractor's target pack made no mention of her New Zealander boyfriend.

The PRIMAL operatives had set up the contractor's laptop on a table in the tiny kitchenette. Next to it an iPRIMAL tablet was connected to the local Wi-Fi network. A secure communicator app reached back to the Bunker on Lascar Island through a series of onion routers, remote servers, and firewalls. 'Flash' Gordon, the vigilante organization's electronic intelligence specialist had designed the sophisticated network to be as secure as possible.

"Ready to dial in?" asked Bishop.

They'd already given the team in the Bunker, PRIMAL's operations center, a verbal heads-up on the attempted abduction. They knew Flash was keen to get access to the online contracting system.

"Ready when you are," Saneh said as she sat beside him.

He pressed the icon to phone PRIMAL's intelligence team. The call connected after a few seconds.

"Hi guys." Flash's voice was tinny through the speakers on the tablet. "Good to see you've taken another holiday and turned it into an opportunity to shoot bad guys."

Bishop shook his head. "Hey mate, it's not my fault, and we didn't shoot anyone."

"No, you're alright, you're just a shit magnet. OK, well let's get this rolling. What I need you to do is plug the cable from your tablet into the USB port on the laptop."

Bishop followed his instructions. "Done."

"OK, now I need you to logon to that website."

Saneh checked the password and entered it in the website on Hunter's computer. "OK, Flash, we're logged in."

"Yep, cool, I'm just waiting for the connection to establish." There was a pause. "OK, I'm in."

Bishop and Saneh watched as Hunter's computer began operating like it was possessed. The cursor danced over the screen exploring the contracting system.

"This is very cool," said Flash.

"There's not actually much there," Bishop said. "The account appears to have only limited access but I'm guessing you can pull it apart."

"Yeah, so what I'm going to do is route my IP through an address in Kruger. Once I do that I'll ghost his laptop's MAC address onto a machine here and access it remotely. That way I can work from this end and you guys don't have to stay online."

Bishop turned to Saneh and shrugged. "Sure, sounds good. Can you put us through to Vance?"

"Sure thing, brother. I'll let you know when you can shut down at your end. Flash out."

The communicator app muted for a moment before Vance's voice sounded from the speaker. "Well if it isn't Mr. and Mrs. Smith. I swear you two cause more goddamn trouble than anyone else in the whole outfit." Vance was the Director of Operations for PRIMAL, effectively their boss.

Bishop rolled his eyes. "Is Chua with you?"

"Yes, I'm here," said the Chief of Intelligence, Vance's counterpart.

"So have you got any more intel? Is GES part of this online contracting site or is someone else after us?"

Chua replied, "Too early to say. Maybe. Flash needs time to pick it apart but at this stage it looks to be bigger than GES. Someone else may have taken an interest in Christina for all we know. Our theft from the private equity firm also could have attracted the attention of others. The CIA may have–"

Bishop interrupted, "So basically you're saying you don't know. Have you had a chance to discuss our idea?"

"We have," said Vance.

"And?"

"We think it's risky."

Bishop shook his head and Saneh leaned forward to speak. "I can deal with the risk. The contractor won't compromise us. We have both his computer and his phone. There's no way he'll be able to contact these people, not before we're on to the next link in the chain."

"Look, I appreciate you putting yourself on the line like this, Saneh. What I'm trying to say is this is high risk no matter how you look at it." Bishop made to speak but Vance continued, "However, considering the threat to PRIMAL as a whole we cannot afford to not take action. Chua will find out who's behind the website as a priority and assess what threat it poses to us. All our other collection operations are suspended until this is dealt with."

Bishop raised his voice. "Chua's got nothing. This is our only lead right now, a fleeting chance to–"

"And," interjected Vance, "that's why we've authorized your proposal. Mirza and the CAT will leave in the next hour to support you. Your mission is approved."

Bishop leant back in the chair and grinned. Vance had just authorized the release of PRIMAL's Critical Assault Team, a four man assault and recovery asset trained and equipped for high-risk operations. He glanced at Saneh. Her lips were pressed together and she wore an intense expression that reminded him she was going to be the one taking the most risk. "We're going to need to plan the hell out of this one."

"I couldn't agree more. I'll take advice from Chua and Flash on the best course of action and we'll consult with you once we've put together the details."

"Understood, we'll stand by here for tasking."

"Get some rest; things are going to get interesting."

"Will do." He terminated the call and turned to Saneh. "You sure you're OK with this?"

She smiled. "It was my idea, of course I'm OK with it."

He kissed her. "Right, now we've got to turn you from a Persian warrior goddess into a wide-eyed hipster photographer."

"Oh you'd like that, wouldn't you?"

"Nope, give me my goddess any day of the week."

"Oh, so you didn't find Christina attractive when she threw herself at you in New York?"

Bishop grinned sheepishly. "I knew getting you two together was a bad idea."

CHAPTER 4

BOSTON

Howard checked the Redemption site again as he drummed his fingers on his desk. Fast food wrappers and empty coffee cups littered the office. It had been over twelve hours since the operative in South Africa had reported identifying Objective Blue Jay and Howard had left his apartment only once since then. Surely it didn't take that long to grab a skinny journalist and stuff her in a trunk, he thought. He checked the activity log again. Hunter had checked in a few more times but hadn't updated his status. The locations were all within Kruger National Park so maybe the contractor hadn't had the opportunity to kidnap Christina yet.

He checked the other task he'd posted. An interrogation team, with a safe house in Gwanda, Zimbabwe, had taken the job and were standing by to receive the girl. They would conduct initial questioning and facilitate her transfer to Larkin's new facility, if required. He sent them a message that the abduction was still pending. As he hit send the unclassified computer on the other side of the desk pinged. He slid across in his chair and unlocked the screen.

In the last week he'd exhausted all his official sources in the hunt for the second key person of interest; Wesley Chambers. Frustrated, he had turned to one of his online hacking buddies for help. Strictly speaking he had breached protocol by going outside Redemption. However, this guy was top-tier, and unlike most government employees, actually knew the meaning of discretion. Howard had sent him all Wesley's details and now, less than twenty-four hours later, he had a response.

The message was short.

Located your boy in New Zealand. 9-month visa. Staying in Queenstown. Residence unknown. Send 30K in bitcoin.

Howard jumped out of his chair and punched a fist in the air. First Christina and now Wesley. He ran a Google search on Queenstown and read the Wikipedia entry. Located on the South Island of New Zealand it was a small resort town renowned for adventure sports and a vibrant nightlife.

He slid his chair back to the Redemption laptop and updated Wesley's target pack. The banker's location had been unknown since he'd been kidnapped. Howard had dubbed him Objective Mariner. He was convinced Wesley had collaborated with the terrorists in stealing close to a billion dollars from his former employer.

With the target pack updated he listed the rendition job in Redemption. As he worked, the indicator for Christina's mission changed. His pulse quickened as he opened the menu.

Target Secured. Enroute to RV.

Howard grinned like a Cheshire cat as he spun in his office chair. This had been the most productive morning in his entire intelligence career. He picked up his smartphone and used a communicator app to dial Larkin.

The OSP director answered immediately. "How's my favorite analyst tracking?"

"Good! Christina has been captured and I've got a fix on Mariner."

"Who?"

"Sorry, Wesley Chambers."

"The banker who worked for Pollard?"

"That's him, the dude who got kidnapped."

"Excellent. I take it you've already put the job out for bidding?"

"Yes, sir."

"Fantastic, I know someone who will be very interested in that. Nicely done, Terrance. I do believe you've met the criteria for a bonus. I'll have it wired through to your account."

Howard pumped his fist again. "Thanks, sir."

"Keep up the good work." Larkin ended the call.

He resisted the urge to dance and instead made another call. It was time to treat himself.

"Hello, Piggy," said a sultry voice.

A shiver ran down his spine. "Would you be available tonight, mistress?"

***

GES FACILITY, VIRGINIA

The buzzer sounded and King reached for the custom Colt 1911 on his hip. As he turned he drew the weapon, flicked off the safety, and thrust it forward in a two-handed grip. The three metal plates rang as he fired off three double taps in quick succession. The slide locked back, he reloaded, and fired three more double taps.

"Seven point eight seconds. Nice work, boss," said Matt.

King loaded a fresh magazine and holstered the weapon. "A little rusty but nothing time on the tools won't fix."

They removed their hearing protection and walked back to the ammunition bench. "How's the jaw, Matt?"

"Good now the swelling has gone down." The former Green Beret had been knocked out during a confrontation with an operative from the Major League Network. "Damn lucky it wasn't broken."

"Still, being injured saved your life," said King as he thumbed .45 ACP rounds into an empty magazine. Anger flashed in the younger man's eyes and he immediately regretted the words. Matt had been scrubbed from the mission that had wiped out the rest of his team. "We'll hit back at them, bud."

"I know, just make sure I'm on any job that goes down."

"You will be." King finished reloading both magazines and slid them onto his belt.

"How's the family going? That boy of yours coming down for a shoot any time soon?"

"When his grades improve."

"Oh, like that is it?"

"Yeah, the kid's good at everything except school work."

"Maybe he's destined to follow his dad's footsteps."

"His mother would kill me." King's phone buzzed in his pocket and he glanced at the screen. It was a notification; a new job had been posted on the Redemption Network. He needed to get to the computer before someone else beat him to it. "We might have our chance. Bud, I've got to run. Can you sort out the ammo?"

"Yeah, boss."

He dashed for the all-terrain buggy parked on the gravel behind the range. He spun the wheels and raced along the path leading to the holding area. Flying past the sheds he continued through a dense pine forest to his residence. He skidded to a halt and headed directly to his office.

Unlocking the computer, he brought up the Redemption site and tried to remember his password. He entered it incorrectly twice. "Goddamn it." A third time would lock him out for an hour giving someone else the opportunity to bid for the mission.

Tentatively he gave it one more try. Success! There was only one new job. As he accessed it his heart nearly stopped. The contract was for another Major League rendition, this time in Queenstown, New Zealand. The target was Objective Mariner, an unfamiliar code name. The mission profile was minimal risk and the notes indicated the target was unlikely to be armed. It also assessed that Mariner was unlikely to maintain a low profile and recommended a small team for the search and abduction.

King smiled, he could guess exactly who Mariner was. With a shaking hand he punched the 'bid' button. The website asked him to input the names of the team. He typed in his own, Hammer's, and Matt and Chris, the survivors from their last encounter with Major League. Entering the minimum bid price he hit submit. Now all he needed to do was wait. As he turned to walk outside the phone on his desk rang. It had to be Larkin.

"What the hell are you doing?" barked the OSP director.

"Look, I'm the best person for the job. I know Wesley better than anyone. I worked with him for three years, for God's sake."

"You're the CEO of a company not a ground pounder."

"I've only got twenty operators, Thomas. I'm not exactly overwhelmed with office work. This is a simple job. I'll be in and out in 72 hours. You need me to do this."

"No, you think you need to do it to somehow redeem yourself. Wake up, you're not a shooter anymore."

"Give me this and it's all I'll ask for."

There was a pause before Larkin replied. "Fine, but you take Wesley directly to the designated facility and you secure him there. You want to be in on this mission, you can see it through to the end."

"Agreed."

"Call me when you have him." Larkin hung up.

**

LASCAR ISLAND

King wasn't the only one monitoring the Redemption system. Seven thousand miles away deep underground on a Pacific island, 'Flash' Gordon was remotely connected to the network through an IP address in South Africa. The intelligence analyst wore a black T-shirt that bulged over his stomach, skinny jeans, and a snapback cap. He chewed his lip as he worked furiously to find a backdoor into the system. Frustratingly it had layer after layer of security measures designed to mislead, block, and even destroy any program that tried to burrow through the code layer.

He had been unable to increase his permission level beyond 'contractor' or gain access to other areas of the system. Whoever had built it had used similar techniques to those he'd employed to defend the iPRIMAL network.

He spotted the new task as soon as it appeared in the contracting menu. "Holy shit," he mouthed. The job was in

Queenstown, New Zealand. Leaping from the chair he bolted out of the intelligence office through a sliding door and into the operations room.

"Vance, we've got a big problem, a big, big problem."

Vance, a hulking African American in his late fifties, sat in the command chair in front of a wall of screens. In front of him stood Frank, one of the watchkeepers, and Chen Chua, PRIMAL's Chinese American Chief of Intelligence. He turned his bullhead toward Flash and frowned.

"Buddy, we're right in the middle of something. Can it wait?"

He shook his head. "Someone posted a new rendition on the network; it's for Queenstown, New Zealand."

Vance looked puzzled for a moment then glanced at Chua. "Wesley Chambers?"

Chua nodded. "That's where he's currently hiding. He likes the nightlife." Both Chua and Flash had worked closely with Wesley in bankrupting his former employer.

"Do we have comms with him?"

"Unfortunately not. Once he got to Queenstown he stopped answering his phone. Shouldn't be hard to find him though, he was a banker. He'll be frequenting bars and chasing girls."

Vance glanced up at the screen that showed the locations of the PRIMAL operatives. All were currently assigned to the mission in South Africa in support of Bishop and Saneh. He checked another screen that showed the inside of the underground hangar two floors above. Also carved from rock, the upper levels of the former-World War Two base housed the organization's aircraft: Sleek, a Gulfstream business jet, Dragonfly, a tilt-rotor, and the Pain Train, a massive Il-76 transport and special operations support platform. The Pain Train was waiting for clearance in front of the camouflaged doors that hid PRIMAL's headquarters from the outside world. "Frank, hold them there. I'm going up top. Flash and Chua, come with me." He prised himself out of his chair and strode through the sliding doors to the elevator.

"Flash, are we any closer to find out who's running this contracting system?"

"Sorry, boss. Permissions on this account are limited and I haven't been able to find anything that points to a government agency. I've tried to trace the IP address but I'm getting nowhere. All I know is that they call it Redemption."

"Whoever set this up is top-tier, yeah?"

"Yes, their security is as good as ours. I'd say they're American." Flash had previously worked in the National Security Agency, which, along with the Israelis, was a world leader in cyber-warfare. He still discreetly maintained contact with a number of NSA geeks, staying abreast of the latest developments.

The elevator arrived and they stepped in. Vance stabbed the button for the hangar. "Chua, do you agree?"

"I'd go one step further," said Chua. "The level of technology, the organizational skills, and types of contracts all point to a CIA-sponsored project. The only question is whether it's privately run or a legitimate government entity."

Vance frowned. "That possibility is why we can't afford to expose ourselves any further."

The elevator shuddered to a halt and the doors opened. The stench of aviation fumes and the high-pitched whine of jet turbines filled the hangar. Vance paced across the floor past the business jet and tilt rotor.

Flash and Chua jogged after him.

The Pain Train faced the hangar doors; a sliding false-rock wall that had yet to be retracted. The aircraft's ramp was up but the side door was open. Mitch Freeman, PRIMAL's tech guru and lead pilot stood in the opening under the vulture-like wings. "What's up?" he yelled over the engines in his British accent. "We've got a twenty minute window to get airborne or we're going to have to wait for the next satellite pass." PRIMAL monitored satellite traffic over the region to ensure their aircraft were not compromised.

Vance climbed up into the transporter as Mitch retreated inside. Chua and Flash followed. In the back of the jet the

Critical Assault Team sat on the fold-down side seating with their equipment bags strapped to the floor. The four operators, Mirza, Kruger, Pavel, and Miklos, were ready to deploy to Africa.

Mitch ducked into the cockpit, the engine noise dropped to a soft whine, and he reappeared.

"What's going on, Vance?" asked Mirza, a former Indian special forces soldier and the leader of the CAT.

"Flash just informed me that a rendition for Wesley Chambers has been added to the contracting network." The PRIMAL team had already been briefed on the new threat. "And it's looking increasingly likely that it's a CIA system."

The grim expression on everyone's face confirmed they understood the severity of the problem.

Vance continued, "I know some of you worked with Wesley and feel like we owe him. We need to remember that our policy regarding the CIA has always been to avoid confrontation where possible." The statement had extra weight coming from Vance; he was a former CIA paramilitary officer. "Additionally, we're fully committed to ensuring the safety of Saneh. That's our priority."

"We have to go and get him," said Mirza. "If we don't it goes against everything we stand for."

"I agree," said Chua. "And, from a counter-intel perspective, Wesley has been exposed to a number of us. We can't afford for him to be interrogated."

"Alright, it's settled. We'll split the team. Mirza, can the CAT do without you?" Since losing two pilots in Ukraine Mirza was the only other PRIMAL operative qualified to fly all their aircraft.

Mirza glanced at Kruger who nodded. "They'll be fine. And they'll have Bishop. Where are we going?"

"New Zealand, grab your bags."

Vance left through the side door with Chua, Flash, and Mirza in tow. As he strode back to the elevator Chua caught up with him.

"You want me to come too?"

He shook his head. "No, I need you to run the Bunker and find out exactly what we're up against. I've got no doubt someone in the CIA is responsible for Redemption and has us on their radar. I want to know who that someone is and I want to know who else is exposed to it."

"Copy, we'll know more once Bishop and Saneh finish their op."

Behind them the rumble of the huge false-rock sliding doors announced the imminent departure of the Pain Train. The pitch of the engines increased in ferocity forcing them to cover their ears. The transporter lumbered forward into the old rusted hangar that hid the entrance to PRIMAL's lair.

"I've got a bad feeling about this," said Vance as the doors shut with a thundering boom.

"We're ahead of the curve," said Chua. "At least we've got some insight into the Redemption system and now we can stay one step ahead."

Vance grunted. "I hope you're right, buddy."

CHAPTER 5

POLOKWANE, SOUTH AFRICA

One of the good things about Africa, thought Bishop, as he stood alongside a recently hired white Pajero four-wheel drive, was the wide-open space. It made constructing airfields easy and as a result every town had one. Of course finding one that was capable of taking a hundred-ton four-engine behemoth was more of a challenge. Fortunately, they'd located a suitable dirt strip in a nature reserve only an hour's drive from Polokwane. He and Saneh had enjoyed a relaxing breakfast before driving out to meet the team.

"There she is," said Saneh from where she waited in the shade of a baobab tree.

Bishop squinted in the direction she pointed. "You've got eyes like a hawk." He still couldn't see the jet. He focused on the sky directly above the end of the eight hundred yard packed earth strip. Finally he spotted it, a tiny speck that grew larger by the second. He walked across to Saneh and placed his hands around her waist. Pulling her in close he locked eyes with her. "You sure about this?"

She nodded, leant in, and kissed him softly. "Stop being over protective. This is what we do, Aden."

The roar of the Pain Train's engines caught their attention. Dust spiraled out behind the jet as it touched down on the red earth. It screamed as the thrust reversed and the nose dipped almost as if bowing in acknowledgment of its impressive landing. Bishop and Saneh shielded their eyes as a cloud of dust rolled over them. Once it dissipated they were confronted by the presence of the hulking airframe an arms length away.

The side door slid open as they walked toward it.

"*Guten Morgen*," said Kurtz as he lowered the steps. The tall German was still recovering from being tortured by CIA contractors. Unable to join the rest of the team in the field and previously qualified as a light aircraft pilot, Mitch was now training him to fly the Pain Train.

Bishop grasped his shoulder as he followed Saneh into the aircraft. "You're looking well, mate."

Kurtz flashed a smile and pointed to his near perfect row of teeth. "Compliments of Tariq, *ja*." A series of medical treatments in the UAE had included extensive dental reconstruction.

Saneh and Bishop greeted the other members of the team in the cargo hold of the aircraft. Kruger handed Bishop a large kit bag. "Good to be back in Africa, big man?" asked Bishop.

"*Ja, ja*, good to be out of the damn jungle," said Kruger. "I thought I'd never see the bush again."

"Well for the time being you're going to have to stay airborne. The plan is I'll follow Saneh on the ground after the drop off. You guys stay airborne and track her. Once we go firm I'll identify a drop zone and you jump in. That way we stay flexible in case I lose her." Bishop glanced around. "Where's Mirza?"

Mitch's bearded face appeared from the cockpit. "He got called off for another task, mate. Heading to New Zealand with Vance to find Wesley Chambers. The banker popped up on the Redemption Network."

"They found him?" asked Saneh.

Mitch nodded as he shook Bishop's hand and gave her a hug.

Bishop unzipped his kit bag and checked the contents. It contained his armor, Tavor assault rifle, pistol belt, and helmet. "We need to get moving on this. Could be our only chance to track these pricks back to the source."

"We're all good to go," said Mitch.

"I want to modify your plan slightly, though," said Kruger. "I think Pavel should travel with you on the ground. Miklos and I can maintain the airborne contingency."

Bishop nodded. "Works for me." He turned to Mitch. "Do you have the tracking gear?"

"As requested." Mitch placed a grey backpack on the floor and opened it. He took out a cell phone and passed it to Bishop. "Hand this over with Saneh. They can take out the battery but it will still transmit a signal. They'll want to keep it with her for exploitation. There's also a transmitter hidden in the backpack."

"And if they don't keep the gear with her?"

Mitch took out a capsule and passed it to Saneh. "This is our backup."

She held up the half-inch cylinder and frowned. "You want me to swallow this?"

"Yes, it's only got a range of a few hundred yards but it might mean the difference between finding you and..."

"OK, got it." Saneh tipped back her head and swallowed the microtransponder.

Mitch handed Bishop a credit card-sized device. "This clips onto your iPRIMAL. It's more accurate than the sensors on the Pain Train but you'll have get within a hundred yards."

"OK, the plan's solid. I'll contact Flash and let him know we're good to go. The RV is an hour away, up on the border near Musina. How are you for fuel?"

"We refueled in Johannesburg and apart from big oaf Kruger we've got bugger-all weight onboard. I can give you just under nine hours of endurance."

"Excellent." Bishop glanced around at the team. "Let's get this show on the road."

***

MUSINA, SOUTH AFRICA

Musina wasn't much to look at. A mining town with a population around 20,000, it was a mix of seedy hotels and truck stops surrounded by sparse scrubland. Situated near the border of South Africa and Zimbabwe, the highway that dissected the town was busy with sixteen-wheelers transporting goods between the two countries.

"Nice part of the world," Bishop said dryly as he drove through the center of town.

"It's sad," replied Pavel in his Russian accent. "So flat and hot. Even the shops are dying."

Bishop had to agree. There were very few people on the streets. Probably because it was mid-afternoon and hotter than hell itself, he thought. Roller shutters secured many shop fronts, some covered in graffiti.

Saneh didn't get an opportunity to see the town. She was bound hand and foot in the trunk.

Bishop activated his iPRIMAL, modified with Mitch's receiver module. "Pain Train, this is Bishop. Can you confirm that the transponders are working?"

"Roger, no change from the last three tests. The gear is working perfectly. Stop getting wound up, mate," replied Mitch from the Pain Train.

Easy for you to say, thought Bishop. You're not the one putting the love of your life in danger. "No problems." His hands were clammy on the steering wheel of the Pajero. He tried to convince himself it was because of the heat not his nerves.

"We're near the RV," said Pavel as they passed a gas station.

"OK, keep an eye out for the yellow sign." The instructions gleaned from the Redemption website had been very specific. They were looking for an abandoned motel three miles out of town.

As they left the town center Bishop was surprised to see a newly constructed gated community of brick homes. It was probably where the miners and their families lived. The wealth didn't seem to be trickling down to the rest of the community.

"I think this is it," said Pavel as they approached a line of shabby brown buildings on the side of the road.

Bishop signaled and pulled off the tarmac onto the gravel. A tall sign covered in peeling yellow paint proclaimed that they had arrived at the Sunshine Motor Inn.

"I'll stick to the Novotel," said Bishop. "Saneh, we've arrived. Standby."

A noise from the trunk acknowledged him.

Bishop felt sick in his stomach as he spotted another vehicle. Three shorthaired athletic-looking men stood alongside a grey Toyota Land Cruiser with dark tinted windows. He reached down and checked that the Beretta was on his hip as he parked a dozen yards away. Turning the engine off he opened the door and stepped out into the heat.

"Which one of you is Derick?" he asked in a convincing South African accent.

A tall, blonde man with a square jaw stepped forward. "*Ja*, that's me. You Hunter?"

Bishop nodded. "I've got a package for you in the trunk. I just need to confirm your order number."

The man read a number from the back of his hand and Bishop checked it against the one from the Redemption site. "All in order. I'll drive over so you can transfer her."

He climbed back in the Pajero, drove past the Toyota, and reversed until the rear of the two vehicles faced each other. He climbed out and opened the trunk. "Bit hot, yeah."

Derick nodded as he looked over Saneh, who was zip-tied and gagged. She appeared unconscious. "Give you any trouble?"

He shook his head. "No, I gave her a mild sedative. She should come-to soon." He handed Derick a bag. "This is all she had when I grabbed her."

"OK, good."

He fought the instinct to lash out and kill the men as they lifted Saneh into the back of their vehicle. They slammed the trunk shut and the tinted windows blocked her from view.

"OK, bro, might see you round some time," said Derick.

Bishop shook his hand and watched as the interrogation team jumped in the Land Cruiser and drove onto the main road. The four-wheel drive headed north toward Zimbabwe.

"Pain Train, this is Bishop, transfer complete. Please confirm you have eyes on and beacons are live," he transmitted.

A moment later Mitch responded. "Roger, we have eyes on and beacons are pinging loud and clear."

"Acknowledged, we'll give them ten minutes head start."

"Roger, Pain Train out."

"So, it's all going to plan," said Pavel when Bishop climbed back in the driver's seat.

The Russian's attempt to reassure him didn't help. Bishop started the engine. "OK, let's go."

"You said ten minutes."

"Fine, we'll head back to the gas station and wait there."

***

GWANDA, ZIMBABWE

Bishop pulled the Mitsubishi over and killed the headlights. It was an hour after nightfall and he and Pavel had been tailing the grey Land Cruiser across Zimbabwe for almost two hours. They had crossed the border twenty minutes after their quarry. A wad of cash and false passports secured passage with no questions asked, and more importantly, no vehicle search. From there it had been a case of tracking the Land Cruiser using the camera feed being relayed from the Pain Train.

When they reached the outskirts of Gwanda things had gone awry. The Land Cruiser had driven through the central built-up area and out into a sprawling township. As it weaved between the tin-roofed shacks and derelict buildings the Pain Train had lost visual and was now relying on the transponders. The problem was accuracy; from the air they could narrow the search to a few hundred yards but within the shantytown that could include dozens of makeshift dwellings and hundreds if not thousands of people.

"Bish, if we leave the car here someone is going to steal it," said Pavel. The transponders had stopped moving; Saneh wasn't far away.

"OK, you stay with the car and locate a drop zone on the far side. I'll go forward for a recce." They were parked at the edge of the slum. He wanted to avoid the sort of attention that a new vehicle would attract. They could see locals in the distance clustered under the streetlights along the main road.

"Bishop, this is Pain Train, we're launching a Seeker," Mitch's voice crackled over his earpiece. The Seeker was a fixed-wing drone with a high-resolution camera and tracking sensors. Stealthy and silent, it could fly close to the target without revealing the presence of the transport aircraft.

"Acknowledged, I'm going in on foot. Pavel will stay mobile on the outskirts and ID a suitable DZ." Bishop strapped his iPRIMAL to his wrist, checking Mitch's receiver module was active. He jumped out of the car, opened the trunk, and unzipped a gear bag. Stripping two spare pistol magazines from the armor he slid them in the pockets of his jeans. He donned a hoodie from his backpack and pulled it over his holstered Beretta.

"You need backup, just call," said Pavel as he strapped on his armor, racked his Tavor assault rifle, and slid into the driver's seat.

"Should be fine, brother. I'll scope out the location and meet you on the other side."

Bishop scrambled down the bank of an irrigation ditch. Slipping back the sleeve of the hoodie he accessed the menu for the tracker. He set up an audio warning, so his earpiece would let him know when he was getting closer.

As he climbed the other side of the trash-filled ditch he swallowed, his mouth dry. He wasn't afraid for himself; he was terrified something would happen to Saneh.

Pulling the hood low over his face he hunched and walked along the side of the dusty main street. He was grateful that half the streetlights were blown. It helped hide what was probably the only white face in the township.

A group of teenage youths were chatting boisterously in front of a dilapidated corner store. They drank from a single plastic bottle and eyeballed him as he walked past on the opposite side of the street. He should have packed a can of pepper spray, he thought. Glancing over his shoulder he was relieved to see they'd lost interest in him and returned to their conversation.

He hadn't walked another dozen yards when a dog launched itself at a tall metal gate. Jumping backward he stumbled on the curb and almost fell. "Get your shit together," he whispered as he steadied himself and continued walking down the street. A soft beep in his ear reminded him that Saneh and the interrogation team was close by.

"Bishop, we've got a hit from the drone. You need to take the next left," Mitch's voice came through in his earpiece.

"Roger," he whispered.

The turn that Mitch instructed him to take led down a dark narrow alley with sheet iron shacks on either side. It stank of urine. He gagged as he paused, letting his eyes adjust to the gloom. It was the perfect place for an ambush. Exhaling he touched the butt of his pistol and stepped off into the darkness. The only other reassurance was the constant beep in his ear that told him Saneh was close.

A hundred yards down the lane he reached a street where a cluster of run-down commercial properties rose above the makeshift shacks. Bishop checked the receiver app on his iPRIMAL. Saneh's transponder was pinging from the direction of an old two-story warehouse. A wire fence surrounded the building and curtains covered the windows on the second floor. "I've got eyes on, Mitch. Two-story warehouse. Cinder-block construction. Eight-foot mesh fence with razor wire." The beep in his ear increased in tempo with every step.

"That's it. You need to get back to Pavel. Kruger and the boys are inbound."

***

Saneh hoped that the façade of fear she had created was believable. So far Derick and his two associates hadn't shown any signs of suspicion. Once they'd parked the Land Cruiser inside the empty warehouse she had been taken upstairs into a small windowless room and strapped to a chair. The tape had been gently removed from her mouth and she'd been offered water.

Without a doubt they were professionals. That in itself was intimidating, however, it also gave her some confidence that they wouldn't employ any of the violent torture techniques commonly portrayed by Hollywood. Yes they created pain and looked spectacular but they rarely produced reliable results in a situation like this.

Her main concern was that her cobbled together disguise held out for at least another half hour. Her hair was dyed a deep red to match the journalist's. Contacts changed the color of her eyes and, much to Bishop's chagrin, a bruised cheek, self-inflicted, drew the attention from her more angular features. Christina was slightly shorter but she didn't think that would matter. The biggest issue was the rose tattoo on her neck. Bishop had found a tattoo parlor in Polokwane but with only a few hours to draw a semi-permanent copy it was, how did he put it, shoddy.

She looked around the bare dusty room. Two cameras had been bolted to the ceiling at opposite corners with cables taped to the walls. There were no windows and the only furniture was two cheap plastic seats. She sat on one and across from her Derick sat on the other smoking a cigarette.

"You sure you don't want a smoke?" he said offering her one.

She shook her head.

He shrugged and put the cigarette away. "I've got lots of questions for you, Miss Munoz," he said in a thick Afrikaans accent.

"Who are you?" she whimpered.

"No, I don't think you've quite got it. I'm the one asking the questions. How about you tell me everything you know about Aden."

"I don't know any Aden."

"Come now, Christina, we both know that's a lie. You were down in Mexico with him and his pack of merry men." He dropped the cigarette butt and ground it into the floor. "Now listen up, Miss Munoz. You need to be very honest with me and answer all my questions. If you do I can help you. I can tell the people I work for that you were very helpful and maybe they will go easy on you. They may even pay you for your time and let me take you back to your friends at Kruger."

Saneh sighed and pretended to consider the offer. Derick was smart; giving her a way out before he threatened her. He had offered her the carrot. Now she waited for the stick.

"But, if you don't help me, I can't help you. They will take you from here to a place where you don't want to go. A place filled with pain and suffering. They will make you talk and they will use anything to achieve that. They will take away your sleep, they'll take away your food, and they'll hurt you. They'll shock you with electricity and half drown you." He leant in close so she could smell the stench of cigarettes on his breath. "They'll rape you."

Saneh had no doubt that he was telling the truth. However, if everything went to plan she would not be hanging around that long. All she needed to do was fabricate a story that would keep Derick amused for the next twenty minutes or so. She took a deep breath. "OK. I will tell you what I know."

Derick smiled, flashing his nicotine-stained teeth. "Go on."

"Let me start from the beginning. In New York…"

PRIMAL REDEMPTION

CHAPTER 6

THE PAIN TRAIN

Mitch hunched over the Pain Train's sensors and weapons terminal, located behind the cockpit. The little alcove was the control node for the aircraft's sophisticated array of cameras, electromagnetic receivers, drones, and precision munitions. He played the bank of laptops like a maestro on a piano. One screen showed the feed being transmitted from the Seeker drone; another displayed a map of the town below. A chess piece icon showed Bishop's location and a rapidly shrinking bubble indicated Saneh's probable position.

"Kurtz, how are you doing, mate?" he asked as he checked the outputs from the aircraft's electronic warfare package. The sensors were sniffing the sky for communication transmissions in their search area.

"Autopilot is working fine." The lanky German sat in the copilot's seat monitoring the aircraft's automated systems. Mitch had retrofitted the jet so a crew of two could comfortably fly it.

"OK, we're looking pretty good here. Bishop has a solid fix on Saneh and I'm sending in the drone for a closer recce of the building." Mitch felt a hand on his shoulder and glanced up at the big South African, Kruger.

"How's it, bro?" In his black carbon-nanotube armor the assaulter was an imposing sight, even without his full-face helmet.

"You're going to want to see this." He angled the infrared camera on the drone at the building where Saneh's transponders were pinging. As the UAV circled, it beamed back an oblique shot that revealed the structure was two stories high and surrounded by a wire fence. "Bishop's confirmed this warehouse is the objective. It's cinder-block construction, windows on the top floor, with an eight-foot wire mesh fence."

65

"Got it. We're going to need to breach, *ja*," said Kruger. "Have we got a drop zone yet?"

Mitch pointed to an open area a few hundred yards to the north. "Here." He panned the camera in the nose of the Pain Train so they could see where the Pajero was parked. "Pavel is ready and waiting. Bishop is returning to his location now."

"Good, let's get on the ground, get Saneh back, and find out what these assholes know."

"Sounds like a plan." Mitch jumped out of the chair. Leaving Kruger, he ducked into the cockpit. "Kurtz, can you control the drone and check on Bishop? I'm going to bring us around for the drop."

Kurtz left the cockpit and replaced him at the sensors terminal.

He strapped into the pilot's seat, flicked off the autopilot, and took positive control. "OK, Kruger, Miklos, you ready back there?" he asked into his headset mike.

"Let's do this," Kruger confirmed.

"OK, here we go. Coming in on our final run." Mitch banked the massive transporter. As he leveled out he hit the control for the ramp. The big jet shuddered as the additional drag slowed their airspeed. "Thirty seconds." He monitored the navigation system. "On my mark… GO, GO, GO!" He glanced at the screen for the cargo bay camera and watched as two black figures disappeared into the night sky.

He closed the ramp and reprogrammed the autopilot. The computer would gain altitude and hold the jet in a highly fuel-efficient circuit at 40,000 feet. At that altitude they would remain undetected to anyone on the ground. He joined Kurtz in front of the sensors and weapons alcove. "All call signs, this is Pain Train, we are on-station and monitoring. Pavel, ETA of air deployable assets in your location is four minutes."

"Roger," replied the Russian.

Mitch glanced over Kurtz's shoulder at the feed from the drone. "Here's trouble." The fixed-wing UAV's camera was slaved to Bishop's iPRIMAL, tracking his movement through the slum. "Bish, you've got three possible hostiles on your six and two more at your twelve. I recommend you take evasive action."

"I'm on it," Bishop's voice came through at a whisper.

"Do you want me to bring the drone in closer?" asked Kurtz.

"Yeah, worse case scenario you can use it to scare Bishop's new friends."

***

GWANDA, ZIMBABWE

Bishop drew his compact Beretta and held it in the pocket of his hoodie. The three men following him had probably caught a glimpse of his white face and now, like hyenas, they were circling for the kill. They might have thought he was a junkie trying to get a hit or perhaps looking for a cheap hooker. Bishop didn't really care if they got between him and recovering Saneh; firing his Beretta was unlikely to compromise the mission. Life was cheap in the townships and he assumed gunshots were commonplace.

"Bish," Mitch's voice came through in his earpiece. "There's a side alley just ahead, it should get you around the other guys in front of you."

"OK," Bishop said as he saw another four men ahead. They were clustered in the dark shadow cast by a two-story shack.

Behind, a voice called out, "Hey white boy, why you running away, man? We just want to talk."

The situation took Bishop back to one of his first experiences in Africa. As UN Peacekeepers in Sierra Leone, he and Mirza had gone head to head with a gang of drugged-up rebel fighters. He turned down the side alley and had only taken a few steps when more men shuffled out from the shacks and blocked his way. A dog snarled and yellow eyes glared from the darkness. "Shit!"

Backing out of the alley he turned to face the two men following him. Both were tall and lean, with ebony skin. One held a baseball bat against his shoulder and the other wielded a long bush knife. He pulled his pistol from the hoodie, aiming it from the hip.

"You a big boss man, are you?" one of them leered, unperturbed by the weapon. "Going to shoot us all with your pop gun?"

Bishop glanced around. There were now half a dozen approaching from all sides.

Facing the armed men he whispered, "Mitch, what have you got?"

"Standby."

There was a strange noise behind him and he spun in time to see a black-clad figure drop from the night sky. A parachute flapped from where it was snagged on the power lines.

"Batman's here," Kruger snarled as he released the chute.

The armed hoodlums dropped their weapons and fled. The other men stared at the dark helmeted figure then scattered.

Bishop couldn't blame them; in full CAT rig Kruger looked like a total bad-ass. The South African strode toward him, his compact Tavor assault rifle held ready.

"Nice landing."

"I nearly hit the fucking power lines." His voice was metallic through the helmet's ventilation system. "Scared the shit out of those punks though."

"I owe you big time."

"Follow me. We need to move fast. One of those scumbags could be an informant." Kruger led him down a side alley.

A minute later they reached a wider street. Pavel was waiting in the SUV with Miklos. Both were suited-up and Miklos was loading grey tear gas rounds into a six-shot grenade launcher.

Climbing in the back, Bishop threw on his armor. Pulling off his covert communications earpiece and mike he snapped his fully-enclosed helmet in place, donned a pair of gloves, and racked his Tavor. "What's the assault plan?"

Kruger held up a breaching charge. "Knock, knock!"

"Who's there?"

"Fucking Batman. We breach the fence quietly, blast through the door, roll gas heavy, thermal on, fight till we find her, and then exploit."

Bishop gave the black knight a nod. "Sounds good. Let's rock'n roll."

***

Derick left the girl in the makeshift detention cell and joined the others next door. They had setup the former office as an observation room. Two laptops on a table recorded the feeds from the CCTV cameras and microphones that had been installed in the interrogation room. "What do you think?" he asked.

"She's feeding us total shit," replied one of the men, tall and middle-aged, with cold grey eyes.

"*Ja*, she's had training, been coached," said the other, a shorter man with a thick black beard. "Give me five minutes in there with a hot iron and I'll make that bitch talk."

Derick shook his head. "No, the instructions were clear, she's not to be harmed. We've got eight hours before we hand her off. She needs to stay in one piece."

The guy with the beard bit his lower lip. "Derick, bro, there's an extra hundred grand if we get her to spill the beans. That's twice what we're getting for delivery."

"Hey, she talked. It's not our fault it's all crap."

"What if she's not the right person?" said the older man.

Black beard shook his head. "The other guy wouldn't have dumped the wrong chick on us." He pointed at the screen. "It's her, she matches the photo, got the rose tattoo and everything."

Derick sat in front of one of the laptops. "Hang on." He opened the target pack they'd been provided through the contracting website. He studied the photo of Christina, then pulled up an image of their captive. At first glance they looked to be the same person but something wasn't right.

The photo they had of Christina Munoz only showed a glimpse of the rose tattoo on her neck. He frowned. On closer inspection it looked slightly different from the tattoo on their captive. "Gents, I think we've been fucked."

He opened the chat window on the contracting site and checked to see if the contact that had posted the job was online. He was, some guy called Slayer. He wrote him a message.

Have concerns that detainee is not Munoz.

He hit enter and waited for a reply. It came a moment later.

Send photo.

Derick dragged an image taken earlier to the chat window. It transmitted and a moment later a response came through.

Not her. Enhanced interrogation techniques authorized. Find out who this woman is and what she knows.

Derick let out a low whistle. "Well, looks like you're going to get a chance to use that hot iron after all." At that moment the lights flickered and the room was plunged into darkness except for the soft glow of the laptop screens. "Bloody Zimbabwe. Someone get the generator going."

All three men felt the floor shudder followed by a muffled explosion. A window shattered as something punched through the curtain and bounced across the floor. A loud hissing emitted from the corner of the room.

"Gas! Someone's breached the lower level!" Derick yelled as he drew his pistol.

***

The breaching charge tore the heavy steel warehouse door completely off its rails. Kruger tossed a tear gas grenade through the opening and stormed in after it. As the gas billowed his helmet's thermal sensors came online, giving him near perfect vision. The ground floor of the building was empty except for a parked Land Cruiser. In the back corner a staircase led up to the next level. "Going deep," transmitted Kruger as he followed the right hand wall toward the stairs.

"With you," responded Pavel.

They moved as a pair with suppressed Tavor assault rifles held ready. Lasers on the weapons were superimposed in their helmets. They heard a number of dull thuds from outside; Miklos firing more gas into the upper level.

Reaching the staircase Kruger lobbed another grenade into the upper level for good measure. He waited for the gas to billow before pacing slowly upward. He was confronted with shouting and coughing from further back in the building. With Pavel at his shoulder he crested the staircase and scanned the next floor.

Shots rang out and a bullet ricocheted off the wall above his head. He spotted a heat signature through the thick gas. The figure held a pistol. His Tavor spat twice and the target dropped. The dead hostile lay at the far end of a main corridor with rooms on each side.

"Tango down. Moving," said Kruger. He rolled through the building like death, sweeping along the corridor. With Pavel beside him they cleared the first set of rooms. He glanced back. Bishop and Miklos were right behind them.

From the far end he could hear more coughing and spluttering. Two doors down a tall man tried to raise a submachine gun as he entered a room. Kruger left him dead on the floor with a third eye. He stormed back out, past Bishop, and into the next room.

Moving smoothly through the unlocked door he spotted a female figure kneeling with a chair tied to her back. She had a male figure pinned to the floor by his arm. Kruger caught a glimpse of a pistol being raised and he fired a shot into the man's head.

"What took you boys so long?" spluttered Saneh as she rocked back on the chair. "And what's with all the gas?"

Kruger fired two more shots into the body. "We stopped off for Mexican," he said as he cleared the room. "Building secure. Pavel, standby for evac. Miklos, grab anything that might be of intel value."

Bishop dashed to Saneh's side. Kruger watched as he slipped a mask over her face, placed the oxygen bottle in her lap, and cut the zip-ties attaching her to the chair.

"Hey, keep your eyes closed. Are you injured?" asked the Australian.

"I'm fine." She shook her head and he directed her toward the door. She stopped once to cough before they disappeared through the gas.

Kruger retrieved a phone and wallet from the corpse then pushed open the door to the next room. Miklos was stuffing two laptops into his backpack.

"That's it," the Czech said as he threw the pack over his shoulders. "There's nothing else here. I'd say this place was only set up in the last few days." He pointed at the network cable taped to the wall. "This isn't a permanent facility."

"OK, let's go."

They trotted downstairs out to where Pavel had their four-wheel drive running. They piled in as buildings along the street lit up. The little shantytown would soon be crawling with people.

"Go, go, go!" Kruger said thumping the dash.

Pavel raced the four-wheel drive along the main street and drifted it around a corner onto a dirt track.

"The airstrip is about ten minutes down the road," Kruger said.

As they raced away from the township Saneh leant against Bishop's shoulder and took steady breaths from the oxygen mask.

"How are you feeling?" asked Kruger from the front seat.

"Not too bad." She coughed. "The gas was a nice touch. What did you get off the target?"

"Two laptops and a phone."

"Well I hope it's worth it because my sinuses are screwed and this hair color is outrageous."

The cabin was filled with laughter. They bounced over a ditch and the headlights lit up a long dirt airstrip. As they sped down the runway the hulking shape of the Pain Train gradually materialized from the darkness. Kurtz stood guard under its wing with a submachine gun.

Pavel skidded the truck to a halt and they all piled out. Gear was quickly stowed inside the aircraft as they climbed inside through the side door. Kruger tossed a time-delay thermite grenade through the window of the four-wheel drive and boarded.

The hundred-ton aircraft began to roll down the dirt strip as the side door slammed shut. The engines spooled up to full throttle and a rocket pod under each wing ignited in white-hot flame. The transporter lurched forward, blasted into the air, and climbed skyward. Below in the darkness the four-wheel drive exploded in a shower of phosphorescent sparks and flames.

"This is your pilot speaking. We're tracking direct to Pretoria where we're going to refuel before heading home," Mitch transmitted over the intercom. "I suggest you get your feet up and relax with our inflight entertainment. As requested by Aden 'Romeo' Bishop, here is one of the immortal hits of the Beatles." The lyrics of 'I want to hold your hand' blasted over the speakers.

Bishop laughed as he used an eye bath to rinse the last of the tear gas from Saneh's eyes. "Let's not do anything like that again."

"Why is that?"

He shook his head. "I can't handle the stress."

She laughed. "Now you know how it feels."

***

BOSTON

It was early morning in Boston and Howard hadn't left his apartment to wander down to Starbucks for his regular coffee. He felt like crap. His eyes itched, his brain was numb, and his skin felt like it had ants crawling under it. He contemplated cracking the can of energy drink in the fridge but decided against it. As soon as he got a response from the interrogation team in Zimbabwe he would go and get a coffee.

Howard had been awake since five in the morning waiting for Derick and his men to send through the video and sound files from their interrogation. So far he had a photo of a woman resembling Christina Munoz. Someone had gone to the trouble of using a body-double and he wanted to know exactly who and why.

When Derick's chat line had gone dead he initially put it down to a bad connection. It had been unresponsive for over thirty minutes now. He picked up his cell phone and used the secure app to call the number linked to the South African's profile. The call rang out.

He checked the profile of Hunter, the contractor who had kidnapped the body-double. The account had been used in the last few minutes but was offline. A phone call to the number also went unanswered.

Howard leant back in his chair and reviewed the facts. Someone had replaced Christina Munoz with a body-double and two of the contractors involved in the rendition of that individual were now out of contact. However, one of their accounts had recently been accessed. "Oh shit!" He grabbed his phone again and called Larkin.

***

LANGLEY

Thomas Larkin rarely used his office in the CIA complex at Langley. His pretty assistant, Marlene, usually took messages and forwarded them. In fact he spent more time in his company jet than any fixed location. It was part and parcel of managing the specialized contracted solutions delivered to the National Clandestine Service.

Larkin was thankful that his responsibilities didn't include the numerous day-to-day contracts that kept the CIA running. A department of accountants and pencil pushers handled that side of the business. As Director of the Operational Support Program, or OSP, Larkin had a much more sensitive role. He provided the deniable contracted capabilities directly to his boss, the Director of the National Clandestine Service. The NCS director controlled all of the CIA's covert collection and action operations. With tightening manpower constraints he was increasingly dependent on Larkin's services.

When the phone rang Larkin happened to be in his office at Langley. He'd been scheduled to attend a meeting with his boss and was in the middle of reviewing his presentation. Glancing at the phone he saw it was Howard and hit the speaker button. "Terrance, how's the op going?"

"Dude, we've got a problem. I think the network's been compromised."

He stopped looking at his computer screen and picked up the handset. "Come again?"

"Someone's accessing the network. It's probably Major League."

"Not possible. Redemption is secure, there's no way they could have gotten inside."

"Christina was replaced with a body-double and both the contractors have been taken down. I can't reach either of them but one of their accounts has been online. You need to lock it out, ASAP."

"If they've got his logon they've only got access to the tasking tool. I'll have the contracting front-end purged." Larkin clenched his fist and slammed it down on his desk. The program had only recently gone live and now was in jeopardy. He couldn't risk the possibility of his other contracts being compromised.

"At least there was only one other op running. The Queenstown job against Wesley... Oh shit!"

"Oh shit is right. I've got to go." Larkin terminated the call and dialed Charles King. The GES boss answered immediately. "When are you going to be in Queenstown?"

"We just landed."

"Right, be aware it's possible Redemption has been compromised. There's a chance that Major League knows you're moving on Wesley. You need to pick him up ASAP and transport him to a rendition site in Alaska. I'll send you the details over secure email. Until further notice all contracts will come direct from me."

"Got it. Does this have something to do with the African job? I told you my boys should have done it."

"Then they would be just as dead as the team that were compromised. Get Wesley and move him to the facility. Do not underestimate this threat."

"Maybe you should take your own advice."

Larkin terminated the call and dialed his IT technician in Dead Land. He needed to get Redemption contracting offline and purged. Once he'd that done he would focus all his resources on finding and destroying the Major League Network.

CHAPTER 7

QUEENSTOWN, NEW ZEALAND

Mirza taxied PRIMAL's Gulfstream jet off Queenstown Airport's runway and parked it in front of the private terminal. There was already a row of business jets on the apron. He wondered if one of them belonged to a CIA rendition team.

He shut down the engines as Vance lowered the stairs and stepped out. Mirza followed him into the cool embrace of an early alpine evening. He glanced up at the Remarkables mountain range that towered above them. The setting sun bathed the jagged rock face in a soft glow. "Amazing. You ever been here before?" he asked Vance as they walked across to the terminal.

"Once, a long time ago. I came here with my wife."

"I didn't know you were married."

"For a little while. She wasn't real big on the CIA."

"Right now, the feeling's mutual," quipped Mirza.

They cleared customs and picked up a hire car. Mirza punched a lat-long coordinate into the GPS and drove them out of the airport through a large industrial complex. They swept downhill toward a river and turned off onto a gravel road. A minute later he parked beside some woods directly underneath the approach to the runway.

Mirza switched off the engine and opened the door. "I'll get it." He walked into the trees, pulled out his iPRIMAL and activated a tracking app. It took him a few minutes to find the thermos-sized pod they had dropped from the jet. He handed it over as he got back in the car.

Vance punched a code into the top of the canister, twisted off the cap, and tipped it upside down. Two Glock 19 compact pistols in concealed-carry holsters and four spare magazines dropped into his lap. He secured a weapon into the waistband of his jeans and pulled the sweater down over it. The second pistol disappeared under Mirza's jacket.

Mirza drove them back to the main road and they headed toward the resort town. The traffic was heavy with tourists. A motor home was travelling at a snails pace and backing up traffic for miles as they cruised alongside the clear blue water of Lake Wakatipu.

They found a park on the outskirts and they walked toward the center of town. On their way in the sun dipped behind a distant mountain and the temperature dropped.

"Keep your eyes peeled for anyone that looks like a contractor," Vance said.

"That shouldn't be too hard." Mirza scanned the throngs of tourists wandering into town in search of somewhere warm to enjoy dinner. The crowd was a mixed bag of young adventurers, Asian tourists, and grey-haired retirees. Anyone well built with a military bearing would stand out. Unfortunately that included Vance.

"So where should we start?" the hulking African American asked.

Mirza pulled a piece of paper from his pocket as they approached a mall lined with rows of restaurants and bars bustling with patrons. "I printed off a list of the more upmarket bars in town. Wesley has money and a taste for quality beverages. He'll be at one of these."

Vance nodded. "Good old fashioned bar crawl. What's the first one on the list?"

"It's called Barmuda."

"I like that name, sounds warm. Lead the way."

Mirza took him down an alley where they found a sign marking the venue. It was a classy little establishment with an outdoor fireplace and a well-stocked bar. He glanced around at the few patrons but didn't spot Wesley.

"Where to next?" asked Vance as they left.

"There's one nearby called The Bunker."

Vance raised an eyebrow. "It would be a little ironic if we found him hiding in there."

He laughed as they walked past a mall, up a flight of stairs, and into a quiet bar. He spotted a photo of the Rat Pack on one wall and on another a print of Sean Connery as 007. This was his kind of bar.

"Evening, lads, what'll it be?" The bearded blonde bartender wore a smart vest and an easy smile. He had a stainless steel cocktail shaker in his hands that he was agitating vigorously.

"Looking for a friend," said Mirza.

"Oh yeah? Been pretty quiet tonight. What does this friend look like?"

"Tall, kind of thin, well dressed, blonde hair, used to be a banker."

The barman popped the top of the shaker and used a straw to test it. "Yeah mate, I know the guy you're looking for. Wes, right?"

Mirza nodded.

"He's in here most nights. Nice guy."

"You know where he's at?" asked Vance.

The barman poured the cocktail into a tall glass. "I'd try the Naughty Penguin if I were you. Down the stairs and to the right, you can't miss it. Once you find him you should bring him up here. I'll whip you guys up something special."

"Sounds good," said Vance.

The Naughty Penguin was exactly where the bartender described, nestled in a cobblestone back alley. It was cosy inside and there were only a few patrons. Mirza spotted Wesley sitting at the bar fixated on the petite barmaid. He pulled up the stool next to him. Vance took a seat closer to the door.

The former investment banker glanced sideways at him before turning his attention back to the barmaid. A moment later Mirza's Asiatic features registered and he swiveled back.

"Holy shit, Mirza, what are you doing here?" His words were a little slurred.

"Wes, the CIA knows you're here. You need to come with us now."

Wesley's eyes went wide. "They're going to kill me."

"Come on, let's go." Mirza placed a hand on his shoulder and directed him toward the door.

"Hey, what about his tab?" said the barmaid.

Vance tossed a hundred dollar bill on the bar. "Keep the change."

***

King had split his team into two pairs to search for Wesley. He checked the bars with Hammer, while Matt remained nearby in the SUV with Chris. With the threat from Major League he wanted the vehicle close for a quick extract or to access their automatic weapons.

He glanced at his watch. It was just after ten and the town was teeming with people heading out for a drink. He stopped and glanced down a narrow alley with a few quiet bars along one side. The street sign identified it as Cow Lane. "Hammer, have we been down here?"

Checking the tourist map he was holding, Hammer could have almost passed for an adventurer taking advantage of the region's plethora of extreme sports. He had the athletic build, tall and wiry, although his searching gaze didn't quite match the wide-eyed wonder of most of the tourists. "Not yet, there's a couple of spots here we haven't checked."

As King stepped off down the lane he noticed two men leaving a bar half way down. His hand moved to the .45 pistol concealed under his shirt as he recognized Wesley Chambers. "Hammer, that's him."

"OK, boss, let's sit tight. We don't know who that other guy is or who else is around."

King checked himself as he recognized the other man; it was the Indian investment banker he'd met at Pollard's house. The overweight businessman was now lean and moved with purpose. Major League had beaten them to it.

"We've got at least two others with him. The Indian looking guy and the big bald black guy," said Hammer as he glanced over his map. "We might be able to block them at the other end of the alley. It turns right and hits Beach Street."

A boisterous group of young backpackers spilled into the alley from another bar. King waited for them to block the view between him and his quarry before hitting transmit on his radio. "Matt, we've found them. Can you block the end of Cow Lane where it intercepts Beach Street?"

"On it," transmitted Matt.

"Be aware he's with at least two heavy hitters, an Indian and a big black guy."

King and Hammer walked through the group of intoxicated backpackers, following Wesley around the corner. They were only a dozen yards away when Matt's SUV screamed into view and screeched to a halt. King's jaw dropped as the Indian drew a pistol and dropped five rounds on the vehicle in the space of a second. The volley of shots echoed off the buildings as the black man produced his weapon almost as quickly and spun toward them. King dove behind a parked car as he went for his own piece. Tourists screamed as Hammer managed to snap off a round.

The shooting stopped and King glanced around cover in time to see the two shooters rushing Wesley inside a shop. Hammer sprinted in hot pursuit.

He ran to the shot-up SUV. Matt and Chris cautiously appeared from where they'd taken cover behind the console. They were uninjured but the windshield was bullet riddled. "Chris, with me. Matt, shadow with the car." King entered the store where Hammer was waiting.

"They've gone out the front," said the lanky operator.

Shoving tourists out of the way King charged out of the store. He caught a glimpse of the three men on the other side of the street and fired a shot. It shattered a shop front. He crossed the street scanning for threats. Out the corner of his eye he spotted Chris bolting down another street to flank the men. More shots rang out as Hammer engaged from the opposite side. Bullets thudded into the car next to him as someone returned fire.

Shrieks filled the air as tourists ran from the gunfire. King spotted the African American operator lumber around a building. He wasn't moving very fast.

Hammer charged across the road and took cover behind a parked car. "We've got them pinned, boss!"

King glanced around the corner of the building. He could see the lake where a jetty stretched out into the inky black water. Lamps lined the wharf area in a picturesque setting. Between the shadows he saw the three men running onto the jetty and taking cover behind a tourism booth.

The wail of a siren caught his attention as a police car appeared in the street near Hammer. The contractor fired a single round at the bonnet of the car and it reversed with a screech of tires. At the same time Matt parked his damaged SUV behind them.

"Chris, where are you?" King asked over the radio.

"To your left. Covering the jetty."

Excellent, he thought. They had them cornered. Time to break out the firepower.

***

"Well we're up shit creek without a paddle," said Vance between breaths as he hunkered down behind the ticket booth. "At least the cops are here."

Next to him Mirza shook his head. "Kiwi police don't carry guns."

Vance's eyebrows climbed up his forehead. "That's the dumbest thing I've ever heard."

A spray of bullets hit the booth blowing chunks of yellow wood over them. "It would seem they now have assault rifles," said Mirza.

"And you guys didn't bring any?" Wesley screamed.

Mirza ignored him and searched for a way out. His eyes fell on the yellow jet boats tied to the wharf below them.

"You think you can get one going?" Vance asked as he fired a single round in the direction of their attackers. A burst of automatic fire stitched the wood next to him and he rolled sideways.

Mirza found the door at the back of the ticket booth and blasted the lock off. Crawling inside he searched the cramped space for a key press. There was one on the wall. Another shot blew the door open and he grabbed a fist full of keys. Gunfire lashed the booth as he scrambled out and snaked down the steps onto the nose of one of the boats.

They were compact bright yellow craft with rows of benches for the passengers. At the front there was a bucket seat, steering wheel, and throttle pedal, not unlike a car. He tried one of the keys. It didn't fit.

"Anytime now would be good!" yelled Vance as he snapped off more rounds.

Mirza finally found the right key and turned the ignition. The engine turned over but didn't start.

More gunfire sounded from above. "They're closing in!" bellowed Vance.

"Come on!" Mirza turned the key again as Wesley jumped down to the boat. The engine coughed but refused to start.

"There's got to be a fuel tap." Wesley reached under the dash. "Got it, try that."

The big engine rumbled to life as Vance jumped from the wharf and landed on the front deck. He grunted and rolled into the boat.

Wesley threw off the tie lines as more shots sounded from above. Mirza stomped down on the pedal and spun the wheel.

The V8-powered jet boat roared and took off like a rocket. Mirza aimed for the green channel marker in the distance. Bullets cracked through the air as they skimmed over the glassy lake. A round sparked off a metal bar inches from Vance's head.

"Son-of-a-bitch!"

Mirza spun the boat around the flashing green channel marker and they belted across the water. "We need to get to the airport!" he yelled over the bellowing engine.

"If we keep going we'll almost run straight past it," said Wesley. "I took a jet boat ride up here last week." The banker looked behind them. "Oh shit, we've got company."

Mirza glanced over his shoulder. In the glow cast by the town's lights he caught a glimpse of another yellow boat, a few hundred yards behind them. A muzzle flashed and bullets snapped through the air.

He jinked the boat from side to side, making it a harder target. The tactic was a catch-22; as it slowed their progress allowing the other boat to catch up. The throttle pedal was already to the floor and the throaty V8 roared like a wounded animal. All it would take was one bullet to find a vital component and the chase would end. Mirza aimed the boat at the other end of the lake, held it in a straight line, and hunkered low.

"Head for those lights on the right," Wesley said pointing to an illuminated complex. "That's the Hilton. There's a bridge then the lake turns into a river. We can ditch the boat there and run up to the airport."

"Guys, I ain't gonna be running," yelled Vance over the roar of the engine. "I fuckcd my ankle."

As the lights grew in intensity Mirza could see the bridge. He glanced over his shoulder; the other boat was barely visible but still on their tail.

"Stay left and watch out for the rocks," yelled Wesley as they sped under the bridge.

In the ambient light he could barely see the outcrops of rock in the river. He eased off on the throttle and weaved between them. More gunshots urged him on, one round striking the engine cowling. Glancing down he checked the temperature gauge. The motor was running hot. Lifting his head he spotted white water boiling over a boulder. He spun the wheel and they narrowly missed the rapids.

"We're getting away," whooped Wesley over the roar of the engine.

Mirza suppressed a grin and sent the boat blasting around a river bend.

"Up ahead we need to go left up the other river. There's a bridge where we can ditch the boat and head to the airport on foot."

He nodded, looking for the turn. They swept around another bend and he spotted the other river. Easing off the pedal, he searched for a way through the rocks.

"There!" Wesley spotted the fast moving flow that had carved a channel.

Mirza angled the boat through the gap as their pursuers approached the fork behind them. He accelerated as Vance fired off the last of his magazine at the bright yellow craft. He must have spooked the driver as the other boat overshot the turn and was forced to double back.

Wesley stood gripping the rail, searching for submerged rocks. "Once we're under the bridge bring us into the bank." The banker's blonde hair streamed in the wind and he wore a broad grin.

He's enjoying this, thought Mirza. As they approached the bridge he glanced over his shoulder. The other boat was nowhere to be seen.

A crack sounded and a round punched through the bow just inches in front of Mirza. He spun the wheel as more rounds impacted. "Shooter on the bridge!"

Wesley cried out and toppled overboard as Mirza wrenched the steering wheel again. More shots rang out until they found cover under the span.

He eased off the throttle and handed his pistol to Vance. "I'm going to take us back for Wes." The roar of another engine filled the air. The other boat appeared out of the darkness. Rounds snapped overhead and Mirza stomped on the accelerator. They blasted out from under the bridge with Vance laying down suppressing fire, emptying the last fifteen-round magazine. There were no return shots as they escaped up river and around a sweeping bend.

"Goddamn it!" Vance punched one of the padded seats.

Mirza was silent as he brought the boat in under a willow that hung over the bank. He knew the contractors wouldn't give chase. They had their prize. He killed the engine as the boat's hull slid up the bank. "That confirms GES is still after us."

Vance stepped out of the boat and limped up the riverbank. "You recognize one of those guys?"

"Yeah, I'm almost certain I saw Charles King."

"Motherfucker."

He offered Vance a shoulder. "Come on, we need to find somewhere to lay low till we can get to the airport. We better ditch the pistols as well."

"Should have topped King in Venezuela." Vance winced as he hobbled up the bank.

"Can't dwell on the past, Vance. We need to focus on defeating our enemies by outmaneuvering them."

"Thanks for the tip, Sun Tzu."

***

Wesley cried out as he was dragged from the water and dumped into the boat.

"Shut the hell up," snarled King.

"Charles, thank God you rescued me," he whimpered cradling an arm drenched in blood. "They're animals—"

King hit the banker with a savage punch knocking him out. He turned to Hammer. "Get a tourniquet on his arm."

"Boss, we going to chase those punks?" asked Chris from behind the wheel.

"No, we've got what we came for and there could be more of them. Head for the riverbank." He pressed the transmit button on his radio. "Matt, you there?"

"Yeah, moving back to the car now."

"Good shooting, son. Meet us two hundred yards from the bridge on the western bank."

"You got it."

As the boat reached the gravel bank King jumped over the side. He heaved Wesley's unconscious form onto his shoulder and carried him to the road. Headlights flashed and he made a beeline for the SUV. Matt had already opened the trunk door and helped load the unconscious body into the back.

"Airport's shut down for the night," said Matt as he slammed the trunk.

King jumped in the passenger seat as the others piled in. "I don't give a shit, we're leaving. Hammer, call the pilot and tell him to start up."

"Copy."

As they sped along the road King phoned Larkin. "We've got the target, we'll exfil immediately."

"Good, I've emailed you the coordinates for my rendition facility. You can refuel in Hickam. You and your team will be staying with the detainee."

"For how long?"

"As long as I need you to. You wanted to play a role in the destruction of Major League, this is your chance."

King paused. "They were here with Wesley."

"Did you kill them?"

"No, they got away. Things are going to get pretty hot here soon, otherwise we could stay and hunt them down."

"Clearly Wesley means something to them. He's the priority. Call me when you're at the facility." Larkin hung up.

King checked his phone as they drove toward the airport. He opened a secure email from Larkin and scanned the contents. It contained a set of coordinates.

"Boss, how are we going to handle this?" asked Matt as he approached the private terminal at the airport. The gate was shut and all the lights were off.

"Hammer, can you open it?"

"That depends, boss."

"On what?"

"On how loud you want to go."

King looked across at their jet. In the headlights he could see the turbines were turning and they emitted a faint whine. "Get it open."

Hammer jumped out with his AR carbine and fired ten rounds into the locking mechanism. He grabbed the heavy sliding gate and wrenched it sideways. An alarm wailed as he shoved it open. When the gap was wide enough to slip through he gave a thumbs-up.

Wesley had regained consciousness so King dragged him from the trunk, buried his pistol between the traitor's shoulder blades, and shoved him through the gap. The others grabbed their gear and jogged toward the waiting jet. Hammer followed up at the rear.

A siren wailed and lights flashed as a police car screamed up to the gates and screeched to a halt. As King shoved Wesley up the stairs to the business jet Hammer gave the cop car the remainder of the magazine from his carbine. Jumping inside the jet, he raised the door shut.

"Let's get the hell out of here!" King yelled at the pilot.

He didn't have to be told twice. The jet avoided the other parked aircraft and rolled onto the taxiway. Rather than use the full length of tarmac the pilot pushed the throttle to the stops and they roared down the runway, leaping into the air within five hundred yards.

In a matter of minutes they reached cruising altitude on a heading toward Hawaii. From his mission planning King knew there was zero chance of being intercepted. The tiny New Zealand Air Force consisted of only transporters and utility helicopters.

"Outstanding job, boys," he gave Hammer a slap on the shoulder.

"Good enough for a bonus?" asked Matt.

"That's up to our new master." He turned to their captive sitting next to him. The former-banker's clothes were soaked and he was shivering. Wet hair was plastered to his head, his right sleeve was bloodstained and constricted with a tourniquet, and his cheekbone had begun to swell. King reached for a blanket from an overhead locker and tossed it to him. "Now Wesley, we're going to patch that arm up and you're going to tell us everything you know about your buddies."

***

LASCAR ISLAND

While Vance and Mirza laid low in Queenstown, the Pain Train had landed at the island. Chua convened a working group immediately. Bishop, Saneh, and Flash joined him in the conference room at the back of the Bunker. This was where most of the organization's key decisions were made. It had a long black glass table and a bank of flat panel screens bolted to the volcanic rock walls.

"Flash, do you want to give us a quick heads up on Redemption and where we're at?" asked Chua.

"Sure." Flash tapped his tablet and the main screen turned on revealing images of the Redemption website. "So early today the contracting website shut down. I've been trying to hit it ever since but the server is offline. I think that whoever's running it worked out that we were inside and killed it."

"Hunter could have let them know," said Bishop referring to the contractor they had left alive in Africa.

"More likely they ran a security check once we foiled their attempt to kidnap Christina. No real harm done. I mean we got in and had a good look. Their security is as tight as ours so apart from an idea of how the system works I'm no closer to knowing where it's hosted or by whom."

"Vance and I concur with the assessment that Redemption is most likely a CIA project," added Chua.

"Yeah sorry, I meant specifically who is running it. The whole system is probably highly compartmented. I'd be very surprised if more than a handful of people know of its existence."

"Is there more to it than just a non-attributable contracting interface?" asked Bishop.

"Yeah, there seems to be some kind of intel functionality that feeds the contracts but I couldn't get into it."

"This has to be off the books," said Bishop. "With all the heat the Agency has been getting over interrogation and exploitation of social media, there's no way they would officially authorize the rendition of two US citizens."

Chua nodded. "I concur."

"So did we actually get anything useful out of Zimbabwe?" Saneh asked. Her eyes were still red from the tear gas.

"Not from the computers but it did lead us to the next link in the chain," said Flash.

"How so?" she asked.

"The phone you pulled off the job received a call literally minutes after you guys left. The other phone, the one you took from Hunter, was hit by a different number a few seconds later."

"Someone checking in on them?"

"Yeah, using both numbers I managed to trace the calls back through a series of gateways and servers to a single point of origin."

"Let me guess," said Chua. "Langley, Virginia?"

Flash shook his head. "No dude, Siargao Island in the Philippines. Whoever's running Redemption has offshored their communications router."

"To the Philippines?"

"Yeah, I looked into it and the island was part of an old NSA radio intercept network. It looks like the Philippines took it over a while back. The CIA probably has a contract with them to secure their comms gear."

"So, if we want more info that's where we need to go?" asked Bishop.

"Yeah, although we can't remote in. These guys are running pretty sophisticated firewalls. I would have to be physically in the server room to crack it."

"Sounds like a plan," said Bishop.

Flash shook his head vigorously. "Nooo, I'm not a field operative. Mitch is heaps better at that James Bond crap than me."

"You did well in Jamaica," said Chua.

"Very impressive," added Saneh with a wink. "Plus, Bishop and I will be there to look after you."

Flash sighed. "Fine, but after this no more field work. I'm a nerd. I belong behind my computer."

The laughter in the room was interrupted by a knock at the door. Frank, the watchkeeper, pushed it open. "Chen, Vance just checked in."

"Everything OK?"

"No, GES contractors got the drop on them and nabbed Wesley. Charles King was there."

The lighthearted mood in the room evaporated.

"Are they OK?"

"Yes, they're airborne and heading home. Vance wants options to hit back. We need to find out where they're taking Wes."

Chua nodded and turned to the PRIMAL operatives at the table. "You guys better get started on your battle prep and planning. We need to hit that server site, ASAP."

CHAPTER 8

SIARGAO ISLAND, PHILIPPINES

Bishop scanned the crowd waiting outside the arrivals gate at Sayak airport. He spotted a sign marked Mr. Wilson and locked eyes with the grinning Filipino who held it. Turning to Saneh he guided her toward their host. "This way, Mrs. Wilson."

As he approach Bishop thrust out his hand. "Hello, I'm Sam."

"Good afternoon, Mr. Wilson, my name is Arvin. I will be your attendant for your stay here in Siargao." He was short with an almost perfectly spherical bald head.

"You can call me Sam, this is my wife Sarah."

Saneh gave him a smile.

"Very good, Mr. Wilson, I will get your bags and we will go to the villa."

Arvin may have been small but he was strong. He unloaded their heavy black dive bags from the carousel, loaded them onto a baggage cart, and pushed it out to a minivan.

Soon they were driving through the lush green jungle on their way to the coast.

Saneh waved at a gaggle of children playing by the side of the road. "Everyone's so happy here."

"Of course they are," said Arvin. "We live in a magical place."

"It looks that way."

Bishop smiled as they drove through a village. Chua had come up with the cover story of a honeymoon and it hadn't taken much to convince him it was a good idea. Poor Flash though, he had drawn the short straw. The intel analyst was posing as a backpacker and staying in a cheap hostel close to their luxury villa.

"How far is the hotel?" Bishop asked.

"Nearly there."

He squeezed Saneh's hand as they turned off the road and pulled up in front of the resort.

"Oh wow," she exclaimed. She'd selected the accommodation online and the pictures had not done it justice.

Bishop was also impressed. The Balinese-style villas were picturesque, with broad sweeping verandahs, crisp white walls, wide-open windows, and thatched roofs. She had chosen well. As Arvin tended to the check-in they explored the lush gardens.

"This way," their guide said as he appeared, pushing their bags on a cart. He led them to their beach hut in a secluded corner. Inside it was clean and modern with polished timber floors and a king-sized bed.

Arvin placed their bags down. "There's a barbeque dinner tonight out on the restaurant deck. Best seafood on the island."

"Sounds great," Bishop said tipping him.

"Tomorrow, I can take you diving. Or perhaps you would you prefer to go surfing?"

"Diving sounds great. Would you be able to organize a boat?"

"Of course. What time would you like to go?"

"After breakfast if possible."

"My friend has a boat we can hire. I will show you all the best spots. Do you need any equipment?"

Bishop shook his head. "No, we brought our own."

"Very good. I will make the arrangements."

Arvin departed and they inspected the apartment. Bishop opened the plantation doors and gazed out over the perfectly manicured lawns to the beach and bright blue waters of the Philippine Sea. He felt Saneh wrap her arms around his waist and her lips brush his ear.

"This is stunning," she purred.

"No, babe, you're stunning. This is only picturesque."

"Wow you're really getting into this honeymoon thing, aren't you?"

He turned and kissed her passionately, grasping her buttocks. "It's important to keep up appearances."

"We should start planning our mission, Mr. Wilson."

Bishop lifted her off her feet and tossed her on the bed. "There's plenty of time for that."

"No, they've abducted Wesley. We need to get onto that island as soon as possible."

He kissed her on the lips. "You're right. I got a little carried away with the honeymoon."

Saneh wiggled out from his embrace. "Like you said, there'll be plenty of time for that." She grabbed her backpack and pulled out a tablet. Sitting on the bed, she checked her messages. "Hey, Chua has sent through an intel pack."

He sighed and climbed on the bed next to her so he could see the screen. "I thought we'd just hire a boat and do a night infil, yeah?"

"Actually, he's recommending we dive this reef here for a recon," she said examining a satellite map.

The reef was only half a mile from their target, which was a linear island containing a cluster of blocky concrete buildings nestled in the jungle. A wooden wharf extended from the southern side with a pair of boats moored alongside. She zoomed in and the image was clear enough to identify them as military-style RHIBs.

"So apparently this reef to the north is spectacular," she continued.

Bishop checked the distance. It would be an easy swim for him and Saneh but challenging for Flash who was less experienced and not as physically fit.

"Good plan. We'll do a recon by day. Then slip in under the cover of darkness and check it out. If we get busted we just pretend we got lost during the dive."

"So no weapons."

Bishop nodded. "Just those highly trained hands of yours." He leant in, kissed the lobe of her ear, and slipped a hand onto her thigh.

"Cut it out, you horny old man." She brushed his hand aside and continued reading the report. "There's a storm due in a couple of days. We'll have to infiltrate tomorrow night."

"We can dive twice during the day, rest up, and go back at dusk."

Saneh raised an eyebrow. "Rest up?"

Bishop smiled as he climbed off the bed. "Just a little decompression, darling. Now, I have to go and bump into Flash at a bar. I'll be back in thirty minutes."

Saneh tossed the tablet on the bed. "So you're going to abandon me on our honeymoon and go drink with a stranger in a bar?"

"Now who's the horn bag?" Bishop winked at her through the gap in the door as he closed it.

***

FORT YUKON RESEARCH STATION, ALASKA

Charles King thought the man who greeted his team in the aircraft hangar was an evil-looking weirdo. The widow's peak, almost jet black eyes, and pale skin reminded him of the vampires in the movies his daughter liked to watch. He had never understood why teenage girls swooned over pasty blood-sucking introverts. That reminded him; at the first opportunity he needed to call home and let his wife know he wasn't going to be back for at least a week, possibly longer.

"Mr. King, gentlemen, welcome to Dead Land. My name is Aaron Small and I run this facility for the OSP." He neglected to offer his hand. "My staff will take Mr. Chambers from here."

King had cuffed the banker and treated his wound but hadn't bothered to hood him. Wesley had spent the entire flight from Hawaii spilling his guts. Now King was confident that he knew everything the traitor had to offer.

One of Small's men slipped a black hood over the prisoner's head. With another guard he pushed him into a wheelchair and they disappeared through a side door.

"He's told me everything he knows."

"We'll see about that. Now, if you will follow me." Small led the GES operatives out of the hangar, through an enclosed walkway, to another building. "These first four rooms are yours," he said as they entered a corridor with doors along each side. "Your men can make themselves at home. I'll brief you now in the ops room upstairs."

King gave Hammer a nod. "Can you unload my gear?"

"Yeah sure, boss."

He followed Small up a set of stairs before entering the operations room. The multitude of screens and terminals reminded him of photos he had seen of NASA mission command, except it didn't have the throngs of personnel. In fact a number of the surveillance systems appeared to be autonomous. All aspects of the facility looked to be covered by high-resolution cameras, from the detention cells through to the icy wasteland beyond the tall security fence. He took a seat and listened as Small began pacing the room and lecturing.

"Director Larkin wants you and your men to focus on security, enabling me and my staff to concentrate on detainee management and interrogation. Now that you've brought me Mr. Chambers, I'm going to have my hands full." Small's thin lips turned up in a sickly smile.

King almost shivered. "If you give me a few hours to type up my report you'll be able to use it in your questioning."

"Yes, that will be useful. I've read the information Larkin sent me but I believe you have intimate knowledge that may assist in the interrogation."

"You could say that. He betrayed me and his work colleagues. Sold us out to terrorists who killed my men and robbed American citizens of millions of dollars."

"You worked with him?"

"Yes, I was a director on the board of a private equity firm. He single-handedly destroyed the company."

Small's sickly smile returned. "Oh your insights are going to be so powerful." He rose from his chair. "Contact me when your report is done. I'll have one of my people brief you now on the intricacies of the security system."

"I need to call Larkin."

"You can contact him via the secure phone here. I'll have one of the techs show you how to connect your phone and laptop to the local encrypted network. Now, if you will excuse me, I need to get to work." Small turned on his heel and strode out of the room.

He reached for the phone and scrolled through the menu. A number for 'OSP Director' was listed and he made the call.

"Sir, we've delivered Chambers to the facility."

"Very good, did you have any problems?"

"No, he came clean on the flight. I've got descriptions and first names for five of Aden's associates. I'll have my post-op report done shortly."

"The picture is building. I'll be interested to see what Small comes up with."

"That guy's nuttier than a squirrel turd."

"He's the best at what he does. I want you to support him with whatever he needs."

King rolled his eyes. "How long do you anticipate me remaining in this frozen hell hole?"

"Until the threat has been neutralized."

He clenched his jaw. "Thomas, I've got a family and I've got other teams to run. You can't keep me here indefinitely, and more to the point, if I'm here I can't deal with Major League."

"Trust me when I say that you're in exactly the right location. You can run missions from the operations room. Now, I've got to go. Get yourself across the defenses and draft your post-op report. I'll be in touch."

As King hung up the door to the operations room opened and a bespectacled man entered. Chris, Matt, and Hammer followed behind him. "Mr. King, Aaron instructed me to bring your team up to speed on our systems."

Hammer dropped into a chair. "How long we gonna be in this dump?"

"A while," said King. "Let's get this security briefing out of the way so we can get our heads down."

***

LASCAR ISLAND

Vance opened a cabinet door in the corner of his office. He pulled out a bottle of scotch and poured a finger in both the glasses on his desk. He stood gazing at the LCD screen on the wall. The swimming fish screensaver did little to calm him.

There was a knock and Chua entered. Vance limped over, handed him a tumbler of scotch, and they sat in the battered leather armchairs he kept for such an occasion.

"How's the ankle?"

"Yeah fine."

"Mirza thinks we should have eliminated Wesley when we had the chance."

Vance grunted. "I know. He's going to sing like a goddamn canary." He took a hefty slug from his glass. "This shit has got me stressed, Chua. You know, Charles King was leading his team personally. I wish we'd offed that prick back in Venezuela. Him and Wesley, the whole lot of them."

Chua sipped from his own glass. "There's no way King and GES alone are responsible for the Redemption Network. It's too sophisticated. We need to find out who's pulling the strings. Then we can decide what we need to do. Bishop, Flash, and Saneh will hit the Filipino comms facility tomorrow night. That should give us a lead."

"What if it doesn't? What then? We might be up against something beyond our capabilities."

"Vance, this isn't like you and it's not what the team needs right now. You need to snap out of it. We're flexible, we're skilled, and we're a tight-knit family. We'll get through this."

"You're right, buddy. I'm just hung up on the Agency potentially hunting us. You know, the CIA may have made some bad calls in its time, but they're pretty damn good at what they do."

"Come on, Vance, our team aren't exactly girl scouts. We've planned for this. We've got contingencies in place."

"Yeah, worse case scenario we shut it all down and disappear for a while. Let's face it, with the tempo we've been running for the last few years, we need a break."

"True, an actual operational pause would be welcomed."

Vance laughed. "We'd just have to make sure Bishop isn't allowed near anyone or anything. That guy's a shit magnet."

Chua smiled and lifted the glass. "To Saneh, Flash, and the shit magnet. Let's hope they stay out of trouble in the Philippines."

Vance raised his glass. "Amen to that."

CHAPTER 9

SIARGAO ISLAND, PHILIPPINES

Bishop carried their gear bags down to the beach and dumped them next to Arvin's boat. A sturdy looking trimaran, it had a sun canopy adorning the long wooden hull and an outrigger jutting from each side.

Saneh was already in the boat. Clad in a white bikini and a sarong, her bronzed skin looked radiant. Turning to face him she caught his stare and gave a wink.

Bishop tried to focus his attention on loading the bags. Mitch had provided them with the latest Divex rebreather rigs. Lighter than a traditional SCUBA setup, the self-contained systems didn't give off a telltale stream of bubbles. He heaved the bags into the boat and Arvin stowed them in the hull.

"Mate, I hope you don't mind, we've got a friend coming with us."

"That's fine, Mr. Wilson. But, are you sure you want to go to Anahawan? There are some good spots a bit closer."

"Yeah, but we really don't want to dive with the other tourists. I've heard the reefs around Anahawan are some of the best."

"Oh, of course. Very nice, and no tourists!" Arvin's grin returned to his face.

Bishop climbed in and slid next to Saneh. "You ready?"

She flashed her teeth in a brilliant smile. "Sam, for this, I was born ready. This place is amazing."

Bishop agreed, they couldn't have picked a better location, even if it was a fake honeymoon. The sand on the beach was pristine and the water sparkled with only the slightest swell. It was a perfect day for diving.

"Sorry I'm late, guys," Flash puffed as he shuffled down the beach, struggling with a gear bag. Dressed in board shorts, a black Ramones T-shirt, and a flat-brim cap, he didn't quite fit the tropical setting.

"No problem, mate." Bishop grabbed the bag and slung it into the boat. He turned to the stern where their guide had started the outboard motor. "Arvin, this is my friend, Ed."

The Filipino gave a friendly wave. "Mr. Ed, can you push us off?"

"Why sure, Wilbur," said Flash in his best imitation of the 60's television character. Bishop laughed but the joke was lost on the others.

Flash pushed off and jumped in as they reversed from the beach. Turning the boat, Arvin gave it a little throttle and angled them away from the shore.

"How are the lovebirds doing?" asked Flash.

"Fabulous," said Saneh. "How could we not be?"

Flash nodded as they skimmed across the glassy water. In a matter of minutes the main island had shrunk to a sliver of green behind them.

"So where are we heading?" Flash asked Bishop.

"We're going to dive on a reef near the island of Anahawan. It's supposed to be one of the best in the area. We'll get two dives in today, come back for dinner, and then head out for a night dive. Sound good?"

"Sounds awesome, dude," Flash said in a sarcastic tone.

Bishop smirked. He knew that Flash was terrified. The PRIMAL geek had only recently learnt to dive and had never been in the water at night. "We're going to have a great time," he said with a wink.

Twenty minutes later the island loomed in the distance. Bishop spotted the tall radio mast and gave Saneh a nod.

Arvin cut the engine and dropped anchor. "We're over the reef now. Perfect diving!" The PRIMAL team was already suited up and once in the water Flash looked more comfortable. It was warm and visibility excellent. The bottom was only sixteen meters so they were able to rapidly descend and explore the vibrant underwater world.

Bishop watched Saneh glide through the water like a mermaid. She was a natural; her buoyancy was perfect and she moved with energy conserving flicks of her fins. Flash on the other hand bobbed up and down struggling to maintain an even depth. He'd taken to hanging onto the reef as he adjusted his buoyancy vest. Bishop hoped that after another dive the computer geek would improve.

He checked his dive computer. They'd been submerged for ten minutes. One of the best things about the Divex Stealth system was the length of bottom time it offered. At sixteen meters they could stay submerged for five hours.

The hiss of a propeller caught his attention and he looked up. A second boat had pulled alongside Arvin's vessel. Bishop recognized the solid hull and rubber skirts of a military-style RHIB. He contemplated surfacing but after a minute the RHIB sped off back toward the island.

They spent another twenty minutes on the bottom. Saneh continued exploring the reef while Bishop kept an eye on Flash as he practiced maintaining an even depth. Once he'd got the hang of it they made their way back to the boat.

Arvin greeted them with his signature smile as they broke the surface. The strong Filipino helped them shrug out of their gear and hauled it in the boat. When they climbed over the side of the hull he had a tray of fresh watermelon and bottles of cold water ready.

"What did your friends want?" Bishop nodded toward the RHIB that was now patrolling around the island.

"They just tell us not to come any closer."

"We're fine to dive again tonight?"

"Yes, of course. We just cannot go any closer. There is an army base on there. Very secret, no one is allowed on the island."

Bishop ate a slice of watermelon. "Fair enough. Lots of pretty fish here, should be great tonight. The weather will still be OK, yeah?"

"The storm will hit in the morning or maybe during the day. We will be gone."

"How long do they usually last?"

Arvin shrugged. "Half a day, maybe longer. We get the big ones in a few months."

He stared at the RHIB as it cruised around the island and out of sight. They shouldn't have any problem making it to the island. The hard bit was going to be getting into the facility and back to the boat before their guide started freaking out.

***

Later that evening Arvin anchored the trimaran at the same spot they had dived during the day. The water was inky black and reflected the star-filled sky. Had Bishop and Saneh not been focused on the mission it would have been very romantic. Helping Flash, they geared up ready for the underwater infiltration. As they were about to depart Bishop handed a plastic zip-lock bag to their guide.

"What is this?"

"It's payment." Bishop glanced over his shoulder at Flash and Saneh as they slipped into the water.

Arvin opened the bag and inspected the contents under the lamp hanging from the awning. His eyes went wide as he saw the wad of hundred dollar bills. "Mr. Wilson, this is too much."

Bishop shook his head. "I want you to wait here for us. We could be a while."

"OK, but you can't stay under for long."

He checked his watch; it was just after 1900 hours. "If we're not back by midnight I want you to return to the resort."

Arvin looked confused. "You can't stay underwater that long."

"Trust me, we can." Bishop slipped over the side and turned to the waiting divers bobbing in the water. "OK, Ed, you follow me. Sarah, you bring up the rear."

Flash gave a nervous nod and jammed his regulator into his mouth.

Bishop returned an OK with his trigger finger and thumb. "Going to be fine, mate. Right, let's go." He adjusted his mask, fitted his regulator, and released the air from his inflator. Sinking beneath the water, he adjusted his buoyancy till he hovered five meters below the surface alongside Saneh. Flash disappeared below them and Bishop waited for him to rise back up to the same level. He checked the incandescent dive computer for a bearing and finned slowly through the water. Every few meters he checked over his shoulder to make sure Saneh and Flash were with him.

It took thirty minutes to reach the beach. When the bottom rose toward them Bishop signaled for the others to stay below the surface before he approached the shore. His head broke through the water a dozen yards from the sand. Touching down with his knees he scanned for any sign of life. The empty beach glowed white in the soft light offered by the stars. The treeline was only twenty yards from the water. Unlike the resort where palms grew everywhere the island was covered in shorter, scrubbier, trees and bushes.

Confident they were alone he submerged and swam back to where Saneh and Flash were waiting. He signaled for them to follow and when they could stand they pulled off their fins and masks and waded up to the beach. Bishop led them across the sand and showed them where to stash their gear beneath a dense clump of bushes. He shrugged out of his equipment and hid it with the rest.

"Good work, mate," he whispered giving Flash a pat on the shoulder.

The geek took a modified dive computer from his vest and slipped it inside his wetsuit. Bishop detached a dry bag from his dive rig.

"OK, let's get moving," said Saneh.

Bishop pulled his iPRIMAL from the bag and activated it. The GPS locked on and he got his bearings. "The facility is about three hundred meters north." He sniffed the air. "Can you smell that?"

Flash nodded. "Grilled fish."

"I'm guessing the security detail is having their dinner, perfect time to make our approach."

Bishop shouldered the dry bag and walked slowly into the scrub. Dressed in black wetsuits they blended into the darkness.

Ten minutes later they could hear voices and the dull drone of a generator. Bishop left Saneh and Flash crouched in the undergrowth and went forward to reconnoiter the target. He crept through bushes and past trees till he a found a spot where he could see into the military camp.

It was pretty much as he expected. A squad of soldiers had been given the task of securing the communications facility and they didn't take it particularly seriously. Their accommodation consisted of a dilapidated weatherboard barracks. Light shone from a number of the windows and in front of it a fireplace glowed where two soldiers cooked fish on the coals. Others were sitting on benches drinking beer and chatting. He saw only one weapon, a rusty M-16A1 propped against the wall.

Beyond the camp a tall mesh fence blocked the way to a cluster of concrete structures. The radio antenna he had spotted from the boat jutted up into the night sky; the old intercept tower. He spotted a satellite dish on top of one of the buildings. It also had a row of shiny air-conditioning units bolted to the wall. He smiled, servers needed to be kept cool or they would burn out. On the way back to the others he followed a route that avoided the barracks.

"How does it look?" Saneh asked when he returned.

He gave them a quick run-down on what he had seen.

"Did you spot any security systems?" asked Flash.

"There's no exterior security except for the fence. Saneh and I can get you to the building but you'll have to deal with any interior alarms."

Flash gave him a thumbs-up.

"OK, team, let's do this."

***

Flash's heart pounded as he followed Bishop through the bushes. He could hear the crackle of the soldiers' fire, their laughter, and he could smell the fish they were cooking. This was the closest he had ever been to a real threat; his first time truly in the field.

In front of him Bishop stopped and knelt. Flash followed his lead and slowly crouched. His mind raced, had Bishop spotted one of the soldiers? Were they in danger?

Bishop rose and continued through the undergrowth. Flash wiped his sweaty palms on his wetsuit and followed. He emulated Bishop's actions, methodically scanning ahead as they walked. Every shadow and every noise could have been a Filipino soldier laying in wait ready to take his life. He was so fixated on spotting the enemy that he nearly collided with Bishop.

"Wait here," the PRIMAL operative whispered.

Flash crouched and glanced over his shoulder to check that Saneh was behind him. Her white teeth flashed in a reassuring smile.

A moment later Bishop reappeared. "I've found a way in."

The dull thrum of a generator grew louder as Flash followed Bishop to the edge of a clearing. In the starlight he could make out a tall chain-link fence and the squat concrete buildings behind it. The closest structure had a satellite dish and microwave array on top as well as the telltale air-conditioning units. No doubt about it, this was what they were looking for.

"Flash," Bishop whispered as lifted the bottom of the fence. "Under."

He scrabbled through and waited on the other side. Saneh joined him with Bishop bringing up the rear. They moved to the side of the target building up to a heavy steel door with an electronic lock.

"Can you open it?" Bishop whispered as he handed over a compact flashlight.

Flash inspected the keypad; it was a model he was familiar with and knew he could hack. However, hacking took time and wasn't always the best option. The keypad was worn, to the point that the numbers on four of the buttons had been rubbed smooth. He studied them for a second before trying a sequence. A red light flashed. Reversing the sequence he tried again. Once more the light flashed. Changing the sequence slightly he tried again. Green light, the lock clicked.

"Nicely done," said Bishop as he gently pushed the door ajar. A faint glow emitted. They quickly ducked inside, closing the door behind them.

The space was cramped and gloomy, with rows of tiny lights blinking from the server racks. The air-conditioners maintained a chilly room temperature and the floor was a metal grid. Using the flashlight Flash inspected the racks.

"Hey, buddy, we want to minimize our time here, OK." Bishop was standing next to the door with Saneh by his side.

"Yeah, no problems," Flash muttered as he found the server he wanted and inspected it. The rack had a USB port in the front. He took the dive computer from inside his wetsuit and plugged it into the port. He and Mitch had modified the electronic device so it would hoover all the content it could from the server. They called it a 'vacuum drive'. First he needed to run a diagnostic test to ensure there were no security protocols that would detect his meddling.

"How are we going, Flash?" asked Bishop.

"Good, just give me a minute."

"Is there anything I can do?" Saneh asked.

"Give me a minute, alright?"

The device gave him the all clear and he pressed the button that would begin the file transfer. He watched as a progress bar showed the drive filling up. As it worked he examined the other servers.

"What do they all do?" she whispered.

"These are mostly communications routers. The one we're stealing from is a little bit sneakier. Numbers come in and it reassigns them a different IMSI before sending them out."

"So it masks the origin of the call?"

"Yes, that's exactly what it does."

"But none of the Redemption data is held here?"

Flash shook his head. "No, they've got that hidden somewhere else. The information we get from here might lead us to the person who checked in with your contractor buddies, hopefully."

A bellowing alarm sounded, reverberating throughout the room.

"What did you do?" said Bishop from the doorway. "Grab your shit, we've got to go!"

Flash's hands shook as he checked the dive computer. The progress indicator showed it was only halfway through. "I need more time."

Saneh grasped his shoulder. "We go, now!"

He disconnected the drive and slipped it back inside his wetsuit. Saneh dragged him through the door after Bishop and closed it behind them.

Outside, a blue light flashed on the side of the building and a deafening siren wailed. Flash charged after the two operatives as they ran back to the fence. Bishop held up the wire and waved them through. Saneh slid under then dragged the analyst through by the collar of his wetsuit. She ran him into the bushes and they crouched, waiting for Bishop. As he reached them shouting could be heard from the buildings.

"Hopefully they think it's a false alarm," said Bishop.

Flash shook his head. "Not if they had some kind of remote monitoring system that I didn't detect."

Bishop glanced at Saneh. "We need to get the hell off this island." He led them through the darkness, trusting his instincts to get them back to the beach and their dive gear. They went wide, avoiding the military camp. More agitated yelling could be heard through the trees.

While it had taken almost an hour to stealthily infiltrate to the target building, it took less than ten minutes to rush back to the beach. He spotted their footprints in the sand and found the cluster of bushes. Bishop threw on his dive rig and looped the mask around his neck. He helped Flash with his gear as Saneh sorted her own rig. As he lifted the rebreather over the technician's shoulders he heard the faint sound of outboard motors starting up. "We need to get in the water, now!"

Flash snapped his dive computer into position. "I'm ready."

"Same as before. I'll lead, Saneh will bring up the rear." Bishop led them down the beach into the water. When they were far enough out that he couldn't stand he checked his regulator. The others did the same returning an OK sign. With a gurgle of escaping air all three submerged.

Ever since learning to dive in his teens Bishop had loved the sensation of being fully submerged. The silence, the weightlessness, and the sense of adventure all thrilled him. However, tonight he was simply grateful for the protection the ocean offered. With their fully contained systems there would be no bubbles as they swam a few meters below the surface.

He hoped that Arvin would be still waiting and had been able to convince the soldiers that he was harmless. He checked his watch; they had only been gone for an hour and fifteen minutes. Glancing over his shoulder he confirmed Saneh and Flash were on his tail, and continued finning.

Regularly checking the bearing on his dive computer, he counted his kicks and set a steady pace. Thirty minutes passed before he stopped. By his calculations they should have been directly under Arvin's boat. He signaled for Saneh and Flash to wait and slowly rose. The boat was nowhere to be seen so he cautiously surfaced.

His heart skipped a beat when he spotted two vessels a short distance away. Arvin's distinctive trimaran was anchored a few yards from the wide grey shape of a RHIB. On the military vessel two men appeared to be sitting and waiting.

Bishop formulated a plan as he sank back down to Saneh and Flash. Using the slate and pen on the back of his dive computer, he drew a diagram, illuminated it with a small light, and showed it to Saneh. Her eyes went wide inside her mask but she gave him an OK sign.

Flash swam in close to them and shrugged. Bishop gave him the signal for staying in place then pointed at Saneh and gave her the signal to follow. They swam for a minute then rose through the water together.

When they were below the RHIB Bishop hung underwater for a second until he spotted the shape of a man. Then he tapped Saneh's shoulder, kicked hard, reached up, and pulled the soldier backward over the side. Saneh burst out of the water and grabbed the second man, throwing him overboard. Bishop climbed over the side and hauled Saneh aboard.

One of the soldiers reached up and attempted to climb back into the boat. A swift kick from Saneh sent him back into the inky water. "Where's Flash?" she asked as she tore off her gear and picked up a rifle that had been left in the boat.

"I'm here," said the analyst from behind the engines.

Bishop removed his dive rig and hurried to the rear. "Keep an eye on the guys in the water. I'll help him out." He pulled Flash in before making for the boat's console.

"Mr. Wilson, is that you?" Arvin said, his voice penetrating the darkness. His trimaran was only a few yards away.

"Yes it is, Arvin. Mate, I'm going to need you to help these fine gentlemen out of the water. Then I want you to head back to the resort." As he spoke Bishop inspected the RHIB's console. It had close to a full tank of gas, a built in GPS, and radar mounted on the roof.

"Where are you going?" the guide wailed as Bishop turned over the engines and pushed forward gently on the throttles. The twin 250 horsepower motors rumbled to life and they pulled away from the two soldiers bobbing in the water.

"Just going on a little midnight cruise," said Bishop as he angled the boat east.

Arvin's final words were lost in the roar of the engines as Bishop accelerated away. "Saneh, can you get in contact with the Bunker? We're going to need an exfil plan."

***

Five hours later the seven-meter RHIB was 150 nautical miles offshore and punching through rain, howling wind, and a choppy swell. At the helm Bishop worked the throttles as they rode up one side of the rolling waves and down the other. Spray lashed his face but the wetsuit kept him warm enough. Saneh stood next to him bracing herself against the framework that held up the roof. Flash was sprawled out on one of the seats at the back clinging to the handrail and trying not to throw up.

"I'm hoping we're through the worst of it," yelled Bishop as he glanced at the fuel gauges. They were down to their last third of a tank.

"Mitch won't be able to get to us until it clears." Saneh held her iPRIMAL at arms length in an attempt to get a signal.

"Did you get confirmation from the Bunker?"

She shook her head. "That storm rolled in and I lost comms." They were both using a new model of the iPRIMAL equipped with a satellite communications module. It allowed them to send encrypted text messages in the absence of a local telecommunications network.

"Can you try messaging them again? If we don't get a resup or extracted by dawn we'll be dead in the water."

"I'll try. I'll also ask for some sea-sickness pills." She nodded at Flash.

Bishop looked over his shoulder. The analyst's face was green and he'd just puked down the front of his wetsuit. "Did you stow the computer?"

She nodded. "It's in the dry bag under the seats."

"Good." He turned his attention back to the ocean and wiped the spray from his face with the sleeve of his wetsuit.

"What are we going to do if we run out of fuel?" she asked quietly. "I checked and we don't have much in the way of food and water."

"The Bunker will drop us a resup," said Bishop. "It might take longer than we hoped but they'll find us once the storm clears."

She leant in and placed an arm around his waist. "You don't have to put on a brave face for me, Aden, we're in this together."

He kissed her gently on the cheek. "It's not for you, babe, it's for me and Flash."

***

BOSTON

Howard was leaving his apartment for a coffee when his cell phone rang. He glanced at the ID displayed on the secure communicator app. It was Larkin. "Sir, what's up?"

"We've had another compromise."

"Where and when?"

"One of our communications nodes in the Philippines. My IT guy picked up the hack and alerted the local security force. They interdicted a fishing boat but divers attacked their men and stole a RHIB. I'm sending you everything we have on it."

"Do you think this is related to the Redemption compromise?"

"I don't believe in coincidence, Howard, this has to be Major League. My IT guys tell me Redemption was routing through this node but that there was no way they could decrypt the data or trace it back to our server."

"So they got away with nothing."

"Correct. We've got people heading down there to investigate but they're not going to find much. We need to increase our analytical outputs."

"Did you read my analysis on the Chambers rendition report? I've already got a request in for the CCTV footage from the Queenstown bars but I'll bet my bonus that the bald African American mentioned in the report is Iceman's old partner, Vance Durant."

"That's possible. However, the priority is investigating the Philippines incident."

"I could chase up both if I had additional manpower."

"I'm way ahead of you, Terrance. I'm bringing together my best analysts and you'll head them up for the sole purpose of destroying Major League."

"When do we start?"

"I'll send you the details shortly."

"Looking forward to it. I'll get going on the Philippines."

The call ended.

Howard sighed, walked into the kitchen, and pulled a can of sugar-free energy drink from the fridge. He wasn't going to get down to Starbucks any time soon. Back at his Redemption laptop he opened the email from Larkin regarding the Philippines and scanned over the key points.

Cracking the can of energy drink, he sipped as he plotted the location of the communications facility on an NGA mapping system. The National Geospatial-Intelligence Agency provided wide-area satellite shots on a daily basis. He checked the metadata on the imagery and saw it was nearly twenty-four hours old. He would have to wait until the latest imagery finished uploading.

As he re-read Larkin's email he noted the intruders stole a military RHIB and were seen heading east. He plotted a route from the island out into the Philippine Sea. They would have had to rendezvous with a ship. Shipping data was readily available through an NGA layer that combined open-source transponder tracking with classified space-based sensors. He added it to the map and checked for any possible contenders.

He frowned as he studied the computer screen. There had been no ships in the area for the last twelve hours. In fact a number of tracks had changed course to avoid it. There was only one reason that he could think of why they would do that.

Turning to his personal computer he brought up a real-time weather map. Sure enough a storm front was passing through the exact area the intruders had used to escape. He smiled; storm fronts equaled additional satellite coverage.

Back on his Redemption laptop he opened a form on the NGA website and requested a detailed analysis of all local imagery for the last twenty-four hours. He used a search and rescue justification for the tasking, however, coming from Redemption he knew it would automatically be given highest priority. It might take a day or two to come back but if the

RHIB was out there the NGA sensors and analysts would find it.

As he was about to leave the desk another email hit his inbox. It contained an e-ticket for a flight to Chicago the next day. Why the hell was he going to Chicago, he wondered? He became even more confused when he scrolled down and saw another ticket. This one was for a train called the Southwest Chief. He shook his head as he printed them both. If he was going to be leading the team why couldn't they come to Boston?

CHAPTER 10

PHILIPPINE SEA

Bishop struggled to stay awake as he held the RHIB on its easterly course. His lower back ached and the muscles in his calves were tight from standing behind the helm through the storm.

The weather had cleared an hour earlier. The sea had flattened and the stars appeared in the night sky. Now, as they motored slowly east, the first glimmer of orange streaked the horizon directly ahead.

He glanced over his shoulder to where Saneh lay against the inflatable skirt. She looked peaceful with her head propped up on her inflated buoyancy vest. Flash, however, didn't look so great. His face was still green, his wetsuit covered in flecks of vomit, but at least he seemed to be getting some sleep.

His iPRIMAL pinged from where he had wedged it next to the boat's GPS. They finally had communications. The message was from the Bunker.

Tracking your GPS will conduct resupply ASAP.

Relief washed over him and he relaxed his grip on the steering wheel. When he hadn't heard any response from the Bunker, even after the storm cleared, he had started to worry. The RHIB was almost out of fuel and had been stripped of anything of value. It had zero rations, no emergency locator beacon, and only a gallon of stale smelling water. If their signal hadn't finally gotten through they would have struggled to survive.

"Good morning, Captain." He felt Saneh's hand on his shoulder.

"Hey, we've got comms with the Bunker."

"Good news?"

"Resupply is inbound." His grin was infectious.

They stood in silence watching the orange glow of sunrise ripple across the ocean.

"It's so beautiful," said Saneh.

He nodded in agreement.

From the back of the boat the sound of dry retching interrupted the serenity. "You might want to give him some water," Bishop said.

"Poor Flash." Saneh took a plastic jug of water from the console and headed to the stern.

Bishop glanced down at the GPS and did a rough calculation in his head. They were only two hundred nautical miles from their point of origin. That meant they were nearly a thousand miles from Lascar Island; out of range for extraction by helicopter or tiltrotor, but close enough for an airdropped resupply. Flash was in for a rough few days.

He squinted as the sun nudged its way over the horizon. What he wouldn't give for the sunglasses he had left at the resort.

***

By mid-morning Saneh had replaced Bishop at the helm. He was curled up on the floor getting some much-needed sleep. One of the engines had died and she kept the remaining one throttled back to conserve fuel. They were making the slightest headway east as they waited for resupply. The sun was unrelenting, driving the temperatures up to the mid-nineties. She unzipped her wetsuit and tied the arms around her waist in an attempt to keep cool.

Flash had continued to vomit and his condition had degraded significantly. Severely dehydrated, he'd lapsed into a delirium and she was concerned that if help didn't arrive soon his life would be in danger.

She checked the fuel gauge for the auxiliary tank. The needle was hovering over empty; the primary tank had already run dry. A ping sounded from her iPRIMAL. She grabbed it from the console and read the message.

I see you!

Her heart skipped a beat and she glanced up at the horizon, shielding her eyes with one hand. She couldn't see anything. Scanning she finally spotted a tiny speck above the horizon.

"Aden!" she yelled. "We've got company."

The speck grew in size and for a moment she was confused. Expecting a four engine transporter, the speck grew into PRIMAL's twin-prop AW609 tilt rotor, Dragonfly.

Bishop struggled to his feet as the aircraft's rotors tipped backward and it flared into a hover above them.

Saneh shoved her iPRIMAL into her sports bra and gripped the console as the downwash buffeted them. She spun the wheel and gave the boat a little more throttle to hold it steady as Dragonfly hovered above. Spray and foam whipped through the air.

The pilot of the aircraft positioned it so the side door was over stern of the RHIB. Kurtz stood in the doorway wearing a broad smile.

Bishop helped Flash to his feet and up to the door. Kurtz hauled him inside. Gathering up their bags Bishop tossed them through the open door. "Saneh, you go. I'll burn the boat." He replaced Saneh at the console and she scrambled inside the hovering aircraft.

She watched from the door as he killed the engine, popped the cover on the fuel tanks, and stuffed a rag into it. Looking up at her he showed her the lighter he held.

"We ready to go?" Saneh yelled to Kurtz.

"*Ja!*" She gave Bishop a thumbs-up. He ignited the rag, sprinted across the boat, and leapt through the open door.

"All clear!" she shouted.

The tilt rotor launched skyward as she slammed the door shut. She watched through the window as the RHIB's fuel tank exploded in a ball of flame that engulfed it. She was pressed back in her seat as Dragonfly transitioned from vertical to horizontal flight and gained speed.

"Safe and sound," said Bishop.

"Not quite," Kurtz said. He'd laid Flash on the floor and was administering an intravenous saline bag. "We're almost out of gas. We've got to make it to the FARP or we're in big trouble." He referred to the Forward Area Refueling Point.

Saneh strode into the cockpit where Mitch was in the pilot's seat.

"Hello lovely, you all good?" the Brit asked without his eyes leaving the digital readouts. He gestured to the copilot's seat and Saneh sat.

"We're OK, thanks to you. Flash is very dehydrated but he'll pull through."

"That's ace. Now strap yourself in."

"So what's the situation?" asked Bishop from where he was standing in the cockpit doorway.

"You might want to strap in, mate, we're running on fumes. I'm looking for an atoll that should be almost visible." He squinted through the windshield. "There it is."

Saneh spotted the sliver of white sand as she fastened her harness. It grew in size as they approached.

"Going to be tight. No time for a fly around." He flicked a switch and the landing gear whined as it extended.

Saneh tightened her straps as the land mass grew in size and she realized it wasn't even a real island. It was a tiny strip of sand in the middle of the ocean. At one end she spotted a cluster of black objects, the refueling point. She felt the aircraft shudder as Mitch transitioned it back to hover mode. Out the side window she watched the engines rotate until the blades faced skyward.

They locked in position as the engine warning light flashed and an alarm sounded. "Fuel tank's empty. Hold on!" Mitch announced.

She held her breath as they tipped forward. The island seemed to jump up at them as Mitch used airflow to keep the blades spinning. Right as she thought they were going to crash he hauled up on the collective. Her stomach lurched as they touched down with a heavy thump.

"Bit rough, mate!" yelled Bishop from the back of the cabin.

"Don't listen to him," said Saneh. "That was impressive."

Mitch gave her a wink as he climbed out of his harness. "That's what she said. Now let's get this girl fueled up so we can get you back to base."

CHAPTER 11

LASCAR ISLAND

By the time Dragonfly rolled through the false-rock hangar doors into the PRIMAL complex Flash felt a hell of a lot better. Kurtz had put two bags of fluid into his veins on the flight home and it had revitalized him.

"Hey take it easy, mate," said Bishop as he helped him out through the cabin door. "You might feel pretty good now but you're going to crash hard in an hour or so."

"I'd better work fast then." Flash dashed across to the elevator with the dive computer tucked under his arm, still wearing his vomit-stained wetsuit. His mind raced at a million miles an hour as he descended to the headquarters level. The data he'd pulled from the Philippines wouldn't give them access to the Redemption Network but it might give them a lead. The doors opened and he stormed into the Bunker.

"Welcome home, Seal Team Six," bellowed Vance through the door of his office. He lumbered across and grasped Flash's hand. "Heard you did a damn fine job, bud, well done."

"Thanks, Vance. I'm pretty keen to get at this data." He held up the dive computer.

"Don't let me keep you."

Flash shuffled through a sliding opaque glass door into the PRIMAL intelligence cell. He ignored the other analysts as he slid behind his desk and logged into the terminal. Plugging the modified dive computer into a USB port he uploaded the entire contents to the intel database. He opened the data and began deciphering what he had stolen. It was as he thought; the server he'd hacked took an incoming call, assigned it a new identity, and connected it to the destination device. An advanced form of masking that stopped people from tracking a call to its source.

He entered the two numbers that had called the contractors in Africa. The software took a moment to search the database and link it to the source number; they were both from the same cell phone. It was American. Flash copied the new number across to another application. It was a program that gave him back door access to US cell phone data. He crossed his fingers as he waited for a result.

He frowned as the metadata appeared. Apart from the usual cell-tower locations the device was sterile. No name was associated with the SIM card and location services had been disabled rendering GPS tracking useless. He clicked on the tower location data and brought up a map of the US that revealed the broad locations where the phone had been active. "Been a busy little beaver, haven't you," said Flash.

"What's that?" asked Chua from the door.

He glanced up at the intelligence chief. "Huh? I just managed to track the number that called the contractors in Africa. It's been down in Fort Bliss, Texas, and up to Virginia. Now it's in Boston."

Chua leant over his shoulder and studied the map. "When was it at Fort Bliss?"

"About three weeks ago."

"Right when Bishop was in Mexico. Fort Bliss is where the Joint Task Force responsible for Latin America is based. Where did it go after that?"

"Up to Virginia."

"Near the GES facility?"

Flash zoomed the map in. "Yes, right smack in the middle of it."

"And now it's in Boston?"

"Correct."

"OK, so it probably belongs to a CIA guy who is almost certainly involved in tracking us down. Have you run the number against the ones we pulled from Pershing's phone?" Chua referred to a former CIA officer who had worked for GES. He'd been killed in Brazil when Bishop and the CAT rescued Kurtz.

"Good idea." Flash's fingers raced over his keyboard. "We've got a hit. That cell called Pershing a bunch of times. Mostly when it was located near Fort Bliss."

"Have you got a name?"

"Nope, it's a clean skin. Only got the cell data. We need someone on the ground."

Chua nodded. "I'll talk to Vance about it, but it's certainly worth getting Ivan to investigate. He's in the States now."

"Really?"

"Yes, once he finished up in Venezuela he wanted to take a break. He's touring D.C."

"A Russian secret agent who enjoys American politics and history, interesting."

Chua smirked. "Ivan would argue that to truly understand your enemy you must study every aspect of his existence."

"Well, he's got a new enemy to study now," said Flash. He yawned and realized he still wore the wetsuit coated in vomit. "I need to have a shower and get my head down."

Chua gave him a pat on the shoulder. "You deserve it, good job. I'll run this past Vance and get Ivan on it. This is the break we've been looking for." Chua waited till Flash left the room. "At least it better be," he murmured as he stared at the screen.

***

FORT YUKON RESEARCH STATION, ALASKA

King zipped up the down jacket and stepped out of the accommodation building. An icy gale stripped away the haziness of sleep. He had woken from a well-deserved rest, having completed security familiarization and submitted his post-operation report.

He tramped the forty yards to the underground prison, seeking refuge from the chilly wind. As he reached the stairs he glanced back and spotted a sinister-looking tracked robot drive past the main building. Its machine gun and grenade launchers were aimed past the perimeter fence. On top of the weapons turret a camera swiveled toward him. He gave it a gloved salute. The rest of his team was in the operations room practicing piloting the lethal drones.

The steps were icy and he gripped the handrail as he descended to the heavy sliding blast doors. A smaller pedestrian access point had been installed in the center of one of them. He swiped his card over the reader and glanced at the camera above. The door buzzed and he pushed it open.

King had explored every other aspect of the base, from the aircraft hangar to the drone workshops and the main building. The interrogation facility was his last point of call and one he wasn't looking forward to. He was a soldier not a sadist and had no time for people who took pleasure in another's pain. Better to die from a bullet than scream in agony at the hands of a psychopath, he thought.

Past the entrance was an anteroom with a single steel door that he knew from the briefing led to the cells and what that weirdo Small called his 'lab'. He swiped the security card and opened the door, revealing a corridor with six doors on either side. The one on the right he knew led to an observation room and the interrogation lab. The one on the left, the kitchen and a dormitory. The others were detention cells. He bashed a gloved mitt on the door to the observation room and one of Small's men opened it.

"Mr. King."

He gave the man a nod as he walked in. "What's happening?"

"Not much, Aaron is just putting the new guy through the wringer." He pointed at the monitor in front of him.

King grimaced when he spotted his former-colleague strapped to what resembled a dental chair. Wesley writhed against the straps with a look of pure agony on his face. Small was standing by his head whispering in his ear. "What the fuck is he doing to him?"

The man shrugged. "It's a new technique. He injects capsicum directly into the central nerve clusters. Makes it feel like his entire body is on fire. Once he answers the questions Aaron gives him a little shot of morphine to ease the pain."

King watched in horror as the young man thrashed and screamed, his face contorted with pain. The veins in his neck pulsed as he clenched his jaw, his eyes bloodshot and wide.

He stepped back out to the corridor, slamming the door behind him. Pulling his phone from his pocket he called Larkin using the base's wireless network. The phone seemed to ring for an eternity before the director picked up.

"Speak."

"Your man Small is a goddamn sadist. He's torturing Wesley when we already have everything he knows."

Larkin sighed. "Don't tell me you're going soft. The kid shut you down. Then he partnered up with the people who killed your men. We need everything he knows and I assure you, Small will get it all out of him."

"I picked Wesley's brain for the entire flight. Did you read my report?"

"Yes, it was excellent, for a preliminary interview. My analysts were appreciative of your thoroughness. It confirmed the link between our other detainee and current Major League operations."

"Other detainee?" King glanced down the corridor. "We have more than one?"

"Are you in the facility?"

"Yes."

"Check the cells. There's a prisoner in there they call Iceman. Ten years ago he defected from the CIA with his partner Vance Durant, one of the men you bumped into in New Zealand."

King strode down the corridor. "Why isn't Small working him over?" He glanced in through the observation panel at an empty cell. He moved on to the next one.

"Because he's a shattered wreck. In four years he hasn't been able to remember his name much less his involvement in a terrorist organization."

"So why are you keeping him here?" King peered in through the window of the next door. He spotted a man lying on a bed that was far too small for his frame. He had a shaggy blonde head of hair and a beard. Part of an arm and a leg were missing. "You're going to use him as bait aren't you? That's why you're keeping me here for security. He's your live bait."

"As a last resort, it's an option. That crippled prisoner is my ace in the hole but I don't expect to have to play it."

"You sure about that?"

"If by some miracle Major League come to visit Dead Land, you'll have your chance at vengeance."

"I should be out there hunting."

"It's all joining the dots right now, Charles. If the situation develops I'll consider redeploying you. In the meantime make sure you're ready."

"I'll be ready." He ended the call and slipped the phone into his pocket. "What the hell happened to you?" he whispered as he watched the man in the cell. Turning he strode down the corridor toward the exit.

As he passed the interrogation room a gut-wrenching scream penetrated the wall. He clenched his fists and kept walking.

CHAPTER 12

BOSTON

Ivan abandoned the tour as soon as he received Chua's message. He checked out of his hotel and booked an airline ticket on the way to the airport. Three hours later he landed at Boston Logan International Airport and caught a cab to the search area.

Chua's message had outlined the urgency of the mission so he moved quickly, mitigating risk by time and space rather than intricate planning. He would rely on his fieldcraft and instincts to detect any threat.

The target location was the Boston suburb of Somerville. It was a well-to-do residential area a few miles from downtown. Grabbing his bag, Ivan alighted from the cab on a leafy street lined with white-washed weatherboard townhouses. As the cab pulled away he checked his iPRIMAL. The device placed him directly in the middle of a blue oval that denoted the area where the target phone was active. Chua's analysts had managed to narrow it down to a five hundred yard long ellipse.

He plugged a set of earphones into the device and activated an app. It would search for the target as he strolled through the picturesque suburb and beep when he was close. Picking a street he appeared to be listening to music as he walked. He passed an attractive woman with a dog and regretted not having time to borrow one from a local shelter. There was no better excuse for wandering aimlessly than a hound that needed exercise.

Ten minutes later he heard a single ping from the earpiece. Removing the phone from his pocket he checked the screen. A green arrow pointed in the direction he was traveling. He kept walking and was rewarded with another ping. A dozen yards further and it began emitting a slow beat. The beeps increased in tempo, blending into an almost continuous tone.

When the tone went solid he stopped and casually looked around. He was standing at a main road in front of a two-story weatherboard townhouse with a red-tiled roof. Across the road was a brown brick mall with a Subway and a Starbucks. The target phone was either in the house or the mall. Both sides required a stakeout and that worked best with a coffee in hand. Crossing the road he pulled open the front door of the café and held it for a woman balancing a tray of takeaway cups.

As he entered he gave the room a cursory scan. A half-dozen people were seated at tables or in booths. Sidling up to the counter he ordered a black coffee from the spotty-faced attendant and took a seat in an empty booth. A newspaper lay on the table so he flicked it open and pretended to read. As he assessed each of the customers he continually came back to the overweight thirty-something male sitting next to the door. Dressed in baggy chinos and a rumpled polo shirt he looked like a government employee. A large coffee sat on the table in front of him but he was focused on his phone. Ivan pulled out his own device and checked the tracking app. According to the software his target was active. He glanced around; there were a number of people on their phones. He looked back at the chinos wearing guy.

The man was smiling to himself, completely focused on the device.

Ivan checked the app again. The target indicator pointed directly at the man; the range less than ten yards. No doubt about it, he had found the owner of the target number.

"Sir, your coffee," said the attendant yelled.

"Thank you," Ivan said as he walked over and picked up the cup. On the way back to the booth he snapped a photo of the overweight customer. Taking a seat, he checked to confirm the man's face was visible and transmitted it to Chua. He turned his attention back to the paper and when the man left he checked the app. The target phone was moving away from him. Taking his coffee he followed the man outside. As he strolled along the leafy street his phone buzzed. The message was from Chua.

Maintain contact. Bishop and Saneh enroute.

***

LASCAR ISLAND

Mitch sat in the cockpit of PRIMAL's business jet and watched the onboard systems run through a diagnostic check. With green lights across the board he ticked it off the list of preflight tasks and climbed out of the pilot's seat. The aircraft they called Sleek was refueled and ready for its next mission; deploying Bishop and Saneh to rendezvous with Ivan.

He'd replenished the main gear pod hidden in the rear of the cabin. The carbon-fiber air delivery system contained enough equipment and weaponry to equip four operators. He had also restocked another smaller pod, identical to the one Mirza had used in Queenstown. It now contained a 'snatch pack'; everything Bishop and Saneh needed to subdue and detain a target. As he left the aircraft he remembered one last thing he needed to do. He took the elevator down to the Bunker and knocked on the door of the intel section.

The opaque glass door slid open and Chua glanced up from his terminal. "Since when do you need to knock, Mitch?"

"I wanted to make sure you all had time to put your pants on. You intel guys are always up to weird shit."

Flash spun his chair to face him. "I resent that statement, we're all operators in here," he said grinning.

Mitch laughed. "So that was operator puke I had to wash out of Dragonfly was it?" He dropped into the seat next to the analyst.

Flash shrugged. "Sorry, bro, I'm never great with boats. What can we do for you?"

"I need the target number for the EW package."

"Ah, yes." Flash took a thumb drive from a drawer and plugged it into the computer.

As he loaded the data Mitch glanced at the screen and spotted the photo Ivan had sent from the café. "That our man?"

"Yeah, we think he's a CIA guy. Haven't got a name yet."

Mitch's eyes narrowed; something about the baggy chinos was familiar. "Great dress sense. I thought pleated pants went out in the nineties."

Flash snorted as he removed the drive from his machine and handed it over. "This number is more of a contingency now that Ivan is tracking him."

"Good luck," said Chua from behind his terminal.

He bumped knuckles with Flash and made for the door. He hadn't taken more than a half-dozen paces when he remembered exactly where he'd seen the chinos. It was in Virginia at a gas station near the GES facility. The overweight guy had bought half a dozen energy drinks and dropped his ID card on the floor. He even remembered the surname from the card he'd picked up. "Howard!" He spun back to Flash. "The guy's last name is Howard. He definitely works for the CIA."

"How the hell could you know that?"

"Because Bishop and I ran into him in Virginia."

"Ran into who?"

They both turned as Bishop entered the room.

"This geezer." Mitch pointed to the screen.

Bishop frowned. "Isn't that the douche bag from the truck stop in Virginia, the CIA guy?"

"Bingo!" said Mitch. "Anyway, boys, I'm going make final preparations to Sleek. Bish, wheels up in thirty."

"Roger." Bishop gave him thumbs-up and sat in the chair Mitch had left vacant. "So that's our boy."

"It would seem so," Flash said. "He's recently been based in Boston but before that Fort Bliss and Virginia. Unlike the GES contractors, this guy's almost certainly an insider. If I could get into his computer we could learn everything they know."

"You put together a hack kit?"

"Yep." Flash unzipped a black nylon case on his desk. He pulled out a hard drive. "Here you've got a vacuum drive that will copy everything on his computer. Remember you need to get a logon first. It can't crack the level of security that the CIA system will have."

"OK."

Flash held up a thumb drive. "Now, this little bad boy I can guarantee will get the security systems pinging. I call it the nuke. You plug it in and it will fry everything on a computer and start burning the entire network. Just make sure you and Saneh are ready to get the hell out of there fast."

CHAPTER 13

UNION STATION, CHICAGO

Howard stood on platform eleven at Union Station in Chicago, one of hundreds trying to board the newly-arrived train. He was furious. The tickets that Larkin provided had baffled the attendant. Allegedly they were for a car and a cabin that didn't exist. When he'd demanded to see a manager the attendant had told him it would be sorted out on the train.

"Get out of the way, dipshit." He pushed past an elderly man struggling with two large suitcases and boarded the train. Shoving people out of the way he finally found the conductor. "Hey, can you tell me where to find my room?" He thrust the printed ticket under the man's nose.

"You need to go all the way to the back, past the dining car. I recommend walking along the platform."

Howard swore and pushed his way back outside. He walked beside the train as far as the last carriage then stepped up to the door. It was locked. "For fuck's sake." He hammered on the glass. This time it opened and a gorilla of man dressed in a suit blocked his way.

"Can I help you?"

"Yeah, I need to get on the train."

He shook his head. "I'm sorry, this is a private car."

Terrance glanced at the ticket and then back at the man. "My name's Terrance Howard, does that change things?"

The security guard nodded and ushered him into the entrance. "Can I see your ticket and identification, sir?"

Howard showed him both items.

"Very good, do you have a phone on you, sir?"

Howard handed over the device and the guard placed it in a metallic bag. "If you need it you can come get it. I'm sorry but you are not allowed to use it in this car."

The guard escorted him through a door into a corridor. "This is your cabin," he said pointing out a door on the right.

Howard opened it and glanced inside. It was roomier than he expected with a decent-sized bed. It even had a bathroom in the corner. He dropped his backpack on the floor and went to pull the door shut.

The guard blocked it. "The others are all onboard, sir. They're waiting for you upstairs."

"Oh, OK, let's go." Howard followed him up a narrow staircase to the observation deck of the carriage.

"This is where I leave you, sir."

He tentatively pushed the door open and walked in. The entire level had been converted into an intelligence facility. He smiled as he began to appreciate Larkin's cunning. Unwilling to accommodate his Redemption intelligence team in a government facility, the OSP director had gotten creative. By keeping this new team on the train, he minimized the chance Major League could track them down. Opportunities to expose themselves were reduced and the team would be focused on working full-time to neutralizing the threat.

He scanned the room, satisfied it was suitable for the task ahead. There were desks set up against the walls with good quality office chairs. Multiple laptops were at each workspace and there was a server rack in the corner. Working behind the laptops was his new team; two middle-aged men and a similarly aged woman wearing glasses and a tight white blouse.

"You must be Terrance Howard," said one of the men. He was tall and sported a thick mustache and a comb over.

"That's me. You can call me Terry."

"I'm Andrew." He pointed to his colleagues. "This is Stewart and Heather."

"Hi guys." His eyes lingered on Heather. She was attractive for her age, in a bookish, librarian kind of way. "I'm guessing Larkin briefed you on the task at hand?"

They nodded.

Andrew adjusted his hair. "We're all OSP like you. We've been working on the Redemption program for the last few months."

"Have you been working together?"

"No, this is the first time we've met."

"Cool, have you been read into the Major League Network?"

Once again they nodded.

"OK, well, I'll brief you on the latest developments and then we can get to work."

As Howard addressed the team Ivan stood watching the Southwest Chief rumble away from the platform. PRIMAL's lead Blade had tracked Howard from Boston, managing to purchase a ticket on the same flight to Chicago. Then it had been a case of tailing the cab from the airport to the train station. Boarding the train, however, had posed a problem. Ivan had used a local ticket to follow his target to the platform but had been unable to talk his way onto the Southwest Chief.

As the double-decker train disappeared into the distance Ivan considered his options and rang Chua.

The intel chief answered immediately. "Planes, now trains, you're having a busy day."

Ivan knew his boss would have checked the location data on his iPRIMAL. "I missed the train, unfortunately. Not enough time to purchase a ticket."

He could hear Chua typing. "Southwest Chief, huh? Why on earth is a CIA analyst taking a tourist train? You think he knows he's being followed?"

"No, the target has zero awareness. He's most likely staying onboard."

"What do you mean?"

"He alighted into what looked like a private carriage, complete with blacked-out windows and security guards."

"You think the CIA could have hired the train?"

Ivan searched the platform and found a map for the Southwest Chief. "His travel makes no sense, unless his destination was the actual train. If that is the case it's safe to assume he's staying on board for some time. The Chief goes all the way to L.A., then begins its journey back to Chicago."

"OK, can you get onboard?"

"I can fly to Kansas and board there. Perhaps Bishop and Saneh could meet me?" He checked the map again. "Albuquerque will work. That will give me enough time to assess the situation thoroughly."

"Solid plan. I'll continue to monitor the target's handset and let you know if he gets off the train."

"Excellent." Ivan hung up and walked outside to hail a cab.

***

SOUTHWEST CHIEF

As Ivan flew from Chicago to Kansas City, Howard and his analysts were already hard at work. Following his briefing he'd divided them into two teams. He and Heather had the Philippines lead while Stewart and Andrew went back through every detail of historical reporting.

When Howard logged onto his profile and opened his email he had a message from the NGA. They'd completed his task and uploaded the files to a secure site. He sent the logon details to Heather. "Can you start going through the imagery. We're searching for a RHIB and also anything suspicious."

"What do you mean by suspicious?" she asked.

"Ships in the area, aircraft, literally anything they could have used to escape."

She nodded.

"I'm going to duck out and take care of some admin." Howard collected his phone from the guard at the exit and crossed over into a partially empty restaurant car. He dialed a number as he sat in a booth.

"Hello, Piggy," answered the sultry voice. "I'm looking forward to seeing you soon."

"Yeah, so sorry to do this but I've been called away for work."

There was a pause. "That's not acceptable, Piggy."

"I'm sorry, Mistress."

"I will come to you and punish you."

"You can't, I'm working." Howard remembered the train would pass through New Mexico, not far from Nevada. Maybe he could get Mistress Axera a cabin and they could still play. "Actually, I'm going to try and book you a ticket. I'll email through the details. You'll have to fly to Albuquerque."

"I will be waiting, Piggy." She terminated the call.

Howard smiled as he used his phone to log on to the Southwest Chief website. He booked one of the last remaining cabins, a flight to Albuquerque from Las Vegas, and emailed them to Mistress Axera. All work and no play made Terry a dull boy, he thought as he handed the phone back to the guards and walked up to the intel level. The team was hard at work behind their computers.

"Terry, I've found something," said Heather.

He rolled his chair over to her terminal. "What is it?"

She had an image on the screen. "See this, it's some kind of thermal bloom." She enlarged the object. "Came up on one of the DSP satellites," she said referring to the space-based missile launch detection system.

The infrared shot was grainy but the object was clearly hull shaped. It could very well be their missing RHIB. "I wonder why it's on fire?"

"I wondered the same thing but then I thought they might be burning the evidence."

Howard nodded. "Makes sense."

"I scanned the area around it and found this." She flicked to another image.

He leant closer. The imagery showed a small twin-engine aircraft flying east. "Well done, Heather, that right there is their exfil platform."

"Yes but how did they get off a boat and into a fixed-wing aircraft two hundred miles out to sea?"

"Maybe it's a float plane. Whatever it is it's not going to have a long range. We need to start searching nearby islands."

"NGA ran a search out to three hundred nautical miles. I'm only half way through the imagery."

"OK, I'll start from the other end of the deck." As Howard rolled back to his terminal he took a moment to glance out through the shuttered windows. They were rumbling through flat farmland, on their way to Kansas City. In less than twenty hours they would reach New Mexico. He felt a tightening in his pants as he fantasized about what Mistress Axera would do to him.

Shaking his head he turned to his computer and commenced sorting through the imagery. The NGA analysts were thorough. Each image came annotated with a short description and metadata. Rather than check every one he decided to search using the term 'aircraft'. It returned fifteen matches. The first three were commercial airliners that were transiting through the region. The fourth was very interesting. It revealed an unusual-looking aircraft perched on a strip of sand only thirty miles from where they had found the burning RHIB. Beside it were two black circular objects. "What the hell is that?"

Heather came across and looked over his shoulder. "I have no idea. Andrew, Stewart, do you know what type of aircraft this is?"

The two men joined them and glanced at the screen.

"Looks a lot like a V-22 Osprey," said Andrew. The stationary aircraft had two propellers facing upward like a helicopter.

Howard shook his head. "I thought only the Marines had those?"

"They do but this ain't an Osprey. It's a tilt rotor, yes, but it's too skinny. Has to be some kind of variant." He pointed at the two circular black objects next to it. "If I had to guess I'd say they're refueling."

"OK, thanks guys, that gives us something to work with."

As the two men returned to their workstations Howard walked across to their open source terminal. He typed in V-22 and went straight to the Wikipedia page. An intel analyst's savior, he thought, as he scrolled to the bottom of the entry to where it listed similar aircraft. The only comparable aircraft was an Augusta Westland 609 tilt rotor. He clicked on the link and scrolled down to the images. No doubt about it, the aircraft the NGA had found was a 609.

He checked the listing of known operators. Half a dozen firms and government agencies were listed along with a note that said up to twelve aircraft were owned and operated by individuals. At the bottom of the page he found a link to the aircraft's official site. He clicked through and found a brochure detailing the aircraft's characteristics. One aspect interested him more than any other; the range.

"OK Heather, we've got a solid lead here. This aircraft has a maximum range of 1,100 nautical miles. If they're refueling this close to the extraction location it's because they're working to their limits. We need to extend the search area. If we cut a wedge in the general direction that they were heading we should be able to narrow it down. He opened Google Earth. "What are the coordinates of that island?"

Heather read them out and he entered them. The map zoomed in on the sandy landmass. He dropped a distance measuring point on the map and slid it out 1,100 nautical miles on the same bearing the RHIB was travelling. "OK, so we're roughly searching in and around the Marshall Islands. Let's see what surveillance assets we can get on that." He logged off the terminal and went back to his secure system.

"We could task a Global Hawk. They can do an electronic sweep of the target area in a matter of hours."

"Good call. Work up a tasking request. These Major League guys use some high-tech kit. If they're there, they'll be emitting." He turned to Andrew and Stewart. "Guys, I want you to focus on all the aircraft that have been used by them, not just this tilt rotor. I recall they've used a C-130 before, as well as the business jet. Do a deep dive into them. Tail numbers, previous flight plans, companies they're registered to. Someone has to be supporting or bankrolling them. I want to know names and places. Let's see if we can build out this network." Howard spun back to the screen. "Oh, and how do I get a coffee around here?"

CHAPTER 14

LASCAR ISLAND

Flash threw his hands in the air and released a raging bellow. Realizing he was wearing noise-cancelling headphones he glanced around sheepishly. None of his intel team comrades had paid him the slightest attention. Except Chua, who was frowning at him from behind his computer.

"What's up?" the intelligence chief mouthed.

Flash shook his head and removed his headphones as Chua left his workstation and approached.

"You look frustrated, Flash."

"I'm getting nowhere with Redemption. Every time I think I've found an in, I end up chasing a rabbit down a dry hole." He took off his cap and ran his fingers through his hair as he leant back in his chair. "The guys that built this thing are good, damn good. I can't get a read on their server location, even using the data we pulled out of the Philippines."

"Is it possible to use that intel to work out who else Howard has been communicating with?"

Flash shook his head and reached for the Nerf gun on his desk. "That server's probably one of a dozen that the CIA use to ghost calls. Be like searching for donut at a cop convention. The only reason we were able to trace Howard's original cell is because he made two calls to two different numbers in a very short period of time."

He loaded a dart into the toy gun, racked the slide, and fired it at the glass doors. It slapped against the surface and stuck. "Woo hoo," he cheered half-heartedly.

"So, I guess we wait to see what comes out of the Howard lead." Chua checked his watch. "Bishop and Saneh won't be landing stateside for another six hours. How about you take some time off?" He gave the analyst's shoulder a pat and returned to his desk.

Flash closed his eyes and exhaled. Down time sounded good. Sleep had been elusive since returning from the mission in the Philippines. Every time he lay down he felt the rocking of the boat and the onset of nausea. He might pop a sleeping pill and get his head down, he thought.

As he pushed away from his desk an alert appeared on the screen. He frowned; the message was from Forewarn, a program he'd developed to monitor traffic to certain websites. In particular it watched sites relating to signature PRIMAL equipment like their AW609 tilt rotor, Dragonfly. If certain parameters were met, Forewarn sent out an alert. He opened the program.

Someone had searched for AW609s on a machine that had also been used to access information pertaining to a broad range of contemporary intelligence issues. He tried to ping the IP address to locate the user but it bounced. Not a good sign. Using the IP address he ran a search on its latest web hits. A few seconds later the system returned a detailed report. The computer had recently been used to access Google Earth. His pulse quickened, the search protocol had been a lat-long. He pasted the coordinates into a mapping program. The pin landed 200 nautical miles east of the Philippines. "Chua, we've got a big problem."

***

Chua, Vance, and Flash sat around the conference table with their attention focused on the monitor bolted to the far wall. On screen was the bearded face of Tariq Ahmed, the CEO of Lascar Logistics and their primary benefactor. He, along with Chua and Vance, held veto on every PRIMAL mission. It was rare that the Arab businessman and former head of Abu Dhabi's Police Special Tasks Department involved himself in day-to-day decision-making. Usually his participation was limited to monthly target selection meetings. However, today's situation was far from normal.

"Tariq, can you hear us?" asked Vance.

"Yes, loud and clear. Good afternoon, gentlemen." He flashed a charming smile.

"I'm going to hand straight over to Chua who'll brief us on the situation." He turned to the intelligence chief.

"As you're aware, Tariq, for the last few weeks we've been tracking a significant threat to the organization. Up until this point our adversary has lacked the intelligence to target us directly. We believe this has changed in the last few hours. Flash, if you will."

The analyst leant forward and glanced up at the screen. "Hi, Tariq. Someone, most likely a CIA asset, was able to observe Dragonfly when it extracted our team from the Philippine Sea. I'm not exactly sure how but my guess is they probably relied on surveillance satellites to locate our refueling point. Needless to say they ran an open source search on the aircraft, including its range, and entered the coordinates of the refueling point in Google Earth."

"Have they been able to break through the cover story for the aircraft?" Tariq asked. Dragonfly had been purchased through a Ukrainian arms dealer using an intermediary broker.

Flash shook his head. "No, I think the cover story is intact. What it gives them is a search zone and Lascar Island sits smack bang in the middle of it."

The green-eyed Arab wore a frown. "There's no doubt that the CIA is behind the Redemption Network, is there?"

"CIA personnel are almost certainly involved," answered Chua. "However, given that the only Redemption contracts we've seen so far have involved the illegal rendition of American citizens, it's most likely not officially sanctioned. I assess that only a small number in the CIA have been exposed to the program."

Vance spoke up, "So as you can see we're facing a significant problem. We're in a race to determine exactly who in the CIA is tracking us and shut them down before they find us."

"What leads do you have?" asked Tariq.

"Very few," replied Chua. "The name Larkin has been mentioned and Vance knew a Thomas Larkin responsible for managing contracts when he was in the CIA. Redemption could be one of his projects."

"Is he a viable target?"

"Not at this point," said Vance. "Even if we confirm Larkin has knowledge of Redemption, targeting him is a last resort. Taking direct action against a senior CIA official is not something we should consider lightly. It could bring the entire Agency down on us."

On screen Tariq nodded. "Indeed. What else do you have? What were the outputs from the Philippines?"

Chua answered, "Flash has still been unable to penetrate the Redemption Network, however, we've identified a CIA analyst who was in regular contact with Pershing when he was in Mexico. We've also linked him to the GES site in Virginia. I've tasked Ivan with close surveillance. Bishop and Saneh will take over from him and exploit."

"So what you're telling me, Chua, is currently we have limited fidelity on the threat against us. A threat that has the potential to identify PRIMAL's presence on Lascar Island in the immediate future?"

"That's correct."

Vance interjected, "In consultation with Chen, it's my recommendation that we affect an immediate lockdown of the island."

Chua nodded. "We stay underground, minimize comms, and use our passive sensors to monitor any surveillance activity."

Tariq considered the recommendation. "That makes sense to me. I will initiate security protocols here in case you are required to evacuate."

His statement was met with silence. Evacuation was not something anyone wanted to contemplate. It meant that PRIMAL had been compromised and would essentially spell the end of the organization as they knew it.

"OK!" announced Vance. "Until further notice all movement above ground is cancelled and communications traffic is to be kept to a bare minimum."

"I guess that means I should go?" asked Tariq.

"Chua's team will monitor and give you the all clear when the threat has passed."

"Understood. Tariq, out."

The screen dimmed and they sat in silence for a moment before Vance spoke. "OK, let's make this happen. Inform all deployed elements that comms with the Bunker is for emergencies only. Chua, keep your team monitoring all intel feeds. Flash, no drag racing on the tarmac. We're gonna make like moles and wait this one out."

CHAPTER 15

KANSAS CITY

Ivan waited on the platform for twenty minutes before the Southwest Chief appeared from the darkness. He glanced at his watch. It was 2305. The service was only running a few minutes behind schedule. Impressive considering the debacle that was the national rail system. As the train screeched to a halt he counted the number of cars being towed behind the twin diesel locomotives; there were twelve double-decker carriages.

He rose from the bench and approached a blue-vested attendant who stepped down from the train. The man checked his ticket, grabbed his newly purchased suitcase, and led him to a carriage. Ivan followed him up the steps and along a corridor to his room. He was pleasantly surprised. The Superliner bedroom was small but contained a long bench seat that converted into a bed. It faced an armchair next to the window. There was also a toilet and shower tucked away in a tiny alcove.

After tipping the attendant he made himself comfortable in the armchair and checked his iPRIMAL. He'd received a message from Chua; the Bunker was on lockdown until the threat of detection passed. It meant little to him. As a Blade he mostly worked alone, pathfinding and establishing networks and safe houses for other PRIMAL operatives. Before Saneh and Bishop arrived, he would scope out the train, identifying opportunities and threats in preparation for their pending operation. He'd already booked out the room next to his, ready for them to board in Albuquerque, New Mexico.

The train shuddered as it pulled away from the station and gathered momentum. He kicked off his leather shoes and reclined in the chair. After a short nap he would begin searching for Howard. The train was scheduled to reach Albuquerque late tomorrow afternoon. By then he needed to know everything there was about Howard so he could give

Bishop and Saneh a comprehensive handover. With any luck he could disembark near Las Vegas and hit the blackjack tables. Gambling was a release, an opportunity to escape the calculating world of espionage and leave the outcomes to lady luck.

***

BEALE AIR FORCE BASE, CALIFORNIA

"Hey Brewster, you grown a set of balls and asked that barmaid out yet?" United States Air Force Captain 'Shadow' Cross glanced across at the First Lieutenant who manned the sensor operator workstation.

"Dude, I'm waiting for the right moment," snapped 'Brewster' Smith.

The officers were crewing an RQ-4 Global Hawk drone. Based out of the 9th Reconnaissance Wing in California, they spent countless hours together in the cramped ground control station. Three hours into an eight-hour surveillance mission, they were already bored senseless.

"The right moment? The right moment is right after you order a beer." Cross put on an impersonation of Smith's southern drawl. "Hey, Clarissa, can I grab a beer? Oh and while we're talking, what are you doing this Friday night?"

"If only it was so easy," Smith replied forlornly as he scanned his monitors. The lovesick First Lieutenant was responsible for monitoring the Global Hawk's sophisticated sensor suite. He was currently using the aircraft's electronic warfare package to search for electromagnetic radiation. The CIA had requested a high priority sweep of a search box in the middle of the South West Pacific. "Hey, what exactly are we looking for out here?"

"CIA mission so probably terrorist training facilities," said Cross.

"Terrorists, in the Pacific? Sounds a bit far-fetched."

"That's what makes it such a good place to hide out. You could put Bin Laden on one of these islands and no one would ever know he was there. Screw Abbottabad, if I was trying to hide from the Agency this is where I'd be. Thousands of islands, surf, fish, and all the coconuts you can eat."

"You're full of shit." As Smith studied his console he noted a spike on a bandwidth analyzer. The signal originated from a small atoll located in the cluster that made up the Marshall Islands. "Dude, I'm getting some activity here." He focused the drone's synthetic aperture radar and a grey image of the tropical island appeared on the main screen.

"There you go," said Cross, "probably a bunch of terrorists hanging out on the beach. You want me to set up a loiter pattern?"

"Yeah, would be good to give this a detailed scan." He locked the sensor on the atoll. "Might also be worth sweeping the surrounding islands."

"Affirm." Cross made some subtle adjustments to the drone's navigation system. "Let me know when we're good to move on."

"Hang on," Smith said with a frown. The electromagnetic spike was gone. He looked at the adjacent screen and studied the radar image of the tiny island. He couldn't make out any sign of life. He switched across to the infrared camera and searched for thermal activity. After a few minutes he gave up. "I've got nothing here. Let's start checking out the surrounding islands."

***

LASCAR ISLAND

Flash was taking out his frustration on the shooting range in the lower levels of PRIMAL's underground facility. With the base locked down he wasn't able to race his Triumph Scrambler on the runway, which was how he usually dealt with stress. Instead he worked on his shooting with the organization's South African operative, Kruger.

"The key, bro," said Kruger, "is to focus on being smooth and efficient. Speed comes later, with practice. What we want to do now is get the movements right. Train the muscles and the brain."

"OK." Flash adopted a combat shooting stance. One foot slightly forward, feet shoulder width apart, and slightly hunched forward. He reached to his hip and placed his hand on the butt of the Glock. Sliding it out of the holster he concentrated on smoothly transitioning the weapon from his side up in front of his chest where the other hand waited. He slowly thrust the weapon toward the target as he took up the slack in the trigger. The foresight appeared in his vision and he concentrated on balancing it on the center of the silhouette. When the rear sight lined up he squeezed. A hole appeared an inch below the target's head.

"Awesome, bro. Now you do that a couple hundred times and we can step it up a notch."

Flash returned the pistol to its holster and exhaled. "You're right, this is pretty cathartic."

"I'm down here with the boys at least once a week. You're welcome to join us any time. Right, let's go again."

Flash was reaching for the pistol when the iPRIMAL in the pocket of his shorts vibrated. "Sorry, dude." He pulled it out and checked the screen. "Oh shit, I've got to get back up to the Bunker." He turned for the door.

"Flash, pistol!"

"Sorry." He cleared the Glock, handed it to Kruger, and dashed out of the range. He took the elevator and when the doors opened jogged into the Bunker. Chua and Vance were waiting. "What's going on?"

"The passive sensors have gone off on comms node two," reported Rachel, the on-duty watchkeeper.

Flash sat behind one of the terminals and logged in. When his interface came up he checked the link to their communications relay island. It was offline, shut down when the sensor tripped. He checked the automated message. It had been hit by a synthetic aperture radar. "Guys, there's a surveillance platform up there looking at us. Best guess it's a Global Hawk."

"Could it have sniffed the comms link before it shut down?" asked Chua.

Flash shrugged. "Can't say. It depends on what sort of payload they're running. It's possible but it would have to be the latest generation gear." Another alert popped up on the screen. "We just got swept by the same radar." He glanced up at Chua and caught the concerned look he shot Vance.

"What do you recommend?" asked Vance.

"There's nothing else to recommend," said Chua. "The comms node is offline. We're completely isolated from the outside world. We've still got our passive sensors but can't communicate or access any data feeds."

Vance nodded and looked over at the watchkeeper. "Rachel, is everyone fully prepped for evac?"

"Yes, Vance."

"Alright, if we get confirmation that this facility has been compromised, we're out. Now, get Mirza in here. We need to run through our contingency plan in case the island is attacked."

CHAPTER 16

SOUTHWEST CHIEF

Howard finished reading the 9th Reconnaissance Wing report and glanced out the window at the desert landscape rolling past. The Global Hawk hadn't found anything considered suspicious. Most of the signals had been deemed normal for the region; microwave transmitters, UHF and VHF radio traffic, and a number of cell phone and satellite networks.

The only minor anomaly had been a brief transmission from an isolated island a few hundred miles from Bikini Atoll. The crew had swept the area but had been unable to locate the originator. Apart from an old World War Two era runway on a nearby island there were no signs of habitation. Howard drummed his fingers on the desk as his gaze lingered on the desert. The sun was high in the sky and the harsh terrain looked inhospitable. "Heather, have you finished pulling up the imagery of the islands?" He had tasked her to collate an intelligence deck on the area.

"Yes, it's in your inbox."

"Cool, can you walk me through it?"

"Sure." She walked over and stood behind Howard's terminal.

He opened the document. The first slide showed an overview of the region with red squares denoting the island with the transmission anomaly and a number of other locations of interest.

"I checked the island and the immediate surrounding area. Our communications anomaly emitted from this atoll." She pointed to an island with a red box around it. "As you can see, it's tiny and there is no sign of habitation. But, if you go to the next slide I'll show you something that's really interesting."

Howard clicked to the next slide. It was a detailed image of a large island dominated by an extinct volcano.

"This is a perfect staging area. There's an old runway that still looks usable as well as a large hangar and a bunch of beach huts. You could easily hide a platoon's worth of guys here, maybe more."

Howard enlarged the image. "Did the SAR on the Global Hawk pick anything up?"

"Next slide." Heather waited till he clicked across.

The satellite imagery was replaced by an oblique greyscale shot from the Global Hawk's radar. "As you can see there's nothing interesting. The next slide shows the infrared shot. Same again, nothing."

"Doesn't mean there's no one there, though. Just means they're damn good at hiding. Great job, Heather. I think we need to get someone to check it out." He opened a new email, wrote Larkin a short message, attached the intelligence pack and hit send. "Right, I'm going to go and make a few calls."

He walked downstairs to where the guard manned the exit. "My phone, please."

The guard handed the device over and unlocked the door that led to the dining car. Entering the restaurant Howard nearly collided with a salt-and-pepper-haired gentleman who excused himself in a British accent. Howard gave him a nod and sat at a table.

He sent a text to Mistress Axera. They were only a few hours from Albuquerque and she hadn't replied. The response was almost instant; she had landed and would meet him at the train station. He smiled and waved over an attendant. "Can you find me the manager please?"

The attendant disappeared and a moment later he returned with another man.

"What can I do for you, Mr. Howard?" asked the mustached Conductor.

He leant across and gestured for the man to come closer. "I was wondering if you could move the cabin I've purchased. I have a lady friend joining me at the Albuquerque stop and I'd like somewhere discreet to spend some time with her. As close as possible to the rear of the train."

The Conductor nodded. "I will see what I can do."

Howard tipped him and returned to the intel car, leaving his phone with the guard. When he logged back on to his terminal he already had a message from Larkin. The director was organizing a team of top-tier contractors to search the islands. Excellent; he finally felt like they were making headway.

***

LANGLEY, VIRGINIA

Thomas Larkin was at Langley for the second time in a week. He'd been summoned by his boss to run through the numbers on a contract in Libya. Briefing complete he'd returned to his office to arrange a Redemption contract. As he was about to pick up the phone a senior CIA officer, Brian Masters, barged into his office.

"Thomas, how are you?"

"Busy."

"I've got an issue I want to discuss. It'll only take a moment."

Larkin knew the only reason the official would be approaching him was to help with a delicate matter. More specifically he would have a problem that could only be solved by someone willing to bend the rules.

Technically an employee of the US Government was, under Executive Order 12333, prohibited from conducting assassinations. As far as Larkin was concerned that was a joke. What the hell were drone strikes if they weren't assassination? Another one of the CIA's archaic and hypocritical policies, he thought.

He leant back in his chair and addressed the man who outranked him. "Brian, let's cut to the chase. Exactly what do you need from me?"

"One of my agents has gone rogue. He's feeding intel to the Saudis."

"And why don't you deal with this in house?"

"Because, technically he's an American citizen."

"Oh, and you want me to take care of it."

"If you could."

"I most certainly can. But you're going to have to do something for me."

"What?"

"Come now, I asked you for it yesterday. Don't tell me you've already forgotten."

Brian clenched his jaw and fixed Larkin with an icy stare. "We're the only ones who have authorization for its use. I'll let you have it but you need to run any of your plans past me first."

Larkin had absolutely no intention of complying with the demand. "Deal, do you have the agent's source number?"

"I'll have his file sent up."

Larkin shook his head. "No, I just need his name or number." He pushed a notepad across the table.

The officer scribbled the name down.

"And the information I asked for?"

He sighed, pulled out a notebook, flicked to a page, and copied the details across to Larkin's pad.

"Consider it done. Now, if you don't mind I've got a problem of my own to deal with." He waited for the man to leave and dialed King. "Charles, I need a short-notice team for a recon."

"Where?"

"An island in the South West Pacific."

"Does this have anything to do with the Major League Network?"

"No," Larkin lied. "A short-notice job. I need some heavy hitters." As he talked he logged on to his laptop and opened the target pack from Howard.

"There's a firm based out of New Orleans. They've got their own aircraft and can pull together at least a handful of guys at short notice. They're hard up for work so you'll get a good price."

"They're experienced?"

"Yeah, you could say that. Been working on and off for the Agency for years."

"Excellent."

"Thomas, is anything developing on the Major League front or am I up here freezing my balls off for nothing?"

"I'll know in the next few days. It won't be long. In the meantime I want you to arrange the guys in New Orleans. I'll send you the details. There's a fifty grand bonus in it if you can get them on target in the next twenty-four hours."

"What's my budget?"

Larkin opened a spreadsheet on his computer and checked some numbers. "Quarter of a million."

"And if I can do it for less?"

"You can keep the difference."

"I'll let you know in the next hour."

"Make it happen. I'll email you the information." Larkin terminated the call and checked that the target pack from Howard contained no mention of Major League. Confirming it was clean he sent it through to King. Work done for the day, he grabbed his bag and left the office.

He was in his car when the GES boss rang back.

"We're in luck. The team is in Papua New Guinea waiting for a job to kick off. They can be on your island within ten hours. That puts them on the ground at 1130 hours local time tomorrow morning."

"Excellent, you've just earned yourself an extra fifty-K, Charles."

"Just get me the hell out of this frozen shit hole."

***

ALBUQUERQUE, NEW MEXICO

Mitch touched down at Albuquerque International Airport and disembarked Bishop and Saneh before flying to Los Angeles to refuel and standby. On his way out he airdropped their snatch pack. He was their only backup now the Bunker was in full lockdown. An automated message had informed the team of the communications shutdown.

In Albuquerque, Bishop and Saneh cleared customs and caught a cab to the outskirts of town. The driver waited as Bishop located their air-delivered pod in a field. Another short ride took them to the train station where they picked up their tickets. Now they sat on a bench at the platform holding hands. Once again they were playing the newlyweds.

Bishop felt overdressed. Albuquerque was more backwater than cosmopolitan and locals dressed accordingly. He wore tailored slacks, a button-down shirt, and a sports jacket. His hair was parted and black-rimmed glasses sat on his nose. Saneh looked cute in a summer dress with her hair up and bright red lipstick. It was an attempt to appear as un-operator as possible. Their combat sneakers and cargos were in their luggage.

Bishop glanced along the platform. There were a half-dozen other travelers waiting, hoping to escape the dust and heat of the drab desert city. A stern-faced Asian woman caught his eye. She wore a khaki wrap-around dress that didn't quite match her high-heeled leather boots.

"Why don't you take a photo?" Saneh dug her elbow into his ribs.

"You jealous, babe?" He kissed her on the cheek.

"Of that? No."

"Good, because you have more sex appeal in your little finger than her."

Saneh glared at him. "Is that all I am to you, sex appeal?"

"Not at all. It's just–" The train horn sounded as the Southwest Chief appeared in the distance.

Saneh pressed her lips to his cheek. "It's so easy to stir you up."

The train approached the platform and they waited for it to come to a complete halt. Bishop gathered their bags and they moved toward their designated carriage. Ahead of them Bishop noticed a familiar-looking portly figure step down from the train. He realized it was the guy from the service station in Virginia; their target, Howard.

He watched as the rotund CIA analyst walked up to the Asian woman in the boots. He tried to take her hand and she frowned, directing him to her bags. Howard hefted them from the platform and followed her up into the train.

"She's got an attitude," said Saneh.

"That was Howard," replied Bishop as he found their carriage.

"Oh, so he's got a lady visitor. Very interesting."

He guided her inside the carriage. An attendant showed them up a set of stairs and along a narrow corridor to a cabin. He unlocked the door and gave them a brief tour of the shoebox. Bishop placed their bags on the floor and tipped him.

"What is this, a cabin for ants?" he said as he closed the door behind the attendant.

"I think it's quaint." Saneh sat in the armchair at the window and opened the backpack Bishop had recovered from the air-dropped pod.

Bishop sat on the bench seat opposite. The carriage shuddered as they pulled away from the station. He checked his watch. "It's an hour till they start serving dinner. You hungry?"

"No, I can wait." She laid out the contents of the snatch pack on the table. Two compact HK .45 pistols were followed by suppressors, holsters, a Taser, two rolls of thick black tape, a bundle of zip-ties, and finally a black case containing syringes, auto-injectors, and pharmaceuticals.

There was a knock at the door. Bishop picked up one of the pistols, racked the slide, and checked a round was chambered. "Who is it?"

"An old friend," said a British-accented voice.

Bishop let Ivan in and shook his hand. "Good to see you, mate."

"You too, Aden." Ivan smiled at Saneh. "Hello, very nice to see you also."

"Likewise. Been a busy few weeks."

The Russian operative ran his eye over the equipment set out on the table. "No rest for the wicked, I see."

Bishop offered him a seat on the bench. "Is your room this small?"

"Exactly the same, my friend. Now, I don't have a lot of time. I'll be leaving you at Flagstaff and I'm guessing you're going to want to make a move on our friend as soon as possible."

"Yep, we're running against the clock on this one."

"Understood." Ivan sat and crossed his legs. "The last car on the train has been booked by a private organization. The lower level is being used as accommodation. Two security guys work shifts providing access control. They're armed with pistols and possibly submachine guns. Upstairs has been converted to an office. According to my source, six orders are delivered at each meal, however, he also says they occasionally eat in the adjacent dining car. It's logical to assess there are four people in the office."

"Have you seen any of them in the dining car?"

"The only person I've seen come and go is the target."

"Howard?"

"Yes, he's smuggled a lady onto the train. They're in the next sleeper, end room."

Bishop chuckled. "I saw the girl. But, how do you know all this?"

Ivan shrugged. "The Conductor is a gentleman and a connoisseur of fine scotch."

"OK, how do they receive the meals?"

"I've seen an attendant deliver them to the door. The guard unlocks it and they pass in the food. If you're going to approach with any semblance of stealth you'll have to convince the guard to open the door."

"Got it. And the dining car has direct observation onto the entrance of the target car?"

"Yes, but it closes at nine. The bar stays open till eleven."

Bishop glanced at Saneh. Both were assessing their options. "OK, so how do you suggest we should run this?"

"That depends. Do you want access to the IT systems they've got in the carriage or do you want access to the information Mr. Howard has in his head?"

"Both."

"In that case I recommend a night approach. That way most of the occupants will be asleep. If you isolate Howard with his lady you may be able to interrogate him with minimal risk of compromise. That way you'll spend the least amount of time in the target car. The armed guard behind the locked door is the primary obstacle."

"What if I go around him?"

Ivan frowned. "We're on a train. Your options regarding terrain are limited."

"I could go over the top and come down behind them."

Saneh rolled her eyes. "Disregard his crazy ideas. He's been watching Bond movies again."

"Come on, it's legit."

"The risk is substantial," said Ivan. "If I were you, I would use Saneh's obvious charms to your advantage."

"All I wanted to do was run along the top of a train."

Saneh put a hand on his arm. "I know, darling, but I've got a better idea."

Ivan nodded. "I have no doubt the two of you will be able to manage this problem. I on the other hand am going to have one last drink with the Conductor."

***

FORT YUKON RESEARCH STATION

King sat in the operations room at a computer reading James Castle's file. The guy was a patriot and a hero, he thought. Castle had run CIA paramilitary operations in Kosovo, Afghanistan, Chechnya, and half-a-dozen other places before faking his death in the UAE. The asshole he was suspected of assassinating was an influential Wahhabi extremist, a sponsor of terrorism, and an all-round scumbag no matter how you looked at it. Then, Castle turns up wounded in Afghanistan working allegedly as a mercenary.

Something didn't add up. Why would someone like Castle turn his back on everything he stood for and start working for cash? What's more, his partner, Vance Durant, also suspected of defecting from the CIA, had a file just as impressive. He glanced up at a screen on the wall that monitored Castle's cell. "What aren't you telling us, buddy?"

He scanned the other camera feeds and paused on the entrance to the detention facility. At the top of the stairs one of Small's guards struggled in the snow with a gurney. On it lay a black body bag. "What the hell!"

He bolted out of the room, down the stairs, and burst outside. Ignoring the biting cold he crunched through the snow to the underground cells. The guard was still struggling with the gurney when he intercepted it. He yanked back the zipper of the bag to reveal Wesley Chambers' waxen face. The former investment banker's eyes were wide open and appeared to stare at him.

King clenched his fists and stormed down into the facility. Small wasn't in the office so he checked the interrogation lab. The creepy little murderer was wiping down his precious chair. "What the fuck did you do?"

Small glanced up at him with cold black eyes. "Your little friend had a heart condition. I couldn't revive him." He returned to cleaning his chair.

"You piece of shit, he'd already given up everything he knew."

"Please, he still had so much more to tell." Small smirked. "Plus, from what he told me, I simply finished off what you couldn't. You tried to poison him. I wouldn't be surprised if that's why his heart gave out."

Small's comment hit home. It was true; he had ordered Wesley's death. But a lot had changed since then.

"Lost for words? That's because you know it's the truth. That's what I do, Charles. I find the truth. Some men like James Castle are good at hiding it but I always find it in the end. Thanks to Wesley Chambers I now have the information I need to break him."

"Larkin told you he wasn't to be touched."

"No, he said he was to remain alive."

"You lay a hand on that man and I'll put a bullet in your sick little head," King snarled.

Small looked as if he would challenge the threat, then simply nodded. "Castle can wait."

King glared at the interrogator before leaving the room. He stopped in the corridor and glanced toward Castle's cell. Something here did not feel right.

CHAPTER 17

LASCAR ISLAND

Chen Chua waited on the porch of the caretaker's hut as the grey Grumman HU-16 Albatross touched down on Lascar Island. It taxied the length of the runway and stopped in front of the rusted iron hangar that contained the hidden entrance to the PRIMAL base.

The island's passive radar network had detected the incoming aircraft but it wasn't exactly what Chua had expected. He'd never seen an Albatross before. The amphibious flying boat was designed in the 1940s and was ancient compared to PRIMAL's modern fleet. He didn't recognize the symbol on the tail. It was some kind of bird sitting on a globe, not particularly subtle for a mercenary outfit. He assumed that's what they were. A legitimate special operations team would have at least attempted to infiltrate covertly.

It was midday and Chua was dressed in a tattered and soiled pair of formerly blue coveralls. His black hair was messy, face unshaven, and there were bags under his eyes. As the old Albatross powered down he took a sip from a battered tin mug and stepped down the weather-beaten steps onto the cracked tarmac.

He strolled toward the twin-engine deep-hulled aircraft as a rear door opened and a ladder slid to the ground. Black boots and cargo pants appeared followed by the torso of a muscular man wearing a black tactical vest over a black T-shirt, topped off with a black beret. The outfit was bizarre and Chua tried not to smirk as he spotted a silver revolver on his thigh.

"Hey, bro, you the guy that looks after this place?" The man's voice was gravelly to the point of being almost unintelligible. His face was weathered, the droopy skin reminding him of a bloodhound. Chua judged the man on the downhill side of fifty but he was in good shape with broad shoulders and veiny forearms.

"Yes I am the caretaker. My name is Han." He wiped a hand on his coveralls and thrust it out.

The mercenary's lip curled as he grasped it in a crushing grip. "So, Han, you got any aircraft in that hangar?" He jerked his thumb in the direction of the rusted shed.

Chua shook his head. "No, it is empty. We don't get many planes anymore."

By now another four mercenaries had fanned out from the aircraft and were poking around the hangar and the caretaker's hut. Like their leader they all wore eclectic black outfits and carried a varied array of weapons.

"That right, huh? Well how about you open it up so I can check it out?"

Chua winced as the man grabbed his coveralls and pulled him close. "OK, OK, no need to get nasty."

"Bud, you haven't seen nasty yet."

Chua shivered involuntarily as he led the mercenary across to the hangar. He opened an access door and gestured for him to enter.

"After you." The brute placed a hand on the grip of his revolver.

"See, no aircraft," Chua's voice echoed as he entered. The space felt like an oven and light streamed in from holes in the tin roof.

The man scanned the hangar, squinting into the shadows. His gaze lingered on the false stone wall hiding the entrance to the underground PRIMAL facility. The crew had taken extra precautions before the lockdown. Dust had been sprayed across the floor removing any trace of aircraft movement.

"What else is on this island?"

"Not much. There are beach huts at the other end of the runway."

"Who owns them?"

"Some rich guy. A Sheik or something. I don't know, I just keep it looking nice."

"Hey boss, there's nothing here." The voice from the doorway was British and belonged to a bald-headed guy with an athletic build.

"You got transport?" the mercenary boss asked.

Chua nodded. "I have a cart outside. The keys are in it."

The boss yelled at the Brit, "Go check out the huts at the other end of the runway. Take the buggy."

"Will do."

Chua followed the mercenary boss out of the hangar back onto the tarmac. He glanced up at the sheer granite cliffs. The receiver lodged deep inside his ear crackled. "Seriously, this guy's old enough to be my dad," transmitted Kruger. The South African was hidden above the cliffs, concealed on the thickly vegetated slope. He and Mirza were watching through the scopes of their sniper rifles. "And what's with the beret and the vest? These assholes step straight out of the 80s?"

Chua snorted, struggling not to laugh.

"What's funny, wise guy?" snapped the mercenary as his men raced up the runway in the buggy.

"Nothing."

"Damn straight nothing, punk!" He strode across the tarmac toward the caretaker's hut and the pier that stretched into the bright blue water of a lagoon.

Chua followed as Kruger continued transmitting, "How old is that airplane? I'm pretty sure Amelia Earhart tried to cross the Pacific in it."

"OK, let's keep it down," interrupted Mirza.

Chua watched as the mercenary inspected the aluminum workboat tied against the pier. Loaded with fishing and snorkeling gear, the twin-engine vessel was mainly used by the PRIMAL team for recreation. The mercenary swaggered back up the jetty grumbling. "Goddamn wild goose chase."

"What are you looking for?"

"None of your damn business."

The buggy appeared at the other end of the runway and raced toward them. The guy with the British accent drove with two men in the back.

"Nothing up there. Couple of nice little condos and that's it," reported the Brit.

The boss scowled. "The Agency isn't getting a discount on this. Let's go check out the other island." He pulled out a satellite phone and dialed as he walked back to the plane.

Chua followed at a respectful distance.

"What do you want?" the Brit snapped at Chua.

"I was wondering if you are going to pay landing fees."

"Fuck off, yeah."

He watched as the men climbed back into the aircraft. Their boss pocketed the phone as he disappeared inside. The engines spluttered to life and it taxied onto the airstrip. With a roar and puff of black smoke it lurched down the runway and took flight. "They're heading to another island," said Chua.

"One of the comms islands?" Vance asked from deep within the Bunker.

Chua watched as the amphibious plane climbed before banking west. "Possibly. If they do they're going to find the comms array."

"They need to be neutralized."

Chua walked back into the old hangar. The cliff face at the rear split with a rumble and he entered PRIMAL's underground lair. "I agree. I'll be in with you in a minute." He rode the elevator down to the Bunker and joined Vance and Frank on the operations floor.

"If we launch an aircraft what's the chance it will give us away?" asked Vance.

"We're in the middle of a surveillance satellite window," said Chua. "We have to assume NRO assets have been tasked to monitor the island."

"OK, how about we use the work boat to infil the CAT?" asked Frank.

"That's a good idea," Vance said. "How long will it take to reach the island?"

"An hour or so," replied Frank.

"Alright. Get them underway. Everyone else needs to prepare for evac on the Pain Train."

"I'm on it."

As Frank left his terminal Chua followed Vance to his office. "I'm not sure we need to evacuate yet. There's no indication that we've been fully compromised."

"They're close enough, Chua, we can't take any more risks. Once the CAT deals with that squad of geriatric mercenary wanabees we're getting the hell out of here."

***

SOUTHWEST CHIEF

The secure phone at Howard's workstation rang and he snatched it off the cradle. "What?" It was well past dinner time and he itched to escape the intel carriage and see Mistress Axera.

"That's no way to answer the phone, Terry," said Larkin.

"Sorry, sir, I'm a little frustrated."

"Well this isn't going to help. The island turned out to be a dry hole. There's an old hangar and some beach huts but no sign of any recent activity. Allegedly it's owned by a Sheik."

Howard scribbled on a piece of paper. "Have they checked out the other island yet? The one with the emissions?"

"No, they're on their way now. I'll let you know what they find."

"OK, thanks."

The line went dead.

Howard spun to face his analysts. "Guys, that was Larkin. He says the team that searched the island with the airfield found nothing of interest. I'm not buying it. I want to know who owns that airfield and what it's used for. Go back through historical satellite imagery if you have to. I want to know if it ties in to any of the aircraft that have been linked to these douche bags."

"Terry, we've already got a lead on the island. It belongs to an air-freight company called Lascar Logistics," said Heather.

"Lascar? That name's familiar. Why?"

"Because a Lascar Logistics flight dropped the refuel on the Nemesis," said the usually softly spoken Stewart. "What's more they have an extensive fleet of business jets that could fit the profile of the one that Major League has been using."

Howard leaned back in his chair and a broad smile crossed his face. "Let me guess, they have AW609s?"

This time Andrew replied. "No, not on paper anyway. It is possible that they have them sitting in a sub-company."

"OK, check that. Also look for 609s on the plane-spotting forums and see if they correlate with Lascar Logistics nodes." The analysts jotted down notes before turning back to their terminals.

Howard glanced at his watch; it was 2206. He wanted to call Larkin but could wait until the director got back to him about the island. Everything was starting to come together. Their Major League prisoner, James Castle, had been posted to the Emirates when he'd faked his death. Lascar Logistics, he already knew, was based in the same location. He was confident that once they delved into Lascar they would start to uncover the support network for Aden and his terrorist buddies.

For an hour Howard fought the urge to make an excuse and leave the carriage. He had been fighting it ever since he'd smuggled Mistress Axera onto the train. He glanced at his watch again. It could take the men on the ground hours to search the island for the source of the emissions. There was no reason for the entire team to stay awake waiting. "OK guys, we've got some very strong leads now. We need to get some rest. Let's turn in for the night and kick off again in the morning. Andrew you can take the first shift. I'll replace you in about two hours."

The mustached analyst glanced up from his terminal. "OK, Terry, not a problem."

Once Heather and Stewart retired to their cabins Howard raced downstairs. The guard unlocked the door, allowing him into the restaurant car. There were only three people drinking as he headed through to the next sleeper carriage.

His pulse raced as he knocked on a door. The latch lifted, he slid it open, and stepped inside. The tiny cabin was dark. He stood in the middle of the room and tried to contain his excitement. "Piggy is reporting for duty, Mistress," he said meekly.

The door slid shut behind him, a lock clicked, and the light snapped on. "Hello, Howard."

He spun and found himself staring down the barrel of a suppressed pistol.

"Take a seat." The man holding the weapon flicked it in the direction of the chair in the far corner of the room. Howard's legs shook as he walked across and sat.

"The girl, where is—"

"She's fine."

The guy with the pistol had intelligent brown eyes and looked strangely familiar. It clicked; Aden, the man in front of him was Aden. "Dude, I've been looking for you."

"I know but it looks like I found you first." He smiled pleasantly. "Don't worry about the... girl. We're not in the business of killing innocents."

"So what do you want from me?"

"First, I want you to answer my questions."

Howard swallowed, his eyes fixed on the pistol leveled at his head. "Are you going to kill me?"

"That's completely up to you. Answer my questions and I'll consider letting you go. I'm not an uncivilized man, Howard. This can be a pleasant conversation between friends or it can be something else."

"What do you want to know?"

"For a start I want to know who you work for."

Howard took a deep breath then exhaled. "OK, his name is Thomas Larkin."

"Go on."

"He's the Director of OSP."

"OSP?"

"Operational Support Program. They run clandestine contracted solutions to the CIA's problems."

"So Redemption comes under OSP?"

"You could say that. Redemption is Larkin's personal project."

***

As Bishop interrogated Howard, Saneh prepared for a mission of her own. She examined herself in the wall mirror as she applied blood red lipstick to her lips. Her hair was down and she had borrowed dark eye-makeup from the Dominatrix's luggage. "I hope you don't mind," she said to the woman trussed up on the bed.

There was no response from the Mistress; five ccs of Midazolam ensured she'd remain unconscious for the next few hours.

She adjusted the tight summer dress that revealed her long brown legs and deep cleavage. She was breaking one of her rules in showing both, she thought as she checked her handbag. The pistol inside was her backup plan.

She locked the door as she left and sauntered along the corridor into the restaurant car. It was devoid of customers. Soft lounge music and the rumbling of the train were the only sounds in the carriage. The clock on the wall said half-past eleven and the barman looked bored. She had already checked him out at dinner: roughly Bishop's size, in his early forties, and not ugly. She shot him a sultry smile and leaned against the counter so he could get a good look at her assets. "Kind of dead, isn't it?"

He smiled. "Yeah, all the retirees went to bed."

Saneh laughed. "Must be pretty boring for you."

He shrugged. "You'd be surprised how many sixty-year-olds hit on me."

She ran her eyes over his uniform. With a bright blue vest and matching bow-tie she thought he looked like a circus monkey. "Some women can't resist a handsome man in uniform."

"Would you like a drink? I have to close up soon but there's still time."

"Why not? How about a dirty martini?" Saneh cringed as she said it. She needed to dial it back a bit and seem a little less desperate.

"So where's the guy you had dinner with?" he asked as he grabbed a shaker.

"I don't want to talk about it."

"OK."

She sat quietly as he finished making the drink, poured it into a martini glass, and slid it across the bar. "There you go, my lady."

"How much do I owe you?" She reached for her bag.

He held up his hand. "No, it's on the house."

She raised the glass to her lips and took a sip. "Very nice. Thank you so much."

Fifteen minutes later the bartender had closed up and Saneh led him down the corridor to her cabin. It was cute how nonchalant he tried to act as she slid open the door, gave him a wink, and gestured for him to enter. Flicking on the light, she stepped in after him and slid the door shut. "Clothes off, please."

The man spotted the hog-tied dominatrix unconscious on the bed. "What the…" His voice trailed off as he eyeballed Saneh's pistol.

"Clothes off."

"Hey, I'm not down with this weird shit."

"If you take your clothes off, you'll get to live."

He removed his vest, tie, shirt, pants, and shoes.

"Good. Now kneel facing the window with your hands behind your back."

He obliged and she secured his hands and feet with cable ties. A syringe appeared from her handbag. She flicked off the cap and plunged it into a vein in his arm. A few seconds later his head slumped forward and she eased him onto the floor. She changed out of her dress into cargo pants, a T-shirt, and trainers.

168

"You kids play nice, OK." There was no response. She gathered up the barman's uniform, flicked off the light, and stepped out of the cabin, securing it behind her. It was a short walk to the room where Bishop was. She knocked on the door and he let her in. Howard sat in the armchair, his forehead damp with perspiration.

"Hello." Saneh smiled as she handed the clothes to Bishop.

"Hi," Howard replied nervously.

"Can you watch him?" asked Bishop.

"Sure." Saneh sat on the bench seat and pulled the pistol from her handbag.

Bishop changed into the bartender's outfit. "No change to the plan," he said, adjusting the bow tie. "I'm going to follow Howard to the car, disable the guard, and you join me with our gear."

"Got it, darling," she replied.

"Now, Howard, if you try to tip off the guards I'll shoot you. Wake up any of your buddies and I'll shoot you. Get past the guard, log in, and you may get to live. Got it?"

He nodded, his eyes wide with fear.

Bishop pointed his suppressed HK at Howard's forehead. "Good, because I really don't want to have to kill you, Terrance. Not now that we've become such good friends." He draped a cloth over his pistol and picked up a covered stainless tray from an earlier meal. "Come on, let's go." He pushed Howard out of the room and they walked along the corridor and through the empty dining car.

As they exited Bishop spotted the burly guard through the next door's window.

The guard saw them approach and unlocked the door. Howard stepped through with Bishop behind.

"What's up, Mr. Howard?" asked the guard.

"Not much." He gestured to Bishop. "I thought Andrew might want something to eat."

Bishop shoved the tray at the guard who clutched it. He raised his suppressed HK. "Hands where I can see them, champ."

The guard frowned.

Bishop read his intentions and pistol-whipped him in the temple as he went for his weapon. The guard collapsed, sending the tray crashing to the floor. Saneh appeared behind them and aimed her pistol at Howard as Bishop dragged the body into a toilet.

Bishop emerged half a minute later having hogtied and sedated the guard. He looked down the corridor at the bedroom doors. There was no noise apart from the rumbling of the train. "OK, let's head upstairs," he whispered.

They climbed to the office level with Howard leading. As they entered Bishop spotted one of the analysts asleep at his terminal. He woke the man with a gentle shake. "Hey, shhhh, yeah."

The mustached analyst woke with a jolt. "What the hell?" Oblivious to the gun Bishop held pointed at his head he stood, staggered from the desk, and made a dash for the back stairs.

Bishop fired twice and the analyst hit the floor with a thud.

"Shit," he whispered. He checked the body before turning to Saneh. She shook her head.

Howard's eyes locked on the corpse. "Please don't kill me," he bleated.

Bishop grasped him by the shoulder and pushed him into a chair in front of a computer. "OK, Howard, let's get this started. I need you to log in. Now."

He sat transfixed until Saneh nudged him with her suppressor. "OK, OK." With shaking hands he typed a password into the laptop. The screen opened to the Redemption Network analytical workspace. He looked up as Bishop reached over and plugged in the vacuum drive. The lights on the slim black box lit up.

Howard glanced at the dead body of his fellow analyst sprawled on the floor. Blood was leaking out of his head onto the carpet. "If I give you a piece of information will you let me live?"

Bishop glanced at Saneh. He had no intention of killing Howard in cold blood but he wasn't about to tell him that. "Depends how good the information is."

"Larkin has one of your people."

"We know, Wesley Chambers."

Howard shook his head. "No, some guy called James Castle."

The name hit Bishop like punch to the guts. "Are you sure?" he said slowly.

"Yes, yes, used to be in the CIA. He rolled with you in Ukraine, right? Got blown up in Afghanistan."

Bishop gritted his teeth. "Where is he?"

"Some OSP site—"

"Get your hands where I can see them!" a man wielding a machine pistol yelled from the stairwell.

Bishop snapped off a shot forcing the guard to duck out of sight. "Saneh get the drive!" he yelled as he continued firing.

As she yanked out the vacuum drive and sprinted for the rear stairs the guard thrust his machine pistol around the wall and fired a spray of bullets.

Bishop flinched as the roar of the weapon deafened him. He fired again and turned to Howard. "Let's go." The CIA analyst didn't respond. He was slumped forward on his keyboard with the back of his head missing.

"Fuck!" Bishop shoved the body aside and jammed Flash's nuke USB into the laptop.

"Covering!" Saneh fired her pistol as he dashed to the rear of the carriage.

"Down the stairs!" Bishop yelled. He reloaded as he hunkered down behind a server rack. The guard entered the carriage again blazing away with his submachine gun. Bullets punched through the aluminum server cabinet causing it to spark and hiss. He grabbed the metal box and pulled it over in front of the stairs. The case split and he caught a glimpse of something that didn't belong. "Holy shit!"

Bishop skidded down the stairs and saw Saneh advancing down the corridor with her pistol ready. She was going to work around behind the guard. "We need to go!" he yelled as he ripped open the emergency exit. The tracks raced away from the carriage as the train climbed a steep gradient; now was the time to jump. "Go!" he screamed as she strode toward him.

"What the—"

"Jump!" He grabbed Saneh and pushed her through the open door.

She leapt into the darkness. Bishop gritted his teeth and followed. Jamming his feet together and turning sideways he hit the sleepers hard and spun over in a parachute roll, his chin pressed to his chest. As he staggered to his feet he called out, "Saneh!"

"I'm over here."

His eyes adjusted to the darkness and he spotted her lying twenty yards further down the tracks. "You all right?" he asked running to her side.

She rolled over and sat up. The darkness didn't hide the anger that flashed in her eyes. "It was only one guard! I had—"

A huge explosion lit up the night sky. They turned and watched as a ball of fire blossomed up from the train.

"Was that you?" she asked softly.

"No, some bastard packed the server with explosives. I think Larkin just covered his tracks." He helped her up. "We need to get the hell out of here and RV with Mitch." He pulled the iPRIMAL from his pocket.

"Where are we?"

"According to this we're not far from Barstow. We can probably get a cab to L.A. and use the comms link on Sleek to upload the data to the Bunker."

"Once they're back on comms."

"Yeah." He slid down the railway shoulder into a dry ditch. "You do have the drive don't you?"

Saneh patted her backpack. "I've got it." She glanced at the train, which was grinding to a halt. The rear carriage was split open like a firecracker and burned fiercely. "Aden, who is James Castle?"

Bishop helped her over a fence. "You know him by another name."

"What's that?"

"Ice."

CHAPTER 18

SOUTH WEST PACIFIC

Mirza had the engines of the workboat running flat out as they raced toward the communications island. The aluminum craft was designed for open water and they quickly ate up the distance to the smudge of green on the horizon. In the back the other three CAT operators readied their equipment. All were dressed in jungle warfare rigs complete with mottled-green nanotube armor. Fully-enclosed helmets had been omitted in favor of short brim jungle hats and, if required, NVGs mounted on head-harnesses. Like Mirza, Miklos and Pavel carried suppressed Tavors. Kruger wielded the heavy metal, a MK48 machine gun slung over his shoulder. In the boat they also had a Barrett .50 caliber sniper rifle, spare ammunition, and a SA-24 heat-seeking missile launcher.

As they closed with the island, Mirza spotted a dark speck on the horizon. It was the Albatross amphibious plane. As it grew in size he realized it was heading toward them. "Guys, he's taking off."

"Not on my watch," said Kruger. The big South African placed his machine gun on the deck and shouldered the missile launcher.

Mirza coaxed more speed from the twin engines. The seaplane rapidly grew in size. "He's coming right for us!"

The water next to them exploded in a mushroom of foam and spray from a large-caliber high velocity shell.

He threw the boat sideways as more rounds hit the ocean, drenching them.

"Fuck," Kruger swore as he was thrown to the deck.

The twin-prop grey seaplane roared over them and climbed.

"If that thing gets around again we're dead!" yelled Mirza.

Kruger was back on his feet at the stern with the launcher on his shoulder. "Hold us steady."

The missile leapt from the tube with a pop and its rocket motor ignited thirty yards from the boat. With a roar it accelerated after the banking seaplane. The lumbering aircraft spat flares.

The PRIMAL team cheered as the heat-seeking missile flew straight as an arrow and detonated in a bright flash. Exaltation turned to despair as the Albatross flew on.

"Shit!" Kruger dropped the empty launcher and hefted the machine gun to his shoulder. The others followed suit as the aircraft continued to bank. A greasy stream of smoke spewed from one of the engines and it burst into flame. It wobbled as the pilot struggled to keep it level. There was a second explosion and the left wing dipped, touched the water, and sent the flying boat cartwheeling into the ocean.

When they reached the crash site all that remained was a scum of oil and some floating debris. They could see the outline of the fuselage through the clear water. It had broken in half on impact and sunk to the bottom.

"That's what they get for shooting at us," grunted Kruger. "What's the chance they were all onboard?"

Mirza scanned the island with a pair of binoculars. "There's no way the pilot could have spotted us from sea level. He got warning from someone on high ground."

"Then we need to clear the entire island. It's going to be dark soon. We can hunt granddad and his geriatric hit squad at night."

"No, Vance wants this wrapped up, ASAP. Let's get this done before sunset." Mirza pushed the throttles forward and they accelerated toward the island.

***

FALLS CHURCH, VIRGINIA

Larkin was in his apartment but couldn't sleep. Instead he was working at his desk on the wording of a new contract for outsourcing surveillance in Pakistan. When his cell phone rang he didn't recognize the caller ID. Who the hell would be calling his private number at four in the morning? He frowned and answered the phone.

"Mr. Larkin?"

"Who is this?"

"My name is Dale, I was working on the train." Sirens wailed in the background.

Now it clicked; this number had been given to the security guards on the train as the primary emergency contact. He glanced at the secure chat link on his computer and saw that Howard and the other analysts were offline. "What's happened, Dale?"

"Some guy jumped me and now…"

"Spit it out, man.

"Now they're all dead! The carriage exploded; the guards, the analysts, they're all dead."

Larkin bit his lower lip. "What about the man who attacked you?" He snatched up the remote on his desk and turned on the TV mounted to the wall. Muting the sound he flicked to CNN.

"I don't know. There were two of them, a man and a woman. They could be in the wreckage. Do you want me to tell the authorities?"

"No, stick to your cover story. You work for a software company who hired the carriage."

"Yes, sir."

"My people will get in touch with you." Larkin terminated the call as the story flashed up on the TV. He watched as fire trucks blasted the shattered carriage with foam. A ticker tape running across the bottom of the screen proclaimed it a terrible accident. The self-destructing server rack would have burnt at close to ten thousand degrees. There would be no evidence linking the CIA to the carriage and its occupants. The authorities would be lucky to find anything to identify them. He picked up the secure phone on his desk and rang his IT guy in Dead Land.

"I was about to call you," the man answered.

"Talk to me."

"Someone tried to hack the network from the train. The deniable security protocols got activated and, well, you can see the results on CNN."

"What did they get?"

"Only what was stored locally. The Redemption intel database was being accessed remotely via the server here."

Larkin drummed his fingers on the desk as he evaluated the damage. "Can you tell me if a specific file was on their system?"

"Yes, sir."

"Search James Castle."

There was a pause. "I've got two files, sir; a personnel file and an interrogation report."

"Is there any reference to Dead Land on the drives?"

The man could be heard typing before he responded. "Yes, Wesley Chambers' detention report."

"And they got it all before the charge tripped?"

"I assume so, sir. Whatever they used to suck up the data was pretty high level. The system didn't detect it immediately. The malware they uploaded almost neutralized the self-destruct mechanism, almost."

Larkin watched the footage of the burning carriage. "Unfortunate for the analysts."

"Sir, do you want me to back up our data to another site?"

He contemplated the idea. If things got out of hand all of that information would need to be destroyed. He couldn't afford any chance that it could be tracked back to the OSP. "No, sit tight. I'll let you know if that's required." He ended the call and flipped open his diary. He found the phone number he wanted and lifted the phone.

"Operations Senior Master Sergeant O'Malley speaking," answered a clipped voice.

"O'Malley, it's Operations Director Brian Masters from the CIA. I need to initiate an air tasking under Global Vigilance."

"OK, sir. Is this an ad hoc mission or a preplanned serial?"

"Preplanned, I have the OPORD number here." He read it out.

"Sir, do you have the approval code for activation?"

Larkin picked up a loose piece of paper from his desk. There was a number written on it as well as a codename. He read them out to the Master Sergeant.

"OK, sir, strike aircraft will be prepositioned within the next 12 hours. The air intercept capability is already standing by. You've got a trigger here for a pre-registered airstrike, do you want to use a codeword for that?"

"Yes, the codeword will be Archangel."

"Roger, I confirm Archangel. Mission is loaded and on your call. Is that all, sir?"

"That's all, Master Sergeant."

"Very well, sir, have a good night."

"You too." Larkin placed the phone back in its cradle. He glanced up at the row of clocks above the television. The time in the Pacific was 1700 hours; the mercenary force had cleared the main island four hours ago. He was about to ring King but instead turned to his computer and logged into a remote viewing portal for Dead Land. He scrolled through the external cameras and noted it was snowing again. When he got to the internal feeds he found the operations room and expanded it to full screen. Sitting in front of the monitors were King and one of his men. The GES boss's presence confirmed that the mission on the islands was still underway. He checked the time again and yawned. He needed to get some sleep. King and the island could wait until tomorrow.

***

SOUTH WEST PACIFIC

Mirza crouched in the treeline with Kruger to his left and Pavel on the right. He'd kept Miklos on the boat for flexibility. The Czech would shadow them from the ocean as they cleared the island, providing options for exfil and fire support.

The island was small, about the size of a city block. Dense tropical jungle covered its mountainous slopes except for a rocky outcrop at one end. That's where the communications array was hidden and where Mirza assessed their enemy would be heading. The best case scenario was that most of them had been on the downed aircraft and were now in a watery grave. Mirza didn't plan for best case; as far as he was concerned they were all on the island and wanted him and his team dead. "OK, let's move."

"More fucking jungle," grumbled Kruger as they stepped off.

"Stay alert, these guys look experienced."

"Experienced or just old?" replied the big South African.

After fifteen minutes of patrolling Mirza spotted the first sign of their prey; fresh boot prints in a patch of sand. He crouched and counted four sets of prints.

"Any sign of wheelchair tracks?" asked Kruger.

"You'll get old one day," replied Mirza.

"No, I'm going to burn bright and go out like a soldier."

Light was fading and he knew there was roughly thirty minutes until sunset. As good as their night vision was he preferred to track with natural light. Mirza glanced to his left and it took him a moment to spot Kruger. The mottled green A-TACS camouflage blended perfectly with the lush vegetation. "Four tangos," he transmitted.

Kruger gave him a nod and the others pressed their transmit buttons in confirmation. They patrolled forward steadily, scanning the vegetation for any sign of the enemy. As they progressed the jungle grew thicker, forcing them to converge. Soon they were in single file with Mirza on point. The ground began to slope upward and the tracks he followed weaved in and out of large outcrops of volcanic rock. As they climbed toward the peak the thick jungle was replaced with more boulders and jagged rock.

"Guys, I've got movement a few hundred yards ahead of you," Miklos transmitted from his position on the boat. He was tracking their progress via the iPRIMAL and manning the sniper rifle. "I don't have a shot."

The higher they got the more rugged the terrain became. Mirza signaled for them to spread out, reducing the risk if they were ambushed.

As he rounded a boulder he caught a glimpse of a black shape crouching. He fired a round and it ricocheted off a rock with a whine. "Contact!"

Gunfire broke out on Kruger's side of the hill.

Mirza spotted a figure leap off the rock above him but not in time to raise his weapon. A savage kick hit the center of his armor sending him smashing against a boulder and sprawling onto the ground.

"You shot down my plane you piece of shit!" yelled the man in a gravelly accent. He wore a black beret with a silver six-shooter strapped to his thigh.

As Mirza scrambled to his feet the mercenary boss charged, knocking his Tavor rifle from his grasp, and shoving him backward.

"You shot down my plane, you killed my friend, and now I'm going to crush you!" he bellowed as he kicked the rifle into the bushes.

Lying on his back, Mirza considered drawing his sidearm. However, the mercenary was already poised, hand over the holstered revolver.

"You think you're fast, kid?"

As Mirza rose to his feet he wondered why the old mercenary kept talking. They squared off only a few paces apart and he lowered his hand till it was only an inch from the butt of the Glock. Drawing it was second nature to him. He'd spent thousands of hours on the range honing his drills.

The mercenary's lip turned up in an ugly scowl. "Go on. I'm gonna take you down, punk."

Mirza drew the Glock and fired as it cleared the holster. His first round caught the muscle-bound thug in the thigh. The second hit him in the stomach as he managed to snatch his revolver from the holster. He grunted as he struggled to raise the weapon, his face a mask of determination. Mirza's sights lined up and he squeezed off one last shot. The bullet punched a neat hole through the man's twisted features and he collapsed to his knees before toppling over.

Mirza searched the body and recovered a satellite phone. He slipped it into a pouch as more gunfire sounded from Kruger's direction.

"Motherfuckers!" roared the South African. "I've got a sneaky little ninja trying to throw goddamn knives at me and two other fuckers behind a rock."

Mirza shook his head as he grabbed his Tavor and moved toward the gunshots. These people were nuts, he thought. Who the hell brought throwing knives and revolvers on a mission? "Miklos, can you work your way around to the other side of the island and provide surgical fire support?"

"Already on the way," replied the sniper.

"Pavel, where are you?"

"On the other side of the peak. I've got eyes on the comms node. No sign of any hostiles," he reported.

"That's because they're all shooting at me," transmitted Kruger. "Anytime you wanna join the party, boys." The suppressed MK48 chattered in the background.

Mirza pushed higher, between the rocky outcrops, angling toward the gunfire. He'd moved a dozen yards when he spotted tracer rounds bouncing off a cluster of boulders. "Kruger, I'm on your flank."

"Good, watch out for the damn ninja. He's dressed in black."

"They're all wearing black!" Mirza scanned the terrain around him. There was no sign of Kruger's assassin. He refocused on the craggy ridge that the South African was engaging. There were at least two gunmen using it for cover. Light was fading fast. He needed to flank them and wrap it up. Something struck the back of his armor and he spun. Crouched on the rock above him was the black-clad ninja. Mirza found himself starting down the barrel of the Asian mercenary's submachine gun.

"Now you die," the Asian said with a smirk.

The smile was blown clean off his face by a .50 caliber round. The body spun through the air and landed next to Mirza with a wet thud.

"Mirza, can you confirm that's a hit?" asked Miklos over the radio.

He grimaced at the headless man. "Yeah, that's a hit. Thanks." With the ninja dead he could now focus on eliminating the final two men that Kruger had pinned. "Miklos, do you have eyes on the last two mercs?"

"Negative."

They were going to have to do it the hard way. "Kruger, how are you for ammo?"

"Got another hundred rounds."

"Pavel, locstat?"

"Right behind you," the Russian replied.

"Pavel, on me. We're going to flank them." Mirza took the lead and they worked their way around till they were almost ninety degrees to Kruger's position.

The firefight was short and intense; the two mercenaries didn't stand a chance. By the time they realized they were being flanked, the PRIMAL operatives' 300BLK rounds were tearing into them.

"Crazy motherfuckers had a death wish," said Kruger as he arrived.

Mirza shook his head as he checked the bodies for intel. "We should be thankful the CIA didn't send in Tier One operators."

"I wonder why they didn't?" asked Pavel.

Mirza shrugged. "Chua and Vance think we're dealing with an element of the CIA that uses contractors to do their dirty work. They would have sent these guys because they're expendable."

"Poor bastards," said Kruger.

"Well, now we have to carry them. The entire site needs to be sanitized. We'll ferry the bodies out to where the plane sank and lay them to rest with the pilot. Then we need to load up the comms relay gear." Mirza glanced at his watch. "Let's get this done ASAP in case there's a follow-on force."

***

FORT YUKON RESEARCH STATION

King dialed the number for the mercenary's satellite phone for the third time in an hour. Once again it failed to connect. "What the hell is going on?"

He tossed the handset on the desk and glanced up at the screens bolted to the wall. The local time in the Marshall Islands was displayed; it was two in the morning there. He'd taken a call from the team leader in the late afternoon reporting they had found nothing. They were supposed to check in every hour. Something had to have gone badly wrong. He ran his eye over the other screens. James Castle was safe in his cell. The interrogator had not gone near him.

"Boss, I'm launching another drone," Chris said from behind his bank of touchscreens.

"Good, I want twenty-four hour coverage."

"You think someone's out there?"

"Maybe, maybe not. We can't take any chances. You remember what these guys did to the mine in Mexico, right? They're playing for keeps."

"Yeah, true."

King watched on a screen as the drone climbed above the facility, crossed the fence, and commenced its patrol route. He picked up the phone and dialed Larkin. "I can't raise my guys on the island."

"I guess that confirms Major League were there."

"Major League? You said this wasn't related."

"I wasn't sure if it was."

"Well, what are you going to do about it? I can have thirty more operators down there within twenty-four hours."

"They'll be gone now, Charles. Our next opportunity is Dead Land."

"What do you mean?" King glanced up at the camera feed from James Castle's cell.

There was a moment of silence before Larkin responded. "They hit my analysts last night. The team working on Major League has been eliminated. We have to assume Dead Land has been compromised and they know we've got Castle."

"Thomas, I read his file, he's a hero."

"These people are goddamn terrorists and now they know we've got Castle and where he is. He's not a hero, he's bait."

"I need more men."

"I'm not willing to expose anyone else to the project."

"Give me the funding and I'll bring another team up."

There was another pause. "Listen to me, Charles, you're in the most secure compound in the world. Each of the Talons are worth a platoon not to mention the towers. A handful more shooters ain't going to make a difference."

King clenched his jaw. "Let me bring in my people. I've only got three men."

"Use Aaron Small and his team."

"That little prick. You know he killed Wesley?"

"I am aware. The detainee had passed his usefulness."

"You people are animals." He slammed the phone down and turned to Chris. "How many of the Talons are online?"

Chris checked the status screen. "Four, the techs are working on the other two."

"Drones?"

"We've got one in the air and five on standby."

"If we gun up everyone how many shooters do we have?"

"Twelve, boss. But I don't know how useful Aaron Small's men will be in a gunfight."

"We need more operators."

"Yeah, about another fifteen if we're gonna hold this place. Set up positions on the perimeter. Otherwise we could fall back to the prison and lock it down. It's only got the one egress point."

King nodded. "Prepare the prison as an alternate position. Get the technicians to install a backup ops room there.

Nothing fancy, just a few laptops that we can use to control the towers and the drones."

"Will do, boss. We'll stockpile ammo, food, and water as well."

"Make it happen and step up the patrolling. I want to know if anybody is out there watching us."

CHAPTER 19

CALIFORNIA

Bishop and Saneh flagged a cab in Barstow and paid the grateful driver five hundred dollars to drop them at Ontario International Airport, east of Los Angeles. On the way they swung past the Starbucks outside the airport and grabbed a coffee for Mitch. It was still an hour to daybreak but both the cafe and the airport were already bustling with travellers.

Mitch was waiting outside the private terminal when the cab dropped them off. "You two have been busier than a one-legged man in a kicking contest," he said as he took the coffee.

"I take it you saw the news," said Bishop as he followed Mitch through the security checkpoint. They were unarmed, their weapons buried in the desert.

"Yeah, they're saying it was some kind of freak accident with computer equipment." Mitch led them across the tarmac to where Sleek was parked.

"Some cunning bastard put a bomb in the bottom of the server rack."

"Not exactly CIA standard operating procedure."

"Nope, Thomas Larkin definitely wants his tracks covered." Bishop sat in one of the aircraft's luxurious seats. Saneh chose the chair opposite and Mitch sat next to her.

"So what now?" the Brit asked.

"I think we should check out the data we stole," Saneh said as she searched in her backpack and pulled out the vacuum drive.

Mitch opened a laptop, took the drive from Saneh, and plugged it in.

"Run a search on James Castle," said Bishop.

The tech's fingers flew over the keyboard. "I've got a few PDFs but a lot of this stuff is unreadable. Looks like it's for a custom analytical program."

"Can I have a look?"

"Sure," Mitch passed him the computer. "You think they've got info on Ice?" Mitch and the former PRIMAL operative had worked together in Kosovo. They were also part of the group that initially formed PRIMAL.

"The analyst I interrogated claimed he's still alive."

"What? No, he died in Afghanistan." Mitch shook his head.

Bishop scanned a document. "Yeah, then why do these bastards have an interrogation report dated 2013?"

"You're kidding me? Where are they holding him, Guantanamo?"

"They were, but according to this they moved him somewhere else. Howard mentioned something about an OSP site."

"OSP?"

"Yeah it's some sort of CIA black ops outfit. Apparently Larkin runs it. He's probably got his own rendition facility."

Saneh leaned over and tapped the laptop screen. "If Larkin has a secret prison wouldn't they take Wesley to it?"

Bishop nodded. "Yes, good point." He ran another search and found a capture report for Wesley Chambers. He skim read it. "No shit."

"What?" asked Saneh.

"The job on Wesley was a GES contract. Charles King's name is on the report. He delivered him to some place called Dead Land. Mitch, is this laptop online?"

"Sure is."

Bishop ran a Google search for Dead Land. "Well, I'm guessing they're not holding him in a haunted house in Tennessee." He continued scrolling through the hits and clicked on a link to a blog. The author was an adventurer who explored abandoned government facilities. This particular entry referred to a US Air Force research station in Alaska in an area the locals called Dead Land. "Guys, this might be it." He spun the laptop so the others could see it. "It's an old USAF base in Alaska."

"That would make a perfect rendition facility," said Saneh.

"Do we have comms with the Bunker?" asked Bishop.

Mitch shook his head. "They're still locked down."

Bishop glanced at Saneh. Her stern expression reflected the gravity of the situation. PRIMAL's island base had never been threatened like this before. "Do we have enough fuel to get to Alaska?" he asked Mitch.

"Yep, and I've still got the operator equipment pod in the back if we need weapons."

Bishop turned to Saneh. "What do you think?"

"Sitting around here is a waste of our time and we can't head back to the island. I vote for checking it out."

Mitch jumped to his feet. "Righto, chaps, let's get this show on the road. I'll lodge a flight plan and get in contact with a mate of mine up there who might be able to help out with transport."

***

LASCAR ISLAND

Vance sat in his command chair in the Bunker with a glass of scotch in his hand. For the first time in as long as he could remember the screens on the roughly-cut stone wall were off. The desk usually occupied by the watchkeeper was empty and the room silent. He glanced at the intel cell as the lights went out behind the opaque glass. A moment later, Chen Chua appeared with a laptop tucked under his arm.

"How you doing?" Chua asked.

He shrugged and grunted.

"You made the right call, Vance. The CAT found a satellite phone on the merc boss. He reported to someone not long after arriving on the comms island."

"Do we know who he called?"

"Flash ran it through the database. We don't know who it is but the number is one that Pershing called a few times," he said referring to the GES contractor they had killed in Brazil.

"It has to be King. We need to track him down."

"We can't do that till we're off the island and connected with our back-up systems in the UAE."

"OK, once Mirza and the boys are back we roll." Vance finished his scotch and placed the empty glass on the arm of the chair. He rose and grabbed his backpack. His other gear was already on the Pain Train. "Let's head up top."

He followed Chua to the elevator, stopped, and gave the room one last glance before he switched off the lights.

"We'll be back," said Chua as they stepped inside the elevator. The renovated World War Two base had been a perfect staging area for PRIMAL operations over the last few years.

"Damn I hope so. The Emirates is a shit hole."

The elevator doors opened to the high-pitched whine of idling turbofans and the stench of jet fuel. The vulture-winged Il-76 transporter's ramp was lowered and the rest of the headquarters team was already seated inside. Dragonfly, the tilt rotor, was shrouded in tarpaulins in the back corner of the cavernous space. With Sleek already deployed in the US, it was the only PRIMAL aircraft that would be left on the island.

"We've got an hour before the next satellite is overhead," said Chua.

The rock walls split with a rumble and the CAT strode in through the gap with weapons slung, carrying an assortment of communications components. Vance greeted each man with a handshake as they dumped the equipment in the corner. "Good work, guys."

With slumped shoulders they climbed the transporter's ramp and took their seats. Mirza continued through to the cockpit to join Kurtz. Inside the cabin the remaining staff sat quietly; Flash, the watchkeepers Rachel and Frank, an assortment of technicians, IT specialists, intelligence analysts, and other support personnel.

Vance followed them up the ramp and took a seat next to Chua. A moment later the ramp lifted a few inches and they slowly rumbled forward through the doors into the ancient hangar that masked the entrance. Behind them the lights in the cavern blinked out.

"You want the honors?" Chua held out a tablet.

"No, I'm good. Let's lock her down and get on our way." He watched as Chua used the tablet to initiate a sequence that closed the immense false-rockface and armed the security system. Unauthorized access would now trigger demolition charges, burying the PRIMAL headquarters beneath hundreds of thousands of tons of rock.

Vance caught a final glimpse of the false wall as the ramp raised shut and the Ilyushin turned onto the runway. With a roar it accelerated down the strip and lurched into the night sky.

"How long till we can contact Bishop and Saneh?" Vance asked Chua.

"Let's give it an hour."

He nodded and turned to gaze out the window as they banked around the dark mass that was the island. It had been his home for the last few years and he had a feeling that he wouldn't be seeing it again anytime soon.

***

PAIN TRAIN

As the Pain Train cruised at 35,000 feet over the Pacific Ocean, Flash sat in the alcove that housed the sensors and weapons controls. He used one of the terminals to access the back-up servers in their hangar in Abu Dhabi. He'd already uploaded the data captured from the mercenary leader's phone; the number he had called looked like a satellite phone. When he entered it into the analysis software his fears were confirmed; without NSA tools he had no way of tracking it.

Thumping the armrest of his chair in frustration he noticed a symbol in the corner of the screen. Someone onboard Sleek, their business jet, was uploading data to the intel dump folder. It has to be Bishop and Saneh, he thought. On cue Bishop's chess-piece icon flashed. He donned a headset and answered the call.

"Hey mate, you guys lifted the comms blackout?" Bishop's voice was tinny and distant.

"Not exactly, we've evacuated the island. We're all on the Pain Train."

"What?"

"A bunch of mercs landed earlier. They found the communications relay. The CAT took care of it but Vance ordered the shutdown as a precaution."

"So where are you heading now?"

"We're going to refuel in Singapore then fly to Abu Dhabi. Where are you guys?"

"We're on our way to Alaska."

It was his turn to sound alarmed. "Alaska?"

"I'll explain. Can you grab Vance, he'll want to hear this. Chua as well."

"OK, hang on a second." Flash dropped the headset on the workstation and strode through the narrow corridor to the door that led to the cargo hold. Most of the team was slumped in the fold-down seats, asleep. Vance and Chua were sitting together talking. He caught their eye and waved them over.

"What's up?" Vance asked as they reached the alcove.

"It's Bishop. He's on his way to Alaska." He handed them a headset each. "Bish, I've got Vance and Chua with me."

"Hi guys, Saneh and I had some success with Howard. We managed to question him and grab some data from his computer. Two things. First, we've confirmed that it's Thomas Larkin who's been hunting us. Second, Vance, they've got Ice."

"What?" Vance shook his head in disbelief. "Ice is dead."

"No, he survived. The Taliban captured him. He was found in Kunar province in 2012 by a team of Rangers. He spent two years being interrogated in Gitmo and now Larkin has him in a facility called Dead Land, which we think may be in Alaska. Wesley's probably there too. Check the files, Flash should have them all by now."

He nodded and glanced up at the Operations Director. Vance's face remained expressionless as he attempted to process the possibility that his closest friend was still alive.

"Bishop, it's Chua, you mentioned Larkin. What have you got on him?"

"Howard gave him up. Larkin is the director of the Operational Support Program. OSP handles sensitive contracted operations for the CIA. The Redemption Network is his baby, a deniable means of conducting illegal black ops."

"How big is OSP?"

"Don't know, but according to Howard, his intel team on the train was the only one working on PRIMAL. He called us the Major League Network and reported direct to Larkin. Apparently we are the OSP's number one priority."

"OK, we can work with this," Chua said excitedly. "So the analysts working on PRIMAL, what is their status?"

"Neutralized, and all the IT equipment and servers on the train have been destroyed."

"Right, knowing how compartmented a program like this would be, if we neutralize Larkin we might be able to contain what they know about us. We'll crunch the intel at this end and come up with a plan to target him."

"Ivan might be useful for that," added Bishop.

"Yes, I'll get him digging."

"Bishop, what's your ETA to Alaska?" asked Vance.

There was a pause. "We'll be wheels down in Anchorage in three hours. Stay overnight, sort out some cold-weather gear, then fly to Fort Yukon."

"And what's your plan once you hit the ground?"

"Mitch has a buddy up there, a dog sledder. He's going to help us recce the facility."

Vance turned to Chua and nodded. "Sounds workable. Let us know if you need anything from our end."

"A follow-on force ready if we confirm the target."

"Give us forty-eight hours to prep the assault package. In the meantime try to keep a low profile."

"Will do. Bishop out."

The alcove was silent as the three men contemplated the information that had been dumped on them. Flash had never met James Castle but like everyone else in the organization he was familiar with his story.

"Is it possible?" Vance broke the silence.

Chua sat at the spare terminal and started browsing the new intel. "It is possible. But, this could also be a ruse. We shouldn't rush into things."

"They've got Ice." Vance's tone indicated the mission wasn't up for negotiation.

"And probably Wesley," Flash added.

There was silence as they thought through the problem. A hostage recovery was a seriously complex undertaking. A hostage recovery in the middle of a frozen arctic wasteland took it to the next level.

Vance spoke first. "The CAT is going to need some specialist equipment. I'll get Mirza to send a list through to Tariq."

Chua looked up from the screen. "Arctic warfare kit might be hard to come by in the UAE."

"He runs one of the largest air logistics firms in the world. If we need it Tariq will find it."

"And Larkin?"

"Get Ivan on it. We'll crush these bastards. I want you to find Larkin, I want you to find King, and I want them both taken down."

Chua looked hesitant.

"What?"

"Here's the thing, we know the Redemption servers on the train were destroyed and the analysts neutralized. But we don't know for sure whether their intel has been backed up, or who else knows about it. The CIA have been hunting us since our Mexico op and now it seems they've had Ice since 2012. Taking out Larkin and King might not be enough."

"And that's why, bud, once this is all over we're all going to have to lie low for a while."

"I was afraid of that."

JACK SILKSTONE

CHAPTER 20

FORT YUKON RESEARCH STATION

Charles King stood at the door to Castle's cell and watched the invalid lying on the bed. The former CIA operative was a husk of the man described in his file. A shiver ran down his spine as he thought of the agony the poor bastard would have suffered at the hands of men like Aaron Small.

"Hey, boss, we're all set up." Chris stuck his head out of one of the cells.

King joined him in the tiny room. Three laptops were set up on a trestle table pressed against the wall. A hole had been drilled through the thick concrete to the room next door for the cabling. "Good job."

"We'll be able to run all the defenses from here. Got the spare ammo and weapons stockpiled across the hall. And we've filled the storage boxes with dirt for barricades." Chris gestured to the wires running through the wall. "There's a server room next door. Made it real easy for the techs to get it all set up."

"A server in here?"

"Yeah, the tech said it's the Redemption server, whatever that is."

King had never checked the last cell. He'd assumed it was the same as the others. The door was ajar so he pushed it open. A wave of warm air hit him as he entered. Rows of servers were mounted in racks and the hum of cooling fans filled the space. So this was where Larkin was hiding all his dirty little secrets, he thought. As he turned to leave he noticed a compartment at the bottom of each cabinet. He squatted and popped a panel off. Inside were enough explosives to turn the cell inside out. "Chris!"

The man appeared in the doorway. "Yeah, boss."

"There's a shit-ton of bang under here. I need you to see if we can get rid of it."

"Not a problem, I'll get Matt to sort it."

"Thanks, bud." King left the server room and walked down the corridor. He spotted Aaron Small at the far end. The interrogator glared at him and disappeared into his lab. "Piece of shit," mouthed King.

He passed through a gap in the barricade of containers, moved through the entrance anteroom, and up the stairs into the fresh snow. It crunched under his boots and he inhaled the crisp morning air. Beyond the chain fence with its razor wire and automated gun towers a blanket of fresh powder lay across the hillside. Tracks ran over it where one of the Talons had patrolled. The hill was where he would hide if he were looking to recon the facility. The wooded ridge offered covered approaches and the elevated terrain would have excellent visibility over the base.

He glanced up as a surveillance drone appeared in the distance. It grew in size and buzzed over his head, descending toward the hangars. The technicians would recover it and in a few minutes another aircraft would takeoff. The quadcopters had been patrolling 24/7. Confident that all was as it should be he returned to the main building and climbed the stairs to the operations room.

Hammer gave him a nod as he entered. "What's up, boss?"

"Chris has the alternate ops room set up. We'll run a full rehearsal of the systems later today."

"Roger. I've got two 'copters up and Talon out running a patrol."

King glanced at the screens. The tracked Unmanned Ground Vehicles followed a pre-programmed route scanning with their thermal cameras for anything out of the ordinary. If they detected an anomaly they alerted the controller. They could also be set for 'hunt to kill'. In that mode they would autonomously detect and destroy thermal signatures that met set parameters and were not wearing an identifier beacon.

Each of the six Talons was lethal out to 1200 meters; armed with a 7.62mm machine gun and four single-shot high-velocity grenade launchers. The six guard towers sported a similar configuration except they contained an automatic grenade launcher, additional ammunition, and were heavily armored. King estimated that his robot army gave him the equivalent firepower of a company of conventional infantry. However, the static towers lacked flexibility and he doubted the Talons could sustain much damage. He needed more men. "Has Larkin called back?"

Hammer shook his head. "Negative, boss, no calls."

King picked up the phone and dialed the OSP director's number.

The call rang for what seemed like five minutes before connecting. "Charles, you can't have any more men."

"I thought you might change your mind considering I'm up here with all your secrets. That's right, I found the Redemption server."

"Listen, you're not on your own. I've managed to secure a reaction force from Joint Task Force-Alaska. They have two F-22s on five minutes notice-to-move. They can be in your location in under half an hour."

He took a deep breath. "Can you send through the call sign and comms details?" The F-22 Raptor was not the optimal platform for a close air support mission but it was better than nothing.

"They'll be in contact." The call ended.

King dropped the phone. "He's given us a goddamn interceptor based out of Elmendorf. How's that supposed to help defend this facility? Screw that guy."

"CIA assholes are all the same, boss. You can't trust the fuckers."

***

LASCAR HANGAR, ABU DHABI

While Sleek was being refueled in Alaska, the Pain Train reached Abu Dhabi International Airport. Non-essential staff had been already dismissed in Singapore with a healthy bonus and orders to maintain a low profile. By now most of them would have boarded flights to their home locations. Only Vance, Chua, Flash, Frank, and the CAT remained on the transporter as it touched down with a thump and a screech.

They taxied across to the Lascar Logistics cargo depot and parked beside an identical-looking transporter. It was a little after midnight but the airfreight terminal was still busy. Abu Dhabi was the international hub of Lascar Logistics operations and the base for its fleet of aircraft.

Vance hit the button that lowered the ramp. It dropped slowly, revealing a gentleman with a trimmed black beard, dressed in an immaculate blue pinstripe suit. Tariq Ahmed's stern features broke into a smile as Vance strode down the ramp and reached for his hand. Instead Tariq threw his arms around the PRIMAL director and hugged him.

"Welcome to Abu Dhabi, my brother. What's mine is yours." His voice was as clipped and regal as his Savile Row suit.

"Tariq, despite the circumstances, it's good to see you."

Chua shook Tariq's hand and received an equally enthusiastic hug. As the three leaders of PRIMAL exchanged greetings the remainder of the team filed out and across to the hangar.

"Come, I've made some additions to your old home. I was able to get most of the equipment you requested. The other items will arrive tomorrow." Tariq, Vance, and Chua joined the team inside the cavernous maintenance hangar. Large enough to house a 747, the space officially belonged to an arm of Lascar Logistics called Priority Movements Airlift, the cover organization for PRIMAL.

It didn't seem to have changed much from when Vance had first used it back when PRIMAL numbered only five men. A row of shipping containers served as an armory and a workshop. Beside them a number of transportable buildings contained accommodation, a planning room, and a gym. In the far corner a large air-conditioned container housed PRIMAL's backup servers.

Tariq pointed to a new refrigerated shipping container that had been placed at the back of the hangar next to a pile of cardboard boxes. "Next to your arctic warfare supplies is the acclimatization setup you requested. My people installed a projector and weapon simulator so you can train with your new equipment."

"You've out-done yourself, Tariq," said Chua.

"Ah, you have seen nothing yet. For security reasons I've established your intelligence and command facility in another location. The CAT can remain here to prepare for the mission but the rest of you will be staying at one of my homes."

"I'd prefer to stay with the men," said Vance.

"I think Tariq's precautions are wise," said Chua. "Considering the threat."

"Alright, give me a minute with the boys."

Kruger, Pavel, and Miklos had dumped their equipment and were opening the boxes of arctic gear. As he walked across, Kurtz and Mirza joined them with their own bags.

"Team, I don't need to explain to you the importance of this mission."

The five men nodded.

"Bishop will be on the ground in Alaska within twelve hours to confirm the target. For now, assume the facility contains both Ice and Wesley. Personnel recovery is the primary objective. Secondary objective is exploitation of enemy IT systems. As we planned on the flight, we'll be using the Pain Train for precision fire support, and you'll be rolling heavy with the ATVs."

Mirza wore an intense look. He was the only one of his team that had worked with Ice, and had been on the mission when they'd lost him. "When can we expect to be deployed?"

Vance knew the Indian operative held himself responsible. "It's up to Bishop but your team needs to be prepared to move ASAP. The command team will continue to plan the mission from another facility and we'll give you timings once we've worked out the details. Bishop's team will send through intel and the targeting data for the Pain Train. If you need anything you can contact us via iPRIMAL. Questions?"

The men were focused and clearly wanted to start preparing the equipment.

"Alright, kick some ass, boys." Vance grabbed his own bag and joined the others at the door to the hangar.

A black SUV waited outside. Vance climbed in the front and the CEO of Lascar Logistics took the wheel. "Doing your own driving now?"

Tariq flashed him a smile. "We're not going far."

He drove them to the other end of the airport where an unmarked helicopter idled on the tarmac.

"The helicopter will take you to Nurai Island. That's where I have set up your facility." He turned to Flash, Frank, and Chua, who sat in the back seat. "You will find it meets all of your needs."

"You're not coming?" asked Vance.

Tariq shook his head. "No, I would just get in the way."

As the helicopter climbed into the night sky Mirza and the team in the PRIMAL hangar continued tearing open the boxes of new kit. They pulled out down jackets, winter boots, and a range of other extreme cold weather equipment.

"What sort of crazy camouflage pattern is this?" asked Kruger as he held up a set of overwhites. "Looks like lizard skin."

"It's called Kryptech Yeti," said Mirza.

"Looks very cool," added Pavel.

"First rule of Spec Ops," said Kruger. "Always look cool."

"What's the second rule?" asked Pavel.

"I can't remember." The South African grinned. "Something about not forgetting rule one."

"Get yourself sized up: gloves, jackets, pants, overwhites, and boots. Get your rigs adjusted for the extra bulk. Then we're going to head into the cooler and practice our drills," said Mirza. A veteran of the Kargil conflict in the formidable Himalayan borderlands, he was PRIMAL's cold weather warfare expert.

"Is that necessary?" asked Kruger.

"Have you ever operated your weapon in sub-freezing conditions with mitts on?"

"No, but I have been snowboarding."

"Then I guess it's necessary."

***

FORT YUKON AIRPORT, ALASKA

Forty miles east of Dead Land, at the intersection of the Yukon and Porcupine rivers nestled the town of Fort Yukon. The tiny settlement housed a little over five hundred people, who, according to Bishop's research, were predominantly Inuits. The main income sources for the region were trapping, fishing, and logging. Sitting in Sleek's copilot seat Bishop studied the town as Mitch banked the business jet and inspected the snow-covered runway. A single narrow strip had been cleared down its center. "That going to be wide enough?" he asked.

"Yeah, looks good." Mitch circled the jet, lined it up, and brought them down gently on the gravel strip.

The lone hangar was open and a figure waved them inside. It was tight; the Gulfstream had a yard to spare on either wingtip.

"Sure we can trust this guy?" Bishop asked as he left the cockpit to help Saneh with their luggage.

"Who, Sonny? He's rock solid and doesn't ask too many questions."

"Who did you tell them we are? I don't imagine they'd get too many private jets landing here." Bishop checked the weapons cases he'd removed from the aircraft's equipment pod.

Mitch powered down the engines and entered the cabin to grab his own bags. "I told him you two were rich adventurers with more money than sense. Just some weirdoes who want to get a taste of arctic life."

"So in your case, that's pretty much spot on, right?" Bishop opened the hatch and lowered the stairs as the hangar doors were closed behind them. Despite wearing cold-weather gear, newly-purchased during their stopover in Anchorage, he found the cold hit him like a punch to the face. "Holy shit!"

"You get used to it," said Mitch as he joined him in the shed. Saneh followed down the stairs.

The figure that had waved them into the hangar approached and Mitch embraced him in a bear hug. "Sonny, good to see you again."

"Welcome to Fort Yukon, my friends." He was clearly an Inuit; short with a stocky build emphasized by his cold weather clothing. His face was broad and weathered, with almond-shaped brown eyes.

"Sonny, this is Aden and Saneh."

Bishop extended a gloved hand and their guide grasped it firmly.

"I was about to go trapping with my cousin when you called, so the sleds and dogs are ready."

"I hope we haven't messed up your plans too much," Bishop said.

"No, no, it is fine." The amount of cash Mitch had offered Sonny was more than he would make in a year of trapping and guiding.

They loaded their gear bags into the bed of a Ford F150 parked outside. After they secured the aircraft and locked the hangar doors they piled into the truck and rumbled out of the airport.

"Has there been much snow?" Mitch asked as they drove through the tiny settlement.

"Enough, but not too much. You are lucky, it hasn't gotten really cold yet."

Bishop studied the bleak little town through the window. The snow ploughed onto the sides of the road was only a few feet high. "You live here, Sonny?"

"No, my cousin does. I help him out during trapping season. This is his truck and we will be using his teams. He lives just outside of town."

They drove half a mile before Sonny turned onto a narrow track hemmed in on both sides with tall pine trees. The chains on the tires bit into the icy surface and they drove a few hundred yards before pulling up alongside a large log cabin streaming smoke from a stone chimney.

Sonny's cousin greeted them at the door with a broad smile. They could have been twins, only Sonny looked a little younger. "Welcome to my home. Please, help yourselves to some stew, you'll need the energy. I was just heading out to prepare the teams."

Inside it was toasty warm and they stripped off their heavy jackets. A hearty stew was simmering on the wood-fire stove. They sat around a rough-hewn table while Sonny ladled out generous servings.

Bishop and Saneh focused on eating while Mitch laid out a map.

"So mate, we're keen to check out this area here." Mitch indicated a region about thirty miles away. His finger jabbed at a long water feature. "The lake is a must see."

Sonny peered closely at the map and looked at each of the PRIMAL operatives. "This is close to Dead Land."

"Dead Land?" Mitch enquired.

"Bad place. No one goes there. There are UFOs."

Bishop spooned some more stew into his mouth. "UFOs?"

"My cousin has seen them with his own eyes. One of his friends disappeared a few weeks back. We think he was taken."

"Can we go near there?"

Sonny looked pained.

Mitch gripped his shoulder. "Tell you what, mate. You take us near Dead Land and I'll build you up another carbon fiber sled. We don't want to actually go to Dead Land, just a quick peek through the binoculars."

Sonny nodded slowly. "OK, we can go to the lake, and maybe a bit closer. Trappers are sometimes in this area. We can do some hunting and look at Dead Land, from a distance."

They talked through the details while finishing their meal. As they climbed back into their arctic gear the front door opened and Sonny's cousin beckoned them with a grin.

As they left the hut the cold air was filled with the yaps and howls of dogs. Saneh stopped dead in her tracks. There were at least a dozen fluffy canines attached to two long sleds. Excited by the prospect of dashing through the snow they whined and yapped, tugging at their harnesses.

"They're beautiful," said Saneh.

"Beautiful…?" Mitch responded. "These are highly trained athletes! They can run all day." He crunched through the snow to one of the sleds.

"This time you get your own crew." Sonny gave Mitch a thumbs-up.

The PRIMAL tech had joined the Inuit musher for part of the Iditarod race only a month earlier. Bishop could see they had formed a close bond in the extreme environment. Leaving Saneh to help with the dogs, if getting licked was helping, Bishop used his iPRIMAL to send an update to the team on the Pain Train.

A response came back almost immediately; the PRIMAL headquarters element was now fully established in a new location on the outskirts of Abu Dhabi. Update complete he inspected the sled that Sonny was loading. The aluminum runners were about ten feet long with a platform at the back for the handler to stand on. Sonny was lashing equipment to the cargo net strung between the runners.

"You sit in here," said Sonny pointing to a space at the rear of the sled behind the bags. "Your wife will go with Mitch."

"She's not my wife."

Sonny smiled. "Oh, well then maybe your future wife." He winked. "Now, hop in. It's getting late and we have miles to cover."

Bishop sat in the sled and looked across at the other one. Saneh wore a smile and Mitch gave a thumbs-up.

"Mush, mush!" Sonny's yell sent the dogs yapping and yelping as they scrambled to get the heavy sleds underway.

In a matter of seconds they were belting through the thick pines, following a track to the west. Despite the importance of the mission Bishop found himself grinning. Mitch had been right all along; sledding was awesome!

CHAPTER 21

ALASKA

Bishop enjoyed the ride as they sped across the frozen landscape between Fort Yukon and the former USAF research station. The forest was silent, clean, and beautiful, the air crisp and scented with pine. The dogs were impressive, hauling the sleds along at a pace far quicker than he could achieve on skis. What's more they were the perfect cover; no one would expect trappers to be conducting a recon on a highly-classified CIA black site.

The huskies dragged them out of the treeline down onto the surface of a frozen lake. A solid sheet of ice, it stretched at least half a mile across and more than two miles long. As they hissed over the thick blue ice he glanced down, wondering how thick it was.

When they reached the other side Sonny called for the dogs to halt and Mitch brought his sled alongside. Saneh flashed Bishop a broad smile as the dogs yapped and howled.

"Having a good time?" he asked.

"This is even better than the Philippines."

They climbed out and stretched their legs as Sonny tended to the huskies. Using his iPRIMAL Bishop confirmed their location. They were only ten miles from the facility. "Mitch, how thick do you think the ice is?"

"Not sure, mate, but to hold the Pain Train it would need to be at least two feet, three to be sure."

"Sonny, how thick is the ice?"

"At this time of year, over a yard. Difficult to fish."

"Excellent!" Bishop took a few minutes to outline a report for the headquarters in Abu Dhabi. He included the location of the lake, its suitability as an airstrip, and photos of the approach path. Mirza would be flying the Pain Train and ultimately it would be up to him whether or not they used the lake as an airstrip.

"OK, Sonny, we're good to go," he said once the report was sent.

"We should go comms silent from here on in," said Mitch. "We don't know what type of detection gear they have at that facility."

"Good point. I'll let Vance know we're going offline." Bishop punched in the message. A moment later he received a response.

Acknowleged. CAT conducting battleprep. Expect follow-on-force in 20 hours if target confirmed. Landing on the lake is approved. Pain Train will be configured for precision close air support. Sandpit, out.

"They've approved using the lake to land," Bishop passed on. Sonny gave them a strange look but said nothing.

Another message came through, a weather warning. "Sonny, there's a storm front due, is that going to be a problem?"

The musher clapped his gloved hands on his legs. "No, we will build a shelter and wait it out. The storm is good. It will cover our tracks but we need to get to our campsite before it hits."

Bishop clambered back into the sled. "No worries, let's get rolling."

A minute later the dogs were back doing what they loved, dragging the sleds at high speed through the forest. As they skimmed between the trees Bishop had a thought. He turned his head. "Sonny, what exactly are we trapping out here?"

"Mostly bears."

"Oh great." he said scanning the woods. He looked down at the cases strapped to the sled and wondered how long it would take him to access their rifles.

***

207

NURAI ISLAND, ABU DHABI

The headquarters facility that Tariq had established on the island of Nurai was located in an exclusive gated community. The modern two-story mansion was tiled entirely in white and contained six bedrooms, all with ensuite bathrooms. The floor to ceiling windows were coated in a reflective material that prevented anyone outside seeing in. The view was spectacular, over white beaches of imported sand onto the crystal blue waters of the Arabian Gulf.

Upstairs, one of the bedrooms had been converted to an operations room. Vance and Frank had set up shop and were monitoring Bishop's activities in Alaska on the same equipment they used in the Bunker.

"They've gone radio silent," reported Frank. "We're not going to be able to track them till they report in."

"Have you locked in that landing zone?" asked Vance.

"Yes, Mirza approved it. Lascar engineers are making the necessary modifications to the Pain Train."

"Good work." Vance pointed up at one of the screens attached to the wall. It showed a radar feed from the National Weather Service for Alaska. "Keep an eye on that storm. I'm going to head next door and check in with Chua and Flash."

The intel room had been set up in a similar fashion. There were a number of screens bolted to the wall and laptops sitting on a sleek marble bench. On the other side of the room a row of servers hummed. When Vance pushed open the door Flash was sitting at a terminal typing furiously. "How's it going?"

The analyst's eyes were bloodshot. "Not great. I've gone over half the data from the train and I've still got a long way to go. The guys were working on the Redemption intel system but every lead has been a dry hole. I've tried going through the contracting front end but someone's purged everything. Can't find anything on Dead Land..." His voice trailed off but his eyes remained fixed on the screen.

"You've been up all night, son. Might be time for a break."

Flash shook his head. "No, Bishop and the team won't be sleeping so neither am I."

Vance grabbed his shoulder. "That's the spirit, where's Chua?"

"Downstairs making us coffee."

"OK, I'll give him a hand." Vance left the room and walked down the staircase.

The mansion's living area was a combined dining room and kitchen. It led out to a marbled patio with an infinity pool. The folding glass doors were open to let in the early morning breeze.

"Hey, Vance." Chua stood behind a dual head espresso machine. "What will you have?"

"Long black, bud."

A witty comment would usually follow but both men were feeling the stress of the evacuation and the pending mission.

"I went over most of the intel last night," Chua said as he packed the group head with ground coffee.

"Yeah, find anything new?"

"You were right to order the evacuation and dispersion. This guy, Howard, he was pulling us apart piece by piece. Found Dragonfly, found the island, even made the connection to Lascar Logistics."

"The question now is who else has that information."

Chua poured hot water in a glass and added a shot of espresso. He handed the caramel-colored beverage to Vance. "Flash looked into it last night. The links were added to the database only an hour before the server self-destructed. Best case scenario it died on the train with them."

Vance sipped the coffee. "And the worst case?"

"They might have briefed Larkin. The intel could have been backed up. Another team of analysts could've been looking at it."

"I just hope it doesn't come back to Lascar and Tariq. He's the one who's most exposed here."

"I know. That's why I need you to let Flash go all out on this. He needs more manpower to exploit the data."

"What do you mean by all out?"

"Use the forums to get as many hackers as possible working the case."

"Will that draw attention to us?"

Chua began to make another two coffees. "It can't be traced back to this location and Flash can manage it anonymously. Yes, there's a chance NSA will pick up on it which is why the hackers will only be used against the Redemption intel system. We'll keep Dead Land close hold for now so there's no risk of compromising the mission."

Vance stared out over the ocean as he contemplated the plan. "Well, it won't matter if Larkin knows we're trying to hack his intel system. Wouldn't tell him anything new, not after we destroyed his train, right?"

Chua nodded. "Right, and what Larkin knows won't matter soon. Ivan's identified the jet he uses. It's only a matter of time before we've tracked him down."

"OK, tell Flash he can unleash his geeks. Let's ramp this shit up."

***

LASCAR HANGAR, ABU DHABI

Mirza watched as the Lascar Logistics mechanics finished replacing the Pain Train's landing struts and wheels. A consult with Tariq's chief engineer had revealed the big jet didn't need skis to land on a frozen runway. However, he'd recommended a landing gear upgrade with wider cross-section tires and reduced pressure. His people had worked quickly under the critical eye of PRIMAL's newest pilot. Mirza wouldn't let them inside the aircraft so, while the CAT got some much-needed sleep, he oversaw the operation.

"All done." The lead technician handed Mirza a clipboard with a run-down of the work.

He inspected the list and initialed it. "Thank you for working so quickly."

"No problem, have a great trip to the Arctic. Remember to pack some long johns."

Mirza suppressed a smile; they would be packing a hell of a lot more than long johns.

He watched as the Pain Train was towed out of the maintenance facility and across to the Priority Movements Airlift hangar. It was parked facing away from the huge rolling doors. When it came time to load he would have it backed inside.

He punched his pin number into the hangar's side door and almost tripped over a stack of cardboard as he entered. The team was hard at work on three six-wheel drive Polaris buggies in various states of modification. The far vehicle was now a purpose-built arctic assault buggy while the nearest was still in stock configuration. Pavel, Miklos, and Kruger, clad in coveralls, were working on the one in the middle.

He inspected the finished vehicle. The wheels had been replaced with triangular tracks that bolted directly to the wheel hub. They'd also sprayed it white and attached a swivel mount on the front passenger side for a machine gun. A rack of smoke dischargers completed the enhancements.

"They look good," said Mirza as Kruger joined him.

"We also fitted a cold weather pack for the engines. Shouldn't have any problem with them freezing. We've nearly finished with the second one. The third will only take a few hours now that we've got the hang of it."

"Excellent, what about our gear?"

Kruger led him toward the back of the hangar. Mirza inspected the armor that hung on a steel cable. The carbon nanotube rigs and fully-enclosed helmets were usually black. Kruger and the boys had sprayed them white with flecks of grey. The pouches were empty; magazines had been laid out on paper and given the same treatment as the armor. In the corner an assortment of weapons were arranged. In addition to their integrally-suppressed Tavor carbines, three MK48 machine guns and three PAW-20 grenade launchers had also been wrapped with white camouflage tape.

"Great work. They're not going to see us until it's too late."

Kruger picked up one of the helmets. "We couldn't do anything about the lenses." The full-faced helmets sported a mirrored ballistic visor. They were the only piece that had not been camouflaged.

"That's OK. I've ordered transparent white scope tape. It should be here by lunch time."

"Good, by then we'll be ready, *ja.*"

"Did you get any sleep last night?" asked Mirza as they walked back to where the team worked on fitting tracks to the second buggy.

"No, we can rest when we get in the air."

Mirza grabbed a spanner from a toolbox. "Let's get it done then."

***

ALASKA

It amazed Bishop how much light there was considering the late hour. The stars in the clear sky reflected off the snow bathing the landscape in a soft ambient glow. There was no need for night vision goggles as they skimmed across the snow.

He estimated they'd come at least five more miles, over barren rolling hills into another sparsely wooded forest. They had to be in close vicinity to Dead Land. As he turned to ask Sonny when they would be stopping the musher called out to the lead dog. The husky-cross looked back over its shoulder. Despite running for hours the dog still wore a lopsided grin. The crazy canines would run till they died of exhaustion, thought Bishop.

Sonny brought them to a halt in a clearing surrounded by tall pines. Bishop climbed stiff legged out of the sled and stretched as Mitch halted his team alongside.

"We need to get the tent up," said Sonny. "The bad weather will be here soon."

"Saneh and I can do that," said Bishop.

"OK, I will take care of the dogs with Mitch."

"Do they need a tent as well?" Saneh asked.

Sonny laughed. "No, they have thick fur."

It took Bishop and Saneh twenty minutes of fumbling and arguing to get the arctic dome tent assembled. In that time Mitch and Sonny had pegged out the dogs, checked them for injuries, and fed them a high-energy mix of tuna, chicken, and rice.

"Mitch, if you could please organize dinner, I'm going to put out a trapline out," said Sonny as he unloaded equipment from the sled. He shouldered an old lever-action rifle and slung a brace of steel-toothed traps over his shoulder.

"I'll come with," said Bishop. "You two right to make dinner?" he asked the others.

"Yes, darling," said Saneh with a sarcastic smirk.

Sonny tossed him a set of snowshoes and he fitted them over his boots.

He followed the musher from their camp down a slope into the forest. He'd used snowshoes before but it still took him a few minutes before he was comfortable moving in them.

"You weren't serious about the bears were you? Those traps aren't very big."

Sonny gave a hearty chuckle. "No, these are for varmints, fox, beaver, and maybe otter."

They made their way down the hill to a frozen stream. Sonny used a tomahawk to cut a hole in the ice and lowered in a trap. As he did Bishop heard a strange whirring sound over the rustle of wind through the trees. He glanced up expecting to see the navigation lights of a helicopter in the distance. Instead he spotted a small dark object flying directly toward them.

Silhouetted against the starry sky, Bishop recognized it as a quadcopter, an enlarged variant of the four-bladed recon drones that PRIMAL used. It had to be from the USAF facility, and that confirmed it wasn't abandoned.

Sonny unslung his rifle and focused intensely on the intruder.

Bishop pulled his hood further around his face. "No, leave it, Sonny. We'll keep going, just ignore it."

Sure enough the drone hovered over them for a minute before disappearing in the direction it had come from.

"We should get back to camp, bad weather," said Sonny once it was gone. He pointed a gloved hand at the horizon. A section of the sky was jet black with no stars. A storm front was rolling toward them.

They shuffled over the snow as they followed their tracks back up the hill to where they had established the camp. As they climbed a delicious smell wafted on the crisp night breeze. Bishop's stomach growled and he realized he hadn't eaten since the cabin.

When they tramped back into the camp Saneh and Mitch were crouched around a gas burner with a pot of macaroni cheese bubbling on top. "Hey guys, just in time."

"You see the drone?" puffed Bishop, catching his breath as he removed his snowshoes.

Mitch shot him a concerned look. "No."

"A quadcopter. Big one. Had to have come from Dead Land. Watched Sonny and I lay traps before disappearing to the west."

"It won't be back," added Saneh. "The sky is getting really dark."

On cue the wind gusted and the gas burner flickered. Bishop shivered, the inside of his jacket was damp with sweat and the temperature was dropping.

"Let's get this grub inside," said Mitch.

The three PRIMAL operatives climbed into the heavy-duty dome tent as Sonny checked on the dogs. Mitch spooned the macaroni into bowls and when their guide returned they ate in the glow of a compact fluorescent lantern.

"How far is it to the base from here?" Bishop asked.

"Only a few miles," replied Sonny between mouthfuls. "We will prepare your equipment and after you rest I'll take you there. The storm will keep the UFOs away and cover our tracks." He ate another mouthful. "Mitch, you and Saneh will wait here."

She shook her head. "No, we should go together."

"It is too dangerous in the storm for a woman."

Saneh frowned at Bishop.

He shook his head. "We stick to the plan. I'm manning the observation post so there's no point you all coming out. Once I've established the OP and the storm's passed, you all head to the lake. You'll need to message Sandpit to let them know about the drone."

Saneh wore a dark look but couldn't argue with the logic. Mitch gave him a nod.

"I'll get my gear sorted before the storm gets too heavy." Bishop zipped up his jacket and stepped out into the darkness. As he made his way to the sleds the first flakes of snow began falling. He had an inkling that this was going to be arduous so he focused his thoughts on Ice. As tough as the arctic storm might be, it couldn't compare to what his old friend must have been through.

CHAPTER 22

FORT YUKON RESEARCH STATION

The radio on King's nightstand transmitted, "Boss, you there?"

He reached out and knocked it to the floor. Rubbing his eyes he fumbled around before finding it. "King here, send."

"We spotted some trappers a few miles out. Thought you might want a look."

He glanced at the alarm clock. It was 0305. He'd only been in bed for a few hours. "Yeah OK, I'll be right up."

He pulled on pants and a T-shirt, threw on his trainers, and grabbed a down jacket from the hook on the back of the door. A moment later he took a seat upstairs in the operations room where Hammer was on shift. "What've you got, buddy?"

"One of the drones spotted a couple of guys out on the eastern side of the base, 'bout two miles out. I grabbed these stills." He flicked through the images displayed on a screen. Two hunters were laying a trap in a frozen stream. One was carrying a rifle but neither wore a backpack.

"Did you find their camp?"

"Negative." He gestured to the weather map on one of the other monitors. "Bad weather came in so I brought the drone back. Do you want me to send out a Talon?"

King studied the image. One of the trappers stared up at the aircraft, his face hidden by the fur around his hood. The other man pushed a trap through a hole in the ice. They looked like locals. "Yeah, send out a Talon. If it freezes up in the storm we'll recover it tomorrow."

"Copy." Hammer re-tasked one of the unmanned ground vehicles patrolling inside the wire. It would leave via the automated gate and make its way along a programmed patrol route to where the trappers had been spotted. From there they could conduct a search for the campsite.

"Has the facility been secured against the storm?"

"Yeah boss, the techs just locked down the main hangar. All the drones are back and apart from the two Talons on the perimeter we're set."

King yawned. "Good, let me know if anything suspicious happens."

"You got it, boss. Get some sleep. This storm ain't going to ease up any time soon. Any dumb shit that's out in it is going to end up a popsicle."

***

ALASKA

Bishop had never been so cold in his life as he trudged through the storm. The wind seemed to cut through his jacket to the very depths of his bones. He wore a Merino wool balaclava but it did little to stop his face from going numb. Getting one foot in front of the other had become a challenge that required every ounce of his willpower.

They had departed the base camp a little over an hour earlier with Bishop carrying a backpack filled with equipment. Within half an hour he relinquished the heavy pack to the stocky Inuit. Sonny seemed to be completely unaffected by the cold or the storm. He now carried all their supplies and was still as surefooted as a polar bear.

"Not much further!" Sonny yelled over the wind.

"OK," managed Bishop through chattering teeth. He stumbled onward, stepping in the snowshoe-prints of the musher. They trudged for another five minutes and when he'd almost decided he couldn't go any further Sonny turned and guided him to the cover offered by a large pine tree.

Sonny dropped their gear at Bishop's feet and pulled a collapsible shovel from the side of the rucksack. "Wait here!" he shouted then vanished into the billowing snow.

Minutes later Bishop began to get concerned. There was no sign of Sonny and his hands and feet were numb. Suddenly the musher's grinning face appeared. He picked up their gear and gestured for Bishop to follow. They covered a few more yards before Sonny disappeared down a hole in the snow. Bishop dropped to his knees and crawled in after him.

Sonny had tunneled into a natural snow cave formed under the branches of the pine tree, creating enough space to comfortably accommodate them both. The Inuit continued to work as Bishop removed his snowshoes and wrapped himself in a sleeping bag. He hung a camp light from a branch and cleared a space for the Primus stove. In a few minutes he had melted snow in boiling water and added chocolate powder. Filling a mug with the sweet brown liquid he handed it to Bishop. "You will warm up soon."

Five minutes later Bishop had almost fully recovered. His body no longer shook and feeling had returned to his fingers and toes. "So what's the plan from here? How far is Dead Land?"

"Through there." Sonny pointed to the wall of the cave. "You dig a little hole and you will see all the way down to the camp."

Bishop grinned. "You've dug me a little OP. Job well done, mate."

Sonny shrugged. "OK, so I will head back now before the storm passes. It will cover my tracks. You need to make sure you keep the doorway clear or the bad air will make you sick."

"Got it."

The Inuit strapped on his snowshoes, pulled his hood over his head, and crawled through the tunnel into the storm.

Bishop dragged his heavy rucksack closer withdrawing a two-and-a-half foot steel tube; the barrel to a Windrunner sniper rifle. He retrieved the other parts of the weapon and assembled it. The .408 Cheytac-chambered weapon had an effective range of over a mile and fitted with an advanced thermal imaging scope it gave him all-weather surgical strike capability. The backpack also held thirty rounds of ammunition, a dozen energy bars, and a white camouflage oversuit.

Once he'd donned the camouflage suit over his cold weather gear he went to work digging an observation hole through the snow. He started just under the canopy of the tree, using the shovel to dig a tunnel out to the edge of the branches. He tunneled all the way to the outside and before long had constructed a hide that he could lay in.

Almost immediately the vision hole was blocked over by snowfall. Once the storm lifted he would clear the opening and if Sonny was correct he would have direct observation down to the old USAF facility.

With his hide prepared he slid back into the snow cave and pulled out a roll of white camouflage tape he'd bought from a hunting store in Anchorage. He went to work wrapping it around the barrel of the black rifle. Once that task was complete he climbed inside the sleeping bag. Setting an alarm for every half hour, so he could clear the entrance, he lay back and listened to the wind outside. He hoped Sonny made it back to the others OK. Within a few seconds exhaustion caught up with him and he dozed off.

***

Mitch took the first watch allowing Saneh to get some much-needed rest. Considering the weather outside, he thought, they probably both could have slept. There was no way anyone would be out in the storm that was lashing the tent. After half an hour of staying alert the long day of sledding finally caught up with him and he nodded off.

The sound of the tent's zip woke him and he scrambled for his pistol. Before he could find it Sonny's head appeared through the flaps.

"The storm is done," said the Inuit. "I found something on my way back here; a robot from Dead Land."

"Is it far away?"

"No, I can take you to it."

"Great." Mitch struggled with his jacket.

"What's up?" asked Saneh as her head emerged from her sleeping bag.

"Sonny's back."

"Is Aden OK?"

"Yes," said the musher. "He's in a very good spot where no one can see him. We should move back to the lake now while it is still snowing."

"Sonny found a drone," added Mitch as he pulled on his boots. "I'm going to check it out then we can head off."

"OK," Saneh said climbing out of her sleeping bag. "I'll start packing up here. Are the dogs alright?"

"Yes, they are fine."

Outside the tent Sonny handed Mitch a pair of snowshoes. It was still dark and the pine trees blocked much of the starlight. They waddled past the snow-covered dogs clustered around the sled and tramped off through the woods.

The robot was a few hundred yards from their camp. Covered with fresh snow, the golf cart-sized vehicle's tracks were frozen solid and the sensors were iced-over. As Mitch scraped the snow off he identified it as an evolution of the Talon explosive ordnance disposal robot. Unlike regular Talons this one was bristling with weaponry. He paid particular attention to the antennas that crowned the remote weapon station. It was controlled by a satellite uplink. He grinned as he formulated a plan. "Sonny, I'm going to need to grab a few things from the sled."

"Are you going to destroy the robot?"

Mitch shook his head as they set off back to the camp. "No, hopefully we're going to be able to put it to work." As they walked back the dogs had woken and were demanding to be fed. Mitch grabbed his backpack and left Sonny and Saneh to finish packing up the camp and tending to the dogs.

As he retraced his tracks to the frozen Talon it began to snow harder. He worked quickly, using a multitool to remove a maintenance panel. Taking photos with a camera first he then dismantled his iPRIMAL, using the parts to make the necessary modifications to the robot. As he worked snow continued to fall. By the time he was done his tracks were faint. He followed them back to the camp where the dogs were harnessed to the waiting sleds.

"Everything work out?" asked Saneh as she climbed in behind the stowed equipment.

"We won't know for a while. I snapped a couple of photos to include in the package for the lads." He glanced across at the other sled. Sonny had used a spare jacket and some branches to construct a dummy to sit in front of him. "Sneaky," said Mitch.

"Just in case the UFOs come back," Sonny replied as he urged his team forward.

The excited dogs charged off at break-neck speed hauling the sled down the hill. Mitch's team barked excitedly as they followed and shot into the darkness. Behind them, a few hundred yards from the abandoned campsite, the Talon drone had disappeared under a covering of fresh snow.

CHAPTER 23

ALASKA

Bishop slid a gloved hand down the observation hole he had tunneled through the snow. Clearing the entrance he wiggled his body forward till he could see out through the pine needles. Sonny had chosen a perfect location for the hide. He had observation over the entire base laid out in front of him, less than a mile away. The storm had lifted and the morning sun hung low on the horizon. According to Sonny it would soon disappear for another twenty hours.

He had studied photos of the base from the blog he had found online, and also looked over the satellite imagery from Google. The images were a few years old and a lot had changed. Buildings were refurbished and the security fence upgraded. A new hangar faced the airstrip with an enclosed walkway linking it to the main building, a brick-walled two-story structure. Forty yards to the north was the entrance to what appeared to be an underground bunker. Beside that was a shed that had vehicle tracks leading out from it.

The tall chain fence that bordered the facility was topped with razor wire. That wasn't a significant obstacle. His primary concern was the six heavily-armed remote weapon towers situated around the perimeter. He held up his thermal sight and inspected one of them. He'd seen the configuration before on an armored vehicle; a 7.62mm machine gun paired with an automatic 40mm grenade launcher, a lethal combination. Nestled above the weapons was a sensor suite. He knew that the armored housing contained powerful electro optical and thermal cameras that could spot a man from thousands of yards away. The towers were probably automated; configured to kill anyone outside the wire who wasn't wearing a friendly beacon. He watched as the turret rotated back and forth. He held his breath as it seemed to stare directly at him. After a few seconds it rotated and continued its scan of the terrain.

Bishop was using his imager to range all the buildings and towers. The built-in laser-rangefinder and GPS let him calculate a precise location for each of them. The data automatically uploaded to his iPRIMAL where he would annotate it. When the Pain Train came on-station he would send the package to Mitch in a data burst. The modified Il-76 would then destroy the targets with a barrage of guided bombs.

As he finished logging the last tower he spotted a tracked vehicle trundling between the buildings. It bristled with armament similar to the guard towers. "You're shitting me," he mouthed. As if the towers weren't enough, the base was also protected by unmanned ground vehicles. The squat, heavily-armed, Talon patrolled to the fence and began to follow it around the perimeter. This was without a doubt the most heavily defended facility that PRIMAL had ever attempted to penetrate.

He was about to slide back to the snow cave when he spotted someone walk out from the underground facility. He focused the scope on the opening and exhaled sharply. The man standing at the entrance was none other than Charles King. He hadn't seen the GES boss since capturing him in Venezuela but his face was etched in his memory. There was no doubt in Bishop's mind now; this is where they would be holding Ice and Wesley. He watched as King strolled across to the two-story building. In his imagination the thermal scope was attached to his sniper rifle. He triggered the laser range finder and balanced the targeting dot on King's skull. "Bang, you're dead, Charles."

***

FORT YUKON RESEARCH STATION

King had a sense of foreboding as he climbed the stairs to the operations room. He hadn't slept all night. Something about the trappers irked him and he couldn't push it from his mind.

Once the storm had blown over he visited the interrogation cells to ensure Small hadn't used the opportunity to torture Castle. He could have checked the cameras but he wouldn't put it past the creepy little prick to have a workaround to avoid being recorded.

The detainee was untouched and King returned to the ops room with only the trappers on his mind. Chris was on duty sitting in front of the main bank of screens. The operator had his chest rig and carbine next to the desk as per King's orders. His own gear sat in the corner. "Chris, did you get a chance to check out those trappers?"

"Yeah boss, got a drone up first thing. They pushed off early this morning heading back toward Fort Yukon."

"You still got eyes on?"

"Negative, but we've got a 'copter near by."

"Let's check them out again."

"Copy."

King sat at one of the terminals and logged on. He checked the asset status board and noticed one of the Talon's alert lights was flashing. The location map had it out near where they had seen the trappers. "Chris, what's going on with Talon Four?"

"Hammer sent her out to investigate the camp last night. Froze up before she made it. Is she back online?"

"Looks that way." King activated the communications link to the drone. The feed from the camera filled his screen. It was white, covered in snow and ice. He spun the weapons turret in an attempt to clear it. Jiggling it from side to side he managed to dislodge some of snow. Frustrated he hit the return home command. The two million dollar robot would attempt to retrace its path back to Dead Land. He watched the map. After a few seconds the unmanned vehicle's icon began moving back to base. "Number four is on her way home."

"Cool, I've got your trappers on screen now."

He glanced up at the central monitor. It showed the feed from the quadcopter's camera focused on two dog sleds skimming through the forest.

"Can you zoom in on the lead sled?"

Chris made the adjustment and the sled filled the screen.

He could make out a single passenger along with the musher. "Check the other one."

"It's the same boss, two people each, four man trapping party."

King frowned. "Yeah, I guess so." Something still bothered him. He couldn't put his finger on exactly what it was.

"We're off-station, boss, batteries are low."

***

NURAI ISLAND, ABU DHABI

Frank was reading on a Kindle when his laptop pinged. It was a message from Saneh. "Vance, we have target confirmation from the team in Alaska."

The Director of Operations grunted. "Do they have eyes on the facility?"

"Yes, Bishop has established an OP but is comms silent until the Pain Train is on-station. Once it's in vicinity he'll unmask and upload the target set."

"So they've confirmed the base is operational?" asked Vance.

"Bishop would have extracted already if it wasn't a valid target. UAVs and UGVs patrolling confirms it. The unmanned assets would have come from the Fort Yukon facility."

"UGVs?"

"Unmanned Ground Vehicles. Mitch identified them as some kind of advanced Talon. They're heavily armed but nothing we won't be able to deal with."

"Do the others have this information?"

"Yes, they've got it. Mitch has sent through a target pack and some technical details for Flash. Do we have a green light on the mission?"

"Run me through the mitigation strategy for the aircraft at Elmendorf Air Force Base." There was a squadron of F-22 Raptors based there that could make short work of the lumbering PRIMAL transporter.

"We've organized a Lascar Logistics flight plan. We're running mining supplies to a town near Fort Yukon."

"What we're running is a shit load of risk on this one, Frank." Vance paused. "This is hairier than a French chick's armpit."

"There's no way USAF interceptors will shoot down a legitimate civilian aircraft in US airspace. Green light?" asked Frank.

"Green is go."

"Roger." Frank dialed Mirza's number and relayed the order through his headset.

"Pain Train is rolling, Vance. Estimated time in transit to target area is nine hours."

"Thanks." Vance left the operations room and pushed open the door to the intelligence cell. "Chua, what's your take on this UAV, UGV capability?"

The intel chief was studying something on his screen. He looked up from the computer and blinked a few times. "It's a pretty good indicator that there's something there that Larkin doesn't want anyone finding. I've got my money on Dead Land being his secret rendition site and he's using drones to minimize the number of personnel required to run it. You can almost guarantee that no one in the administration knows it exists."

'The perfect place to keep Wesley and Ice."

"Correct."

Vance turned to Flash who was typing frantically on his laptop. "How you doing, bud?"

Flash glanced up from his computer. "Huh?"

"Any luck with the hacking?"

He shook his head. "I've got people scouring the classified networks for anything that might link to Redemption or Larkin. There are over five hundred black hats helping out and no one can find a goddamn thing." He threw up his arms in frustration.

"Did you go through the info Mitch sent? He managed to get hands on with one of their UGVs. Mentioned a special surprise for you."

Flash shook his head. "No. I haven't had a chance to look at it."

"You might want to get on that."

As Vance left the room Flash opened the report from Mitch. He glanced at the attached photo. He read the comments and grinned. "Mitch, you sneaky son of a bitch."

"What has he done?" asked Chua.

"He's given us our in."

***

CHINESE AIRSPACE

Four hours later, cruising at nearly 40,000 feet, the Pain Train was halfway across China. Mirza sat at the helm of the transporter with Kurtz in the copilot's seat. The former Indian Special Forces operative had recently become fully qualified on the Il-76 and was now training Kurtz. This was his second time commanding PRIMAL's special operations support aircraft.

Mirza activated the autopilot. "You OK here?" he asked. "I'm going to make sure the cargo is still secure." Kurtz gave a nod. He left his seat and walked past the sensors and weapons console and through the door to the cargo area. The three white Polaris buggies were strapped to the floor. Alongside them was a Viper Strike guided munitions pod. The other three members of the CAT were sprawled among their gear, fast asleep. They had been training and preparing non-stop since they arrived in the UAE and deserved the rest.

Kruger's eyes snapped open as Mirza walked past him. He was lying on the fold-down side seats with his head on his chest rig. "Any new intel?"

Mirza shook his head. "Not until we're on the ground."

"OK, how long?"

"Another five hours."

Kruger gave a nod and closed his eyes.

Mirza checked the buggies were strapped securely and walked back to the front. He yawned as he dropped into the pilot's seat and checked the navigation computer.

"You should get some sleep," said Kurtz. "I can take care of this."

"You sure?"

"*Ja.*"

"OK." Mirza left the cockpit. Instead of going back to the cargo hold he sat in front of the sensors and weapons console. He brought up the imagery and intel on Dead Land and studied it intently. He wanted to have every detail committed to memory, every possible contingency mapped out in his brain. If Ice was in the facility nothing could stop him from getting him out. His thoughts slipped back to a day almost three years ago. The day that a single action had cost the life of the bravest man he knew. On that day James Castle had sacrificed himself and Mirza had run. He had never forgiven himself for that. But, now he might finally have a chance for redemption.

***

THREE YEARS EARLIER

KHOD VALLEY, AFGHANISTAN, 2012

Mirza rolled onto his side and looked back up the hill through his sniper scope. The sky had started to glow and in the predawn light he could clearly make out a figure standing at the crest, blocking their exfiltration route. It had to be one of the Afghans from the missile site. "Steady, Ice, we've got company. Two hundred meters, top of the cliff, one sentry."

There was a pause before Ice responded. "There's more of them. Below us."

He shuffled around on his stomach and looked down at the Taliban camp. "Looks like a clearing patrol. We can't stay here, once the sun rises they'll spot us."

"Do you think you can make the shot?"

"Yes, I'll drop the guy on the ridgeline and we can withdraw over the crest."

"Solid plan. Do it."

He rose to a knee and aimed his sniper rifle up the hill. He squeezed the trigger, the weapon emitted a muted crack, and the target toppled forward. As the corpse hit the ground, it let off a single round. In the still morning air the shot echoed off the cliffs like a thunderclap.

Mirza dropped prone, realizing his target's finger must have jarred the trigger. Below, yells filled the air.

It would only take minutes for the Taliban clearing patrol to be on top of them. At this distance they needed to maintain the element of surprise. He crawled forward and took up a firing position beside Ice. As they waited for the approaching fighters he pulled out two white phosphorus grenades.

The line of Taliban climbed swiftly. There were almost thirty of them covering a frontage of a hundred meters. The left flank would hit the pair first and initially only a few of the Afghans would be able to engage.

Ice gave Mirza a nod and they fired when the line was fifty meters out. The first two Taliban toppled like bowling pins. The others dove to the ground returning fire.

Rounds cracked above their heads. They waited until the Taliban were throwing distance and tossed two phosphorus grenades each.

Five seconds later the grenades began to burst into a thick cloud of smoke, hurling smoldering phosphorus in a wide arc. Mirza led as they sprinted up the hill, away from the screams of the burning men. Rounds skipped off the rocks as the surviving fighters fired blindly through the billowing white smoke.

Mirza crested the hill and glanced back. Ice was hot on his heels. He pushed on, scrambling over the crest and down into a steep gully. He looked back again. Ice was falling behind.

"You OK?" he yelled.

"Yeah," the big man grunted.

The Taliban were still pursuing, moving around the burning smoke screen, firing blindly. It wouldn't take long for them to get a visual on the withdrawing PRIMAL operatives.

Mirza knelt and took up a firing position. As Ice got closer, reality dawned on him. He caught Ice as the big man stumbled, pulling him behind a large rock. He spotted the hole in the back of Ice's assault vest. Lifting it slightly he slid his fingers under the clothing. The wound was bleeding profusely. A round had punched into the lower back just to the side of the spine. There was no exit wound.

"Lie still," he whispered. Pulling a trauma kit from his vest he plugged the bleeding hole with a wound sealant. He hoped it was enough. Ice didn't make a sound as Mirza worked frantically, wrapping his torso with a bandage.

He glanced back. The Taliban were moving cautiously over the crest just a couple hundred meters away. Scraping a hole in the dirt, he grabbed Ice's assault rifle and placed it down with a grenade underneath. Then he slung his own rifle, heaved Ice's six foot five frame over his shoulder, and shuffled off down the rocky gully.

"Mitch! Mitch!" he screamed into his throat mike, lungs heaving.

"Mitch here. What's going on? Calm down. Talk to me."

"Ice... Ice's been hit."

"How bad?"

"Lower abdomen, it's bad. I'm carrying him."

"You in contact?"

Mirza didn't get a chance to reply. He slid on the loose ground, falling heavily and dropping Ice from his shoulder. He realized he wouldn't be able to outrun the Taliban like this.

Lifting his rifle up he scanned through the optics. A plume of smoke billowed from where he'd booby-trapped Ice's weapon. He snapped off a shot at the magnified image of one of the fighters.

"Mirza," Ice croaked. "Mirza."

He fired another shot. "Don't talk. Conserve your energy."

"Mirza, you have to go."

He fired again before crouching next to the veteran PRIMAL operative. "No! No, I'm not leaving you here."

"Bro, you have to go." Ice coughed, blood dribbling from his lips, his chiseled features contorted in pain. "One of us can still get out of here," he said slowly, "and it's not going to be me. You know what I need you to do."

Mirza locked eyes with his friend and nodded grimly. He pulled a Claymore directional mine from his backpack. Tears welled in his eyes as he stripped the last few grenades from their vests, placing them in the empty Claymore satchel. He wrapped the bag's shoulder strap around the mine and connected the firing device. He handed the bundle and the trigger to Ice.

"I'll never forget this, my friend. You're the bravest man I know," Mirza choked out his words as he grasped the other man's shoulder.

"Just make sure you keep Bishop out of trouble." Blood bubbled from Ice's lips and he gestured urgently. "Go! Get the fuck out of here."

Mirza hesitated.

"I said get the fuck out of here! Go!" Ice coughed and blood streamed down his chin.

He turned and left Ice lying holding the Claymore mine and bag of grenades. He didn't look back, running wildly down the slope, sliding on the loose dirt, and smashing through the shrubs. Thorns ripped at his pants, tearing like the claws of a wild animal. Pain lashed his legs but he ran on, ignoring the bullets cracking through the air. He only slowed when an explosion detonated behind him. His chest tightened, despair almost overwhelmed him, and he knew he was alone.

***

ALASKA, 2015

Bishop blinked and rubbed his eyes with gloved hands. He peered over his thermal scope out through the fist-sized hole in the snow cave. In the darkness the facility looked abandoned. To the naked eye it was a black hole with not a single visible light.

When he looked back through the scope it told a different story. Powerful infrared spotlights swept the perimeter from the remote weapon towers. The patrolling Talon robots emitted glowing heat signatures and scanned the ground ahead with their own infrared lights.

One of the robots was returning from a patrol beyond the fence. It passed through an automated gate and continued to the maintenance hangar. Removing his glove, he typed a note into the iPRIMAL strapped to his forearm. He calculated the tracked unmanned vehicles had an endurance of six hours. He'd already noted that the quadcopter drones had a shorter endurance and were unable to fly in windy conditions.

He tore the wrapper from his last energy bar and munched on the rubbery substance. Fifteen hours had passed since Sonny had left him in the snow cave. He'd spent most of the time preparing the target pack for the Pain Train and the assault force. The shed where the drones and Talons were housed was the priority target. If they were lucky they might take out the connection to the remote weapon towers. With King blind, they could maneuver the ground force to their assault positions in relative safety. Once they were in place the Pain Train would neutralize the towers and breach the fence.

He had counted almost a dozen different individuals moving between the buildings. Most were armed and dressed in tactical gear. The fact that he'd seen Charles King confirmed the presence of experienced GES operators.

Finishing the bar he stuffed the wrapper in a pocket and contemplated climbing back into his sleeping bag and having a nap. As quickly as the idea popped in his head he discarded it. The team would be on the ground soon and they needed to know as much as possible about the facility.

He raised the thermal scope to his eye again. If required he could quickly snap it onto the sniper rifle and bring it into the fight. He'd already ranged the two closest weapon towers and he was confident he could use armor-piercing ammunition to shoot out their sensors. The risk came from the other four towers that faced away from him. If they had acoustic sensors they would locate him as soon as he fired a shot, even if he used a suppressor.

Bishop wriggled his toes to get some feeling back in them. As he lowered the scope his thoughts turned to Saneh. She was going to have a hard time saying goodbye to the huskies. Maybe he could convince Vance to let them have a dog on the island. Sadness washed over him as he remembered that the island was no longer going to be his home base. Perhaps he and Saneh would settle down in his apartment in Sydney.

A flicker of light near the underground entrance brought him back to earth. Raising the scope he spotted a figure standing in the snow smoking a cigarette. This guy was new. He had a narrow face and a dark fringe that hung from under the hood of his jacket. The man stared up at the night sky, dropped his cigarette, and shuffled toward the accommodation block with his hands in his pockets. Bishop added him to his personnel count. He was up to twelve; a dozen men who were about to learn that working for Thomas Larkin didn't pay.

CHAPTER 24

ALASKA

The night sky had cleared and starlight reflected off the frozen lake with a soft glow. Despite the ambient light, Mitch heard the four-engine transporter before he saw it. A deep pulsing rumble reverberated over the hills before a vulture-winged shape appeared in the distance. With navigation lights switched off it swooped down, landing at the far end of the lake. The turbines raised in pitch, screaming with full reverse thrust as they attempted to slow the hundred-ton aircraft over the ice. Twin parachutes blossomed behind the Pain Train and it bled speed, coming to a halt near the middle of the lake.

Mitch waited for the ramp at the back to lower before grabbing his rucksack. The ice creaked over the noise of the engines.

"That doesn't sound good," said Saneh as she helped Sonny calm the dogs.

"It'll hold," Mitch said, unconvincingly.

The nose of a white Polaris buggy appeared from the back of the jet. It rolled off the end of the ramp onto its tracks and scrambled across the ice, engine revving. Two similar vehicles appeared and followed it up the bank into the snowy treeline.

"OK guys, it's time for us to part ways." Mitch gave one of the dogs a pat and hugged Saneh. He shook Sonny's gloved hand. "Thanks for everything, mate. If you'll have me in next year's Iditarod, I'm keen as mustard."

The musher shot him a broad grin. "Of course. I hope you find whatever you are looking for at Dead Land." He shook Saneh's hand and mounted his sled. Both dog teams were harnessed to it, with the other sled strapped to the top.

"Thank you so much for your help," Saneh said as Sonny took off into the darkness, dogs yapping and yelping.

Mitch strode out from the trees and shuffled onto the ice. He half jogged half slid to the ramp of the waiting aircraft. The ice gave an ominous groan as he stepped onto the ramp and hit the button that closed it. Running through the cargo hold he tore off his jacket and continued past the sensors and weapons bay. The door to the cockpit was open and the broad smile of Kurtz greeted him from the copilot's seat.

"We're ready for takeoff, Captain."

"That ice isn't going to hold much longer." He jumped into the seat beside Kurtz, threw on the pilot's helmet, and activated the integrated night vision and heads-up display. "I'm not going to mess around trying to turn. We're going to punch the RATO." Mitch reached up and flicked the switches that armed the rocket system. "We've got eight hundred feet of runway; should be more than enough." He turned and gave Kurtz a wink. "Should be…"

Outside, the three buggies had parked in a triangle under the pine trees, machine guns aimed outward. As Saneh approached, one of the drivers left his vehicle and waded through the snow to meet her. He was dressed from head to toe in white camouflage including a fully enclosed helmet. The nanotube body armor was colored white and grey, along with the Tavor assault rifle that hung from his chest.

"Hello, it's Mirza," he said, his voice distorted through the helmet's respirator. Saneh flashed him a bright smile and threw her arms around his bulky rig.

The roar of the Pain Train's engines caught their attention. The white braking parachutes detached as it gathered speed. Then, as it almost ran out of lake, there was an ear splitting roar and flames shot out from under the aircraft's wings as rockets fired. The big transporter leapt off the lake in an almost vertical climb. The rockets petered out and the Pain Train disappeared into the night sky.

A suppressed weapon chattered and Mirza spun to face the buggies. "What's going on?" he asked calmly over the radio.

"Drone! Fucker was hovering on the edge of the forest. I got it," Kruger reported.

235

He turned back to Saneh. Her backpack was over her shoulders and she had her own Tavor slung by her side. "We've been compromised, let's move. I've got your armor in my buggy."

As they shuffled through the snow Mirza contacted Mitch. "Pain Train, this is Scrambler. We've destroyed a drone. Our infil is compromised. Anticipate assault at earliest possible opportunity."

"Roger, we're locking in the weapon's pod. As soon as we have the targeting data from Bishop we'll commence our run," Mitch transmitted from the Pain Train. Without surprise their best strategy was now to employ maximum speed and aggression.

Kruger had dragged the shattered drone alongside his buggy. Mirza inspected it as Saneh adjusted her equipment.

"There goes the clandestine approach," said the South African as he nudged the bullet riddled machine with the toe of his boot.

"We're still ten miles out. We need to get rolling," said Mirza.

"I'm ready," Saneh said from the passenger seat of his Polaris. She had pulled a set of Kryptech overwhites on top of her jacket and pants and fastened her custom-fitted armor. A fully-enclosed helmet sat on her lap as she checked that the machine gun mounted above the dash was loaded.

"OK, let's move out," ordered Mirza. Saneh donned her helmet and activated the night vision and comms systems.

They set off in a single file, Mirza and Saneh in the lead buggy with Kruger and Pavel behind, and Miklos bringing up the rear.

***

FORT YUKON RESEARCH STATION

King snatched the phone from its cradle and rang Larkin. "They're here, ten miles to the east. Three vehicles and a

Russian transport aircraft." He was in the operations room with Chris and Hammer. The main video screen was blank since the intruders had shot down the drone.

"We knew they would come. Have you alerted Elmendorf?"

"I will."

"I would suggest you do that now. Keep me informed of your progress." Larkin terminated the call.

"Fucking prick," hissed King through his teeth.

"What are we going to do, boss?"

"Put the call through to the Air Force and lock down the facility."

"Copy." Chris lifted the phone and contacted the USAF base. He passed on the required details and hung up. "They're going to interdict the transporter and report for CAS as fuel permits. Aircraft will be on-station in fifteen."

"Good, establish radio contact once they're in range."

"You want us to fall back to the prison?" asked Hammer.

"No, let's control the defenses here and only withdraw if absolutely necessary. If these assholes only brought three buggies they shouldn't pose much of a threat. Where's Matt?"

"He's on his way up now."

"Small and his people?"

"They're getting their shit together."

"Get down there and hurry them up. I want every man carrying a weapon."

Hammer threw on his chest rig, grabbed his carbine, and headed downstairs. King turned his attention back to the screens. "I want another two drones out patrolling for those vehicles. Try to get them to keep their distance this time. How many Talons do we have online?"

"Five," reported Chris. "The technicians are refueling number four. When she's online we'll have six operational."

"Good, I want two patrolling externally and four inside the wire."

"You got it. Do you want me to switch them to kill?"

King pulled on his own chest rig and checked the beacon was operational. "Yes. But confirm everyone has an identifier first. Make sure Small's men have turned them on."

"Guard towers as well?"

"Yes." King folded his arms and stared at the screens. Let them come, he thought. They were ready.

As the team in the operations room prepared themselves a pair of technicians in the maintenance hangar were fueling Talon Four and checking her over. The tracked robot had spent the previous night frozen out in the barren wasteland beyond the fence but hadn't seemed to have suffered any damage. Once the tank was full they powered up the robot, waiting for a panel of lights to flash and confirm it was operational. What they didn't know was there was an additional system piggy-backing off the power supply and data link. Behind a panel a satellite receiver, stripped from an iPRIMAL, searched for a signal.

The technicians slid open the door to the hangar and using a remote control they drove the Talon outside where they handed over command to the operations room. Within seconds the iPRIMAL receiver hidden behind the panel locked on to a satellite in the clear night skies above.

***

ELMENDORF AIR FORCE BASE

"Holy shit balls, I'm bored," said the tall F-22 Raptor pilot, call sign Donk. He sat in the ready room at Joint Base Elmendorf dressed in his flight rig with his feet on a table.

Another three pilots were also waiting. Call sign Groper, his wingman, lay on a tattered couch watching a B-grade action movie. The other two, part of the crew of a B-1B Lancer that only recently arrived, were playing cards.

"Thought you guys would be used to being bored," said one of the Lancer jockeys. "I mean, it's not like anything happens up here."

Groper yawned. "You'd be surprised, man. The Russians have been getting pretty bold. What are you guys doing up here anyway? I thought you only hung out on beaches?"

The bomber pilot shrugged. "Some kind of strategic strike exercise–" He was cut off by a flashing red light on the wall and a wailing siren.

Donk almost fell off his chair. "Hot damn, we're on." He grabbed his helmet and ran for the door with Groper a few steps behind. Sprinting out into the cold night air, they raced across the tarmac toward the two waiting F-22s. The Raptors were plugged into auxiliary generators with their systems powered up and navigation lights on. The cockpits glowed green beneath the raised canopies.

He sprinted up the stairs and dropped into the cockpit while slipping on his helmet. The crew chief locked the canopy down and rolled the staircase back as he strapped in. Moments later the turbofans had spooled up, the auxiliary power unit disconnected, and his chief marshaled him onto the runway with glowing red and yellow wands.

"Tower, this is Cyclon 1-1 and 1-2, request clearance for takeoff on runway 06-24," transmitted Donk.

"Cyclon 1-1 and Cyclon 1-2, you are clear for takeoff," transmitted the tower.

"Acknowledged, tower." He aimed the F-22 down the runway and rammed the throttle forward sending the stealth interceptor hurtling along the tarmac. Within a few hundred yards he was airborne. He banked and circled, waiting for Groper to lift off. When they were in formation he vectored to the heading provided by the tower. "Tower, can you confirm the mission?"

"Roger, Cyclon 1-1, I confirm the mission is to interdict and destroy a hostile call sign in vicinity of the Fort Yukon Research Station. Aircraft is an Ilyushin-76 conducting surveillance activity."

Behind the visor of his helmet Donk frowned. "Tower, can you confirm that the mission is to interdict and destroy?"

"I confirm interdict and destroy, you are weapons free."

"Shit balls, Groper, we're going hunting," said Donk over the internal frequency he shared with his wingman.

"Hell yeah, let's hit the burners and schwack this Russki motherfucker."

The two jets screamed into the night sky trailing white-hot flame, their powerful search radars hunting for their prey.

CHAPTER 25

FORT YUKON RESEARCH STATION

Bishop zoomed out the thermal scope that was now attached to his sniper rifle. Something had spooked the men in the base. In the last few minutes it had come alive with movement. They ran between the buildings carrying weapons and two of the Talon robots rolled out the gate. He watched as a pair of quadcopters lifted off and streaked away into the darkness.

"Shit." There could be only one reason for the increased activity. He looked at the iPRIMAL strapped to his forearm and checked the menu that would alert him to the presence of other PRIMAL assets. It was blank. He was still out of the loop and waiting to transmit the targeting data to the Pain Train.

He contemplated powering up the satellite module of the device. It was risky; if the facility had a signals monitoring capability they could be on to him in a matter of seconds. His observation post was well within range of the automated defenses. Instead he needed to wait until the Pain Train was in range and on-station to neutralize the threat.

Despite the cold his brow was damp with sweat. He used a frosty glove to wipe it and refocused his attention on the scope. He balanced the crosshairs on the communications array on top of the main building. It was one of the targets the Pain Train couldn't hit without risking collateral damage. Until they confirmed the location of Ice and Wesley they would focus on the facility's defenses. The iPRIMAL vibrated and he glanced at it. The Pain Train was online. He initiated the upload of the target pack.

Kurtz was ready when the data hit the aircraft's weapons system. He opened the file and loaded the targets onto a digital map. A quick glance told him Bishop had prioritized them to align with an assault from the west. He wanted the towers and hangars destroyed before breaching the fence for the buggies to punch through.

"How are we looking?" asked Mitch over the headset.

"Everything is in order. I'm sending the target set to the weapons pack," replied Kurtz.

"Roger, as soon as the assault force is in place and Bishop gives the all-clear we can start the run."

Kurtz left the console and moved back through the aircraft's cargo hold. Without the CAT and their buggies the space seemed cavernous. He strode to the far end where a black box the size of a one-ton pallet was attached to the side of the ramp. The pod contained thirty-five Viper Strike GPS-guided munitions. Each of them was now loaded with a set of coordinates from the target deck. In one pass the Pain Train would rain down fifteen hundred pounds of precision devastation on Dead Land. It would leave very little for Mirza and his team to mop up.

"Pain Train, this is Scrambler, we are five minutes from the form-up point," Mirza came through over the radio. Kurtz flicked off the safety bail that armed the Viper Strike pod. He leant across and hit the controls that lowered the ramp. "Mitch, we are weapons hot."

Thousands of feet below, the three Polaris buggies were blasting through the snow. Mirza was at the wheel of the lead vehicle with Saneh sitting beside him manning the machine gun.

"Overwatch, this is Scrambler, we're five minutes from your location," Mirza transmitted to Bishop. There was no response.

"Fucking drones," Kruger said from the second Polaris. The chatter of his MK48 sounded as he stood on the passenger seat with the machine gun pressed to his shoulder. "Like swatting Tsetse flies." He fired a long burst shredding another of the UAVs.

Mirza launched his Polaris over a snowdrift and slid to the bottom of a shallow valley. He gunned the buggy sending up rooster tails of snow. Wiping ice from the iPRIMAL fixed to the dash he kept one eye on the screen as they scrambled up a tree-covered slope. They were only half a mile from the facility now. He skidded the buggy to a halt just short of the ridgeline.

Bishop's target pack had finished uploading to his iPRIMAL. Flicking through the slides, he took a mental snapshot of the layout of the facility. Critically, the two remote guard towers covering their approach were registered to be destroyed by the Pain Train. He thumbed the radio, trying Bishop again, "Overwatch, this is Scrambler, we're at the form-up point. Confirm target, over."

The three buggies were halted in a line, ready to crest the ridge and assault the facility. As they waited for Bishop to reply the team checked their weapons. In addition to the forward-mounted machine guns each vehicle had a PAW-20 grenade launcher loaded with armor-piercing HEAT rounds strapped behind the seats.

"All call signs, this is Overwatch, you are cleared hot," Bishop's voice came over the radio. "I will stay in position and confirm target neutralization."

"Acknowledged. Pain Train, this is Scrambler. Roll on the pain!"

***

PAIN TRAIN

Mitch banked the Ilyushin to line up their final approach on the Dead Land facility. The cockpit's heads-up-display showed him the exact heading required for optimal deployment of the Viper munitions. Once he had lined the jet up he reached across and stabbed a button with a gloved finger. He lifted his hands off the yoke and relaxed back against the seat. The weapon system now had control of the aircraft.

"Forty seconds to launch," reported Kurtz from the weapons station behind him.

"Roger." He keyed the communications set. "All call signs, stand by for impact."

"Thirty seconds." As Kurtz spoke an alarm blared and a row of lights in the cockpit flashed.

"We just got lit up!" Mitch grabbed the Yoke and over-rode the autopilot sending the Pain Train into a dive. He pushed the throttles to maximum power. "Activate all countermeasures!" he bellowed.

"*Ja*, countermeasures active." Below the tail of the aircraft a hidden hatch slid open revealing the Skyshield laser module. Another internal pod activated a jammer that blasted the airwaves with electronic noise.

"What have you got, Kurtz?" Mitch asked as they banked away from their target.

"Nothing, just the initial hit from a search radar and now nothing."

Mitch continued diving, only leveling them out when they were mere feet above tree height. Hugging the terrain he followed a shallow valley. Another alarm blared. "Missile launch!" yelled Kurtz.

"Bloody hell!" Mitch glanced at the countermeasures screen. It was heatseeker as there were no radar emissions. He knew there was no point trying to outmaneuver the nimble air-to-air missile. They were completely dependent on the Pain Train's automated defenses.

Five miles away the AIM-9X Sidewinder streaked away from Donk's F-22 into the night sky. He switched his radar to active mode and watched the missile's rapid progress as it homed in on the target. Running afterburners he would be in visual range when it struck. The seconds counted down as the missile closed at almost 3,000 kilometers an hour. Donk saw the explosion as a flash in the distance. "Splash one bogey."

"Negative, Donk, the target is still airborne."

"No shit! That bad boy's running some seriously advanced countermeasures." He shook his head in disbelief. The AIM-9X used one of the most advanced thermal seekers in the world; it could only be defeated by the latest US and Israeli laser jammers.

"Goddamn, my radar's possessed!" reported Groper.

Donk glanced down and saw his radar monitor was awash with static. They were under electronic attack by the Russian transporter. "Those sneaky motherfuckers. I'm switching to guns, let's finish this fat pig."

Inside the Pain Train Mitch knew they were flying on borrowed time. The jets lurking in the darkness would be USAF F-22s, the most advanced interceptor in existence. Not even their sophisticated Israeli-built countermeasures were going to keep them alive. He glanced at the navigation screen and hauled back on the yoke, bringing the transporter around in a tight turn that put them back on a path over Dead Land. "Kurtz, we're going to finish the run."

"*Ja*, I'm ready."

As they leveled out a streak of tracer flashed. Mitch felt the aircraft shudder and warning lights lit up. "Now we're proper fucked." They began losing altitude as another stream of tracer flashed past. "We've lost two engines. Strap in, Kurtz, we're going down."

He keyed the radio, "All call signs, this is Pain Train. Sorry guys, you're on your own."

Less than a mile away Donk watched as another of the lumbering aircraft's engines burst into flames. "She's done, Groper, I'm peeling off." He aborted his final attack run and pulled away to watch the demise of the target.

"Damn, that guy's got some skills," reported his wingman as they watched the pilot of the Il-76 struggling to line up the burning jet with the airstrip at the research facility. "You think he'll get it down in one piece?"

"I'll put a hundred bucks on it going up in smoke."

There was silence as Groper contemplated the wager. "You got a deal, I'll take that bet."

They circled the burning aircraft as it came in low toward the USAF research facility. "Whoa, that's bullshit," said Donk as the Russian transporter slammed down on the tarmac and slid along the airstrip in a shower of sparks.

"Fair's fair, buddy."

The aircraft's landing gear had collapsed and it slid on its belly, still streaming flames. One of the wings dipped and tore clean off. Fuel spilled out of the fractured tanks, catching fire as it shot off the end of the runway, through a fence, and plowed through snow into the woods. It finally came to a halt with the fuselage intact.

"He got it down. I win," said Groper as they continued to circle the wreck.

"Hey it's not over till the fat lady sings." Donk keyed his radio and reported the neutralization of the target over the command network. As he waited for a reply the burning fuel around the wreckage seemed to abate.

"I think he's good."

"Fine, you win," Donk said. As he spoke a huge explosion tore the aircraft apart and a fireball rolled skyward.

"Too late, you already called it."

"Goddamn."

Another call sign came through over the command net. "Cyclon 1-1, this is Fort Yukon Research Station. Request close air support, over."

Donk glanced down at the fuel gauge. Using their afterburners had burnt through two-thirds of their gas. "Negative, Yukon, we're almost at bingo fuel." He shook his head, wondering why a classified research facility in the middle of Alaska was requesting air support. Not that he could provide it, he only had ammo for a couple short bursts from the 20mm cannon.

"Let's take these babies home, Groper," he transmitted over their internal frequency. As the two interceptors banked and disappeared into the night sky the scattered wreck of the Pain Train continued to burn.

***

FORT YUKON RESEARCH STATION

Bishop watched in disbelief as the Pain Train slammed down on the runway and slid out of view. He frantically shoveled snow with his hands in an attempt to widen the view from the hide. There was a flash and a massive fireball blossomed above the end of the tarmac. He froze. "Pain Train, this is Overwatch," he croaked into his mike. "Pain Train, this is Overwatch. Mitch, goddamn it, answer me!"

"Overwatch, this is Scrambler, what's going on?" asked Mirza.

"Pain Train is down, I say again the Pain Train is down." He paused. "We're on our own."

There was silence from the other end of the radio as Bishop tucked the sniper rifle into his shoulder and sighted it on the closest of the remote weapon towers.

He balanced the cross hair on the tower's optical unit. "I'm neutralizing the closest towers. Standby." He squeezed the trigger and the Windrunner bucked. Direct hit. Working the bolt he adjusted his position and scoped the next tower. "Oh shit." The pod was staring directly at him. He didn't have time to engage as the machine gun muzzle flashed. Rounds zipped through the snow around him as he shuffled backward franticly.

He hunkered in the bottom of the cave as bullets shredded the snow and ice. Projectiles punched through the tree showering him in splinters of wood. The noise was deafening as another tower joined the first in blasting his position. He slid on his chest through the snow almost swimming as he tried to escape. A 40mm grenade impacted the position and the earth shook. Bursting from the hide, he rolled down the slope away from the trees and came to rest against the tracks of a Polaris.

"Holy shit!" yelled Kruger as more ordnance exploded on the ridgeline above them. "What did you do, Bish, bare your ass at them?"

He climbed to his feet and dusted off the snow. Behind him the fusillade of ammunition churning the ridge finally stopped. In the darkness he looked over the three identical buggies. "Mirza?"

The CAT team leader raised his hand. Beside him another operator, smaller but dressed the same, manned a machine gun. He knew it was Saneh.

"Have we heard anything from Mitch and Kurtz?" Bishop asked as he approached.

Mirza shook his head. "No, we have to assume the worst."

He punched the side of the buggy. "Motherfuckers! We need to finish this."

"We can't go up against that much firepower."

"We can with a plan. Have you checked in with Vance?"

"I'm doing that right now," Mirza said as he typed into the iPRIMAL strapped to his forearm.

"OK, who's got my gear?"

"Over here," yelled Miklos.

Bishop checked the back of the buggy and found his equipment bag. He donned his armor and helmet, and slung a Tavor. He inspected the rest of the equipment and grabbed a PAW-20 grenade launcher. "How many of these do we have? We can hit the towers with them."

"Negative," replied Mirza. "Orders from the Bunker. We are to hold here and wait for directions. Flash has got something on the go."

"What? No, we need to hit these bastards now and hit them hard."

"No, Bish. We wait."

He nodded. "OK, let's see what Flash has got up his sleeve." He climbed into the passenger seat of Miklos's buggy, laying the PAW-20 on his lap. "But if we're not rolling in ten minutes we flank the facility and check the wreckage of the Pain Train, OK?"

Mirza nodded. "Deal."

***

NURAI ISLAND, ABU DHABI

Vance burst in through the door. "Where we at, Flash?"

Chua pressed a finger to his lips. "Let him work," he whispered.

He nodded and pulled out a chair.

Flash was hunched over a laptop, his fingers a blur as they raced across the keyboard. His brow was drenched in sweat and he'd tossed his flat brim cap on the bench. He paused, wiped his forehead, and returned his attention to the screen.

Vance gestured for Chua to follow him out to the corridor. "Does Flash know about the Pain Train?"

Chua closed the door. "Yes, he knows the team's success hinges on this."

"Who the hell gives permission for F-22s to shoot down a civilian aircraft?" Vance looked furious.

"Larkin must have seen us coming, but now we adapt and we overcome."

"He didn't see this coming!" yelled Flash from behind the door.

The two men burst back inside.

"I'm in!" said Flash. "And I've got the keys to dad's Mustang." His fingers continued to dance across the keyboard. "And now, I'm inviting all my buddies 'round to play."

"What exactly have you done?" asked Vance.

"Not me." Flash chuckled. "Mitch, that sneaky Brit, gave me a backdoor into their system. It took me a while because of the bandwidth but I managed to get past their firewall and hack their security. Now twenty of my most trusted hackers have the IP address and encryption key to get in and start wreaking havoc." He recommenced typing. "First things first, I'm getting them to take over the Talons. Then we're going to have some fun trying to shoot each other."

"Can you tell me when the all the defenses are down?"

"Sure, won't take long. These guys work fast."

CHAPTER 26

FORT YUKON RESEARCH STATION

King relaxed in one of the ops room chairs. He would've preferred if the Raptors had remained on-station but the fact was they weren't needed. The enemy only had three vehicles and no more than six men. They must have severely underestimated his defenses. Their fire support appeared to consist of a single sniper, who had now been neutralized.

"Have you dispatched a drone to investigate the crash site?" he asked Hammer. All three of his men were now in the room manning terminals. They were coordinating the Talons and drones, leaving the towers on remote to engage anyone outside the perimeter autonomously.

"Yeah, boss, I've got one keeping an eye on the buggies and the other is checking out the crash. It's burning pretty hard down there though. Can't see through all the damn smoke."

"Keep the drone monitoring the buggies at a safe distance. I don't want them shooting another one down."

"Copy."

King studied the tactical maps on the central screens. One showed a layout of the facility and the other a zoomed-out battle map. The quadcopters, Talons, and towers were displayed as icons that updated their status in real-time. One of the towers was offline, disabled by the enemy sniper. The weakness had been mitigated, however, as they had repositioned two Talons to cover the gap.

He checked the video feed from the drone monitoring the buggies. The three compact vehicles had positioned themselves in a line ready to advance. They bristled with weapons but were unarmored. Once they rolled over the hill into his kill zone they would blasted into scrap-metal by his machine guns and grenade launchers.

King shook his head. "These guys are fucked.

"Yep, and with their jet down, they ain't got an extraction plan," said Hammer.

"ETA on the Raptors from Elmendorf?"

"Hour turnaround, boss."

"What I wouldn't give for an A-10 to finish them off."

"Yeah, or even a mortar," added Hammer.

"Let's push three of the Talons north. If they don't make a move we will. I've got Talon One. Matt and Chris, you're with me."

They took control of the robots and steered them out through the access point and around the perimeter fence to the north. King's hands were more familiar with the grip of an assault rifle than a joystick. The idea that a machine would be doing the killing for him was alien. However, he could see that this was the future of combat. He piloted his Talon out from the facility a few hundred yards, crested a hill, then turned in the direction of the enemy.

"I'm in position, boss," said Matt once he'd brought his robot in line with Talon One.

"Me too," said Chris.

"Let's roll up these douche bags," added Matt.

King glanced up at the main battle map. The icons for the three Talons were in a line ready to advance down the flank and engage the buggies. "Hammer, have they moved?"

The lanky operator checked the drone's video feed. "No, boss."

"Good, let's advance. On me." As King pushed forward on the joystick his screen flickered.

"What the fuck?" said Hammer.

"You get that too?"

"Yeah, some kind of interference."

King looked up at the central screens. As he did they flickered twice and the maps were replaced with videos of a fat pug puppy lying on its back. The animal looked as if it was struggling to get back on its feet. "What the hell is this?" He glanced down at the monitor in front of him. His Talon swiveled its turret randomly. "I've lost control."

"Me too," said Matt.

"Oh shit." King's Talon centered its sights on one of the other robots and unleashed its machine gun in a relentless burst.

"This is all screwed up!" bellowed Matt. "Who the hell is shooting me?"

King's Talon shuddered as it launched a volley of 40mm grenades. Matt's robot exploded in a flash of flame and sparks. More gunfire sounded from outside the administration building.

"We've lost control of the towers," reported Hammer. "And the drones."

"What the fuck is going on?" screamed King. One of the feeds from a quadcopter spun crazily then went blank as the drone crashed into the ground.

"Someone has hacked us, boss," Hammer said. "They've got control of the security systems." He pointed to a CCTV monitor that showed the weapon towers blasting each other and everything in sight. They watched silently as two of Aaron Small's men attempted to sprint to the underground prison and were cut down in a volley of grenade fire.

"Jesus Christ!" The building shuddered as a barrage of grenades slammed into the wall. "How the hell do we shut it down?"

Hammer shook his head. "Don't know, boss, we need one of the IT guys."

King watched in disbelief as the remaining Talons blasted the weapon turrets and fired at the facility's buildings. The rate of fire ramped up to a devastating level, as if an ambush had been triggered. Then, within a matter of seconds the weapons petered out and everything fell quiet. Each tower had been destroyed and the remaining Talons drove around randomly, their ammunition exhausted.

"Grab your gear, boys." King dialed Larkin as the men readied themselves.

"Charles, I hear you've been busy," answered the OSP Director. "I've just got word that jets out of Elmendorf intercepted a Russian spy plane close to your location."

"Listen to me, Thomas. Someone has hacked your goddamn super-prison. I've lost control of all the systems."

"That's not possible."

"You should explain that to the men who were just cut down by one of the towers."

"I'll call my IT–"

"Just shut up and listen. The weapon systems are finished. They destroyed each other. I'm moving my men to defend from the prison. I need you to get us air support from Elmendorf, ASAP. Anything moving outside the prison needs to be smoked."

"I will see what I can do. Keep me posted." Larkin terminated the call.

"That cock sucker is going to hang us out to dry, boss," snarled Hammer as he loaded a 40mm grenade into the launcher under his carbine. "He'll try to blow his servers and leave us up shit creek without a paddle."

King grabbed his carbine from where it leant against the wall. "Let's get down to the cells before those buggies get here."

At the bottom of the stairs he ran into Aaron Small and what was left of his men. They carried their M4 carbines awkwardly and wore ill-fitting chest rigs. King smirked as he spotted the look of fear on the interrogator's face.

"We tried to get to the prison. The towers turned on us. Three of my men are dead."

King barged past, knocking him aside. "The towers are down. We're going to the cells."

***

LANGLEY

Larkin slapped the keyboard. He was logged into the Dead Land security network but it had gone haywire. Random images were flashing up on screen; puppy videos replaced the feeds from the towers and Talons. The few CCTV cameras that were still working showed his defenses were a smoldering wreck. "What in God's name?"

Snatching up his phone he dialed the IT guy at Dead Land. There was no answer. "Son of a bitch." He swept the phone off the desk along with his keyboard. The flashing monitor continued to mock him as it cycled between CCTV footage and fat puppies tumbling over each other.

Taking a deep breath he opened his black Redemption laptop. The intel server was still active and he clicked on the self-destruct menu. Entering the codeword to detonate the explosives he looked at the CCTV monitor and waited for the fireworks. Nothing. "What the hell!" Someone must have disarmed the system.

There was a knock on the door. "What?"

His assistant opened the door enough to stick her head in. "There's someone here to see you, sir."

Larkin waved her away. "I'm busy."

"Damn straight you're busy." Brian Masters stormed into his office. "I've got people jumping through their asses trying to work out why we authorized the interception of a civilian transporter in Alaska."

Larkin met the angry director's stare. "Leave it alone, Brian."

"Leave it alone? I told you to run any plans past me! You shoot down a civilian aircraft and now you've got a strategic bomber waiting to hit something else. I've got the Pentagon threatening to shut down Global Vigilance because you're running your own goddamn war!"

"They're not going to do that. These are legitimate targets. I can guarantee there will be no blowback." His lip curled up in a snarl. "Now, has that little problem in Saudi disappeared?"

"That's not what we're talking about."

"Has it?"

"Well, yes."

"Good, now get the hell out of my office."

Brian stood glaring at him. "One day your little house of cards is going to come crashing down, Thomas Larkin, and when it does I'm not going to be there to clean it up." He turned and walked out, slamming the door.

"We're in this together, Brian, don't forget that!" Larkin shouted after him. He recovered the phone from the floor and punched in a number. He waited for the USAF officer on the other end to answer. "Execute Archangel."

"Yes, sir, I confirm Archangel."

"ETA?"

"Forty minutes, sir."

"Good." He terminated the call and tossed the phone on his desk.

There was another soft knock. "What?"

His assistant pushed open the door with her foot and carried in a tray with hot coffee and pancakes. "Sir, I thought you might want something to eat."

He rubbed his eyes. "Thanks, Marlene, you're a saint."

"Is everything OK, sir?" she asked placing the tray on the desk.

He smiled. "Yeah, everything's fine. Just cleaning up some odds and ends."

***

FORT YUKON RESEARCH STATION

The three tracked buggies crested the ridgeline in linear formation. Side by side they slid down the steep slope through the trees. As they hit the level open ground they accelerated across the snow till they skidded to a halt a dozen yards short of the tall chain fence. From the passenger seat of his buggy Bishop trained his machine gun on a lone Talon. The robot was inside the fence and spinning crazily with its weapons aimed at the sky. According to Vance and the crew in Abu

Dhabi all the automated systems had been destroyed or depleted of ammunition, but he was taking no chances.

As Pavel jumped from the buggy with a breaching circular saw he blasted the Talon. Through his night vision his aiming laser bounced as he sent a stream of tracer into the target. The robot sparked and continued spinning like a top. Another burst ended its erratic dance and it toppled over, catching fire.

He turned his attention to the fence where Pavel was cutting through a second support pole. The screech of the saw ended abruptly as a large section of fence collapsed into the snow.

Moments after the fence fell the three buggies roared through the gap. Bishop spotted two figures sprinting from the main building. He swiveled the machine gun and fired a burst. One of the men went down. As he made to fire again his target took cover in the building.

Bishop released the machine gun and grabbed his PAW-20. Before he could fire, grenades from another buggy detonated around the entrance.

"Bishop, you and Miklos clear the main building," ordered Mirza over the radio. "Kruger and Pavel will clear the hangars. I will secure the bunker entrance with Saneh."

"Wilco." Bishop pointed to the opposite end of the building, away from where the gunman had taken cover.

From the driver's seat Miklos nodded and raced the tracked buggy off to the flank. They slid around the far corner of the building and Bishop glanced past the end of the runway. Through his helmet's thermal sensors he could see the burning wreckage of the Pain Train scattered among the trees. His gut twisted in a ball of anger as they skidded to a halt in front of a fire escape.

Bishop grabbed a frame charge from the Polaris and stuck it to the steel fire escape. He gripped his Tavor with gloved hands and gave Miklos a nod.

The explosion blew the door off its hinges and Bishop rushed through the gap. Bullets sparked off the walls as he searched for a target. He caught a glimpse of two men at the end of a long corridor. As he fired they disappeared into a room. "Two hostiles, deep."

"Stairs to the left," reported Miklos.

"Check 'em out. I'll hold here."

Bishop crouched in the stairwell and kept an eye on the corridor as Miklos climbed to the next level. He spotted a weapon poking out from the room that the men had sought shelter in and heard the thud of a grenade launcher firing. "Shit!"

The golf ball sized projectile skipped off a wall and he dove to the ground. It exploded above his head showering him in shards of hot steel. His armor bore the brunt of the explosion and the enclosed helmet filtered the concussion.

"What the hell was that?" transmitted Miklos.

"Ass clowns have a grenade launcher," Bishop replied as he struggled to his feet. The back of his legs burned from where he'd taken a peppering of shrapnel. Through the enhanced hearing of his helmet he heard the snap of the grenade launcher being closed. They were going to try again.

He sprinted down the polished linoleum corridor as the weapon with the grenade launcher appeared. It fired when he was half a dozen yards away. Diving to the ground he felt the low velocity bomb fly past his head. He slammed onto the floor and slid, coming to a halt opposite the doorway. The grenade exploded at the same time he unleashed a full magazine into the two men standing in the room. The bullets found their mark spraying blood and gore across the walls.

"Two hostiles down," he reported as he changed magazines. He climbed to his feet and inspected the dead men. They may have worn similar equipment but to the trained eye they couldn't be more different. One looked like a kid playing at war. His vest was ill-fitting, his weapon fresh out of the box. The other was clearly a professional. His plate carrier was loaded with magazines and grenades, the straps secured with tape. A pair of NVGs tilted up from the latest model Crye helmet.

Squatting he studied the mangled face of the operator. He wasn't sure but he looked like one of the GES contractors who'd chased him in Rio.

"Bishop, top floor is clear. You're going to want to see this."

"On my way." He left the bodies and as he jogged along the corridor he could hear a vicious gunfight raging outside.

Mirza's voice transmitted, "We've encountered heavy resistance at the underground entrance."

"Roger, we'll finish here and back you up." At the top of the stairs Bishop encountered a door with the lock shot out; Miklos's work. The room inside was similar to the PRIMAL headquarters. There were screens on the walls, workstations with joysticks and keyboards, and tactical radios. Most of the monitors in front of the workstations displayed videos of fat pug puppies. His battle buddy leant over one of the few functioning camera feeds.

"What have you got?" Bishop asked as he joined him.

"Look, it's from a detention cell."

He leant close and studied the CCTV feed. There was a man lying on a bed; the bottom half of one leg was missing, and an entire forearm, and his bearded face was scarred. Bishop took a sharp breath and his heart raced. The man's face was one that was etched in his memory. It was Ice. As he watched, the door to the cell opened and a smaller dark-haired man entered. He stood over the prisoner, waving a pistol. Bishop clenched his jaw as the man struck Ice with the weapon and drew a knife. "Let's go." As they headed to the door a tactical radio set crackled and a voice spoke.

"Bone 1-1, this is Elmendorf Tower, we confirm you are clear to taxi."

"Roger, Elmendorf, we anticipate rolling in the next five. Confirm target package Archangel is good to go."

"Bone, you are weapons free on Archangel, I say again weapons free on Archangel."

Bishop sprinted for the door. From his time in the military he knew exactly what call sign Bone was. It was usually assigned to a B-1B Lancer, one of the deadliest bombers in the USAF arsenal. There was no doubt in his mind where that airframe was going to unleash its thousands of pounds of ordnance.

***

King hunkered down behind a makeshift barricade of containers as Chris let loose a burst from a M240 machine gun. He glanced back to where Matt was slumped against the wall with a gunshot wound. One of the IT technicians was trying to stem the flow of blood coming from his abdomen. Aside from Aaron Small, who was deeper in the cells, they were the last of the defenders alive.

The attacking force had breached the heavy outer door and unleashed a maelstrom of high-explosive ordnance into the anteroom. The metal door into the corridor had been riddled by shrapnel and bullets but remained intact.

He fired a few shots through the door as Chris reloaded the machine gun. With their stockpile of ammunition he was confident they could hold off the attackers until close air support arrived. As he changed magazines the phone in his pocket vibrated.

It was Larkin. "I see you've made it down to the cells."

King knew the OSP director would have been watching him over the cameras. "Yeah, I'm down to five men and I've got one wounded that needs urgent MEDEVAC. Where the hell is my air support?"

"Aren't you monitoring the radio net?"

"Not from here." He paused as Chris fired another burst. Grenades detonated against the barricade in retaliation.

"Listen, Charles, what have you done to the Redemption servers?"

"You mean your little back up plan? It was a fucking liability so I binned it."

There was a pause before Larkin replied. "OK, you need to hold your position. Ensure Major League do NOT get access to those servers. A tactical unit will be in your location within twenty. You got that?"

"We're not going anywhere."

"Hold tight, help's on the way."

The line went dead.

King stowed the phone and turned to where Matt sat propped against the wall, his torso heavily bandaged. He crouched next to the wounded operator. "Hang in there, buddy, reinforcements are inbound." Turning to Small's man, a weedy technician, he snapped, "Where the hell is Aaron?"

"He, he's, in with the prisoner," the geek stuttered.

Bullets ricocheted across the ceiling and King glanced back at the barricade where Chris was working the gun. "Get him more ammo!" he bellowed.

The technician stared with a slack jaw before scampering away. King left Matt and crouched low till he reached the door to the cell. It was unlocked so he kicked it open. The interrogator was standing over Castle with a pistol in one hand and a knife in the other. He had flecks of blood over his face, his eyes were wide, and he wore a psychotic grin. King glanced at the invalid on the bed; his face was bloodied and bruised. "What are you doing?"

An explosion rocked the room and the lights flickered.

"He knows these people," hissed Small. "He knows them."

King wrenched the pistol from his hand. "I told you not to fucking touch him. You get out there and fight or we're all going to be dead." He thrust his carbine at the man. "Use this."

Small's eyes were dark with hatred but he took the weapon and turned for the door.

The room shook again as King locked eyes with James Castle. The man's gaze had always been blank but not today. Today defiance flashed in his eyes. King gave him a nod, secured the door, and ducked through the corridor into the cell they had stockpiled with weapons and ammunition. Grabbing a spare carbine, he searched the boxes. He pulled a liner of 7.62mm belts from the pile and loaded his pouches with grenades. He joined the others back at the makeshift barricade and handed the ammunition box to Chris. "Twenty minutes, team. We need to hang on for twenty minutes."

CHAPTER 27

FORT YUKON RESEARCH STATION

Bishop found the rest of the team covering the entrance to the underground facility. "We're running out of time! There's a goddamn B-1 bomber inbound."

Kruger fired another burst from his machine gun. He was at the bottom of the stairs, shooting past the heavy front door that was blown ajar. The defenders replied in turn. "How do you know that?" he yelled.

"Radio in the ops room. Must be Larkin's contingency plan."

"He's going to kill his own people to get to us?"

"I guess he's willing to expend a few more contractors."

"There's another door inside blocking our assault, they're shooting through it," said Mirza. "We've used a dozen grenades and it's still intact."

"We don't have time to mess around." He checked his watch. They had fifteen minutes to get clear of Dead Land before the air strike. "Kruger, you and I are going in."

"No!" Saneh interjected as she handed Kruger a belt of ammunition. "It's too risky. They've got the entrance covered."

"It's the only option," snapped Bishop. "We blast the door with the PAW-20s and assault."

"No, there's another way," she replied. "We give them the opportunity to surrender."

Bishop considered the idea. "That might actually work. Mirza, you're the lead on this one, it's your call."

Kruger fired another burst with his machine gun. The return fire was the only prompt Mirza needed. "We give them one chance then we go in."

***

King fired off a long burst from the M240. Chris was dead, shot through the face. The IT technician was also slain, victim of the constant barrage of bullets ricocheting down the corridor. The interrogator, he, and Matt were now the only survivors. The gutless vampire had proven himself next to useless with a weapon so King had relegated him to running ammunition. He checked his watch; they only had to hang in for another few minutes. He glanced over his shoulder at Matt. The kid's face was white and his eyes shut. "Buddy, you with me?"

The operator's eyes flickered open and he managed a feeble nod.

King fired another blast through the bullet-riddled door.

"Charles King," a metallic voice boomed from the entrance. "We need to talk."

"Go fuck yourself!"

"Charles, we're running out of time."

"No, you are running out of time."

"Your boss, Larkin, is going to blast this place back to the Stone Age. He's got a Bone call sign inbound."

"Bullshit."

"Call him."

King dialed Larkin's number. It rang out. It made sense, he thought. Eliminate everyone in the area. Obliterate the servers. Leave no evidence behind. He sighed.

The voice persisted, "You give us our people and we'll walk away. This is your final chance."

He tried ringing again. There was no answer. "OK, wait." He glanced at Matt then the interrogator. "Aaron, help me with Castle."

Small scowled and gripped his carbine. "No way, you can't hand him over."

"Shut the hell up and come with me." He abandoned the machine gun and stormed down the corridor. The wheelchair they used to move incapacitated prisoners was folded against the wall. He opened it, unlocked the cell door, and pushed the wheelchair into the room.

The prisoner was sprawled on his bloodstained bed. The beating Small had given him was worse than he'd initially thought. "Help me lift him to the chair."

King felt the muzzle of a rifle pressed against his back.

"Take two steps forward and turn around," said Small.

He complied and turned to face him. The interrogator's eyes were wide and his teeth clenched. "You're not handing this piece of shit over to them, you goddamn traitor."

"Larkin's betrayed us, Aaron. You really think he's going to send in SEAL Team Six when he wouldn't give me a handful of guys to defend the place? He's going to level this entire facility."

"Bullshit, I know Larkin. He needs me." As Small's finger tightened on the trigger the invalid sat upright, reached out with his good arm, and grabbed the carbine. It fired as he yanked it clear. The bullet buried itself in the wall as the prisoner used the stump of his other arm to hook Small's neck and pull him in close.

King watched in shock as the bearded prisoner locked his good arm around his torturer's throat.

Small gurgled and clawed at the arm as he fought in vain to free himself. The headlock was brutally effective and within seconds it stopped the blood flow to his brain. His eyes rolled back and he passed out. Exhausted by the effort Castle collapsed on the bed still under the interrogator's limp body.

King threw Small onto the floor and heaved the crippled prisoner into the wheelchair. As he wheeled Castle into the corridor he bellowed, "I want to talk to whoever is in charge!"

"That's me," the voice echoed from the other end of the prison. "I'm warning you, King, if anything happens to our guy we're going to kill you."

King took a deep breath. "One of my men needs medical attention. You promise to take us as far as Fort Yukon and cut us free, and I'll lay down my weapons. I've got your man, James Castle, here."

"What about Wesley Chambers?"

"He's dead."

There was a pause. "Deal, drop your weapons. We're coming in."

King placed his carbine onto the floor and locked the cell door behind him. Small could take whatever it was that Larkin had planned for Dead Land.

***

"OK, Mirza, how do you want to run this?" Bishop asked.

"You and Kruger are on point. I'll stabilize the casualties before we load them and get out of here." He turned to the other three operators. "Saneh, Miklos, and Pavel are driving. I want Ice onboard first."

"OK, let's roll." Bishop shouldered his Tavor and gave Kruger a nod. They moved down the stairs side by side till they reached the ragged opening where the heavy steel door had been blown off its hinges. Bishop took a deep breath and swung into the anteroom with Kruger at his shoulder. Taking a knee he waited for Mirza to bring up the rear.

He glanced through a hole in the shredded interior door and watched as King shoved a makeshift barricade aside. The GES boss was unarmed and a long-haired detainee sat in a wheelchair behind him. Bishop burst through the bullet-ridden door, covering King with his Tavor.

"Where's your medic?" King asked.

Bishop fought the urge to shoot as he approached the GES boss and checked the person slumped in the wheelchair. He was glad the helmet hid his emotions as he laid eyes on Ice. The long lost PRIMAL operative was a shell of his former self. His right lower leg was missing along with half his right arm. His face was a mass of scar tissue bloodied with recent bruises and cuts. "We've got you now, buddy," he said softly.

Mirza snapped out his orders. "Bishop, Kruger, get Ice in warm gear and get him loaded." He moved past to where the wounded GES operative was slumped against the wall. King pushed aside the last of the barricade and went to help Mirza.

Bishop wheeled Ice across the sea of bullet casings and spent link to the bottom of the stairs. The other four were waiting with a collapsible stretcher and blankets. They gently transferred their semi-conscious comrade onto the stretcher, wrapped him tightly in the blankets, and carried him up the stairs.

"I knew you would come," murmured Ice as Bishop lashed him and the stretcher down onto the back of a Polaris buggy.

"Just take it easy, brother. We'll have you out of here in no time." Bishop cracked a handful of heat pads and slid them inside the blankets. The rest of the team returned down the stairs to carry the wounded GES operative. They secured him to the rear of Mirza's buggy on a second stretcher.

"Mount up," ordered Mirza.

Bishop pointed at King. "You're with me." He glanced at his watch. They were almost out of time to get clear of the facility. "We've got to get moving."

Mirza checked the casualties were secure. "Let's roll. We'll head to the crash site first."

Saneh's buggy led with the wounded GES operative strapped across the back. She drove so Mirza could monitor his vitals and keep him stable. Kruger and Pavel were next with Ice strapped to the rear bed. Bishop and Miklos brought up the rear with King wedged between them.

The three buggies blasted around the main building and slid onto the snow-covered tarmac. Their tracks scrabbled on the blacktop as they powered down the runway at nearly forty miles an hour. Bishop glanced up at the sky. The bomber would not be far away.

They were near the end of the airstrip when the sleek B-1B screamed over the top of them. The earth shook as the strategic bomber dumped thousands of pounds of ordnance on Dead Land. Bishop looked over his shoulder to witness the devastation. Even protected by the helmet and arctic clothing he could feel the heat from the blast. He turned to King. "You work for some real nice people."

The GES boss clenched his jaw and watched the destruction.

As the buggies reached the end of the runway they weaved around the debris that littered the scarred asphalt. Bishop choked back the grief that welled up as they drove through a gaping hole in the fence and approached the smoking ruins of the Il-76 transporter. To his front, Mirza's buggy skidded to a halt.

"You're not going to believe this," transmitted Mirza.

Bishop swung out of the buggy, Tavor carbine in hand. As he strode toward the lead Polaris he spotted two figures near the wreckage. They were backlit by the burning airframe. He instantly identified the tall German and the broad-shouldered Brit. It was Kurtz and Mitch.

"We thought you guys had bought the farm!" he yelled.

Mitch wore a broad grin under his shaggy beard. "Nope, takes more than the world's most sophisticated fighter to take down the super-crew."

"Get in, we've got wounded to extract."

Kurtz joined Kruger and Pavel in their buggy as Mitch jumped into the cargo bed of Bishop's vehicle.

"Man, I thought you were toast," Bishop said.

"Toast is the right word. We got out just as the weapons pod went up." Mitch nodded at King. "What's with him? You picking up hitchhikers again?"

"Long story. Larkin screwed him over. He gave us Ice and we agreed to get him out."

"Sounds like a fair deal. So, we heading to Fort Yukon?"

"Yeah, back to Sleek and then we're getting the hell out of here and back home. I need some downtime."

***

It took three hours to cover the thirty miles from Dead Land to Fort Yukon. It was the early hours of the morning and the sun was peeking over the horizon when the three tracked Polaris buggies skidded to a halt outside the hangar. They no longer bristled with weaponry; guns and gear had been stashed before they entered town.

The mood of the PRIMAL team and their prisoner was somber. The wounded GES operator, Matt, hadn't made it. He'd succumbed to his wounds during the long drive out.

Bishop removed his helmet and helped King unload the stretcher. They laid it on the ground outside the hangar. King stared at the corpse and he couldn't help but feel the man's loss. Three hours earlier they'd been mortal enemies. Now, they were two soldiers touched by the hand of death.

King crouched and covered the lifeless face with the space blanket that had been wrapped around the body. "He was a good man. Had a wife and two young kids, two and three."

The words hit Bishop hard. Most of the men he'd killed were cold ruthless murderers. Criminals that deserved the justice they were ultimately dealt. This was different. "I'm sorry for your loss."

King turned to him. "Thanks for trying."

"That was the deal."

"So what now?"

"Now we go our separate ways. I don't recommend trying to find us." The soft whine of turbines spooling up emanated from the hangar. The rest of the PRIMAL team had finished loading their equipment, stripping the buggies of any military hardware. "You've got a chance that many don't get, Charles. You can make good on some of your wrongs."

The GES boss's gaze dropped. "I didn't set out on this path."

Bishop picked up his gear.

"I want you to know that I didn't kill Wesley. The man who did died at Dead Land."

He gave a nod, turned, and left King standing in the cold with the body of his dead comrade. He walked through the open hangar doors and almost collided with Kruger.

"You want me to finish it?" the mammoth South African was holding a suppressed pistol.

268

"No, a deal is a deal. He gave us Ice. Now let's get the hell out of here." He climbed up the stairs to the jet and dumped his gear in the cabin. At the back of the aircraft he spotted Mirza making Ice comfortable in one of the oversized recliners. Bishop walked slowly down the aisle and lowered himself in the chair opposite.

Mirza gave him a nod and headed to the cockpit.

Ice was a mere shadow of the man he used to be. Four years in confinement had wasted away most of the muscle that hadn't been destroyed when he'd lost his limbs. His scarred face was lean and gaunt with a bushy beard that reached his chest. Despite the horrendous injuries and years of torture his blue eyes remained vibrant. Bishop smiled grimly, the big man was still the warrior he remembered.

"Thank you," Ice croaked.

He exhaled. "God, I'm sorry, mate. We had no idea you were still alive."

Ice shook his shaggy mop of hair. "It's not your fault. It's not Mirza's fault. I always knew you would come for me and here you are. So, how's Vance?"

"Vance is good, you'll see him soon in Abu Dhabi."

A broad smile split his ragged beard. "Awesome."

Bishop could see he was struggling to keep his eyes open. The three hours of bashing their way through the Alaskan snow in the buggies had taken its toll. "OK buddy, you rest up. We'll be in Abu Dhabi in about twelve hours."

"OK, hey, Bish."

"Yeah, mate."

"Do you think I could get a caramel milkshake when we land?"

He laughed. "Of course you can, bro. Anything else you want, just ask." He leant back as the jet taxied out of the hangar onto the icy runway. As the engines gained thrust he glanced out of the window and spotted a lone figure watching them from under the eaves of the hangar. Bishop frowned, he hoped like hell he wasn't going to regret letting King live.

CHAPTER 28

MALDIVES

Vance stepped out of the cabin cruiser and strode across the weathered planks of the jetty. At the end of the decking he kicked off his loafers and continued onto the beach. The fine white sand was hot under his feet and he walked quickly into the shade of the palms that grew in abundance on the island. He was dressed in his favorite attire; baggy shorts, an oversized orange Hawaiian shirt, and a Panama hat.

He strolled through the palms, following the sandy trail at a leisurely pace. For the first time in four years he felt relaxed. Bishop and Saneh were tying up a loose end in South America, a walk in the park for PRIMAL's power couple, and Flash and Chua were finishing the warning system that would monitor any undue attention on what remained of PRIMAL.

Once the final tasks were complete Chua would join them in the Maldives for a sabbatical and the rest of the team would disperse. After nearly four years of high-intensity operations it was the least they deserved, he thought.

Pushing aside a wayward palm frond he emerged out of the trees into the island's private resort. There, under a sailcloth shade, Ice lay stretched out on a sunbed, sipping from a coconut that was gripped in an aluminum claw. He wore only board shorts and his bare torso was heavily scarred.

Ice's recovery during the last month in Abu Dhabi had been astounding. Under the watchful eye of a team of the best doctors and therapists money could buy he'd rapidly gained muscle and adapted to his artificial limbs. The wounds on his face had healed and the scars had started to fade. With a haircut and shave he was now transformed from an invalid prisoner back into a semblance of his former warrior self.

Mitch had helped a surgeon to design his artificial lower leg and an interim mechanical hand. The PRIMAL technician was currently in Israel working on what he called the Skywalker Special, a hand that would have similar dexterity to the one Ice had lost.

"Putting on some bulk, buddy," Vance said sitting on an empty sunbed. He groaned as he lay back and stretched out his legs.

"They haven't stopped feeding me since I arrived." Ice smiled as he slurped the last of the coconut water through a straw and dropped the empty husk in the sand. "Tariq had a full gym shipped in. I've been hitting the weights three times a day. I'll be ready to get back on the tools in the next week or two."

"No rush." Vance waved a waiter over and ordered a coconut of his own. "Once Bishop and Saneh finish up we're shutting down operations."

"For how long?"

"I don't think PRIMAL will ever return to what you knew, buddy. We've popped up on the radar of the CIA, and we've left a trail of dead bodies across three continents. We're going to have to make like Al-Qaeda and move to a smaller, more flexible, operating footprint."

"So no more island?"

The waiter reappeared, handing Vance a coconut. He waited for the man to disappear before continuing. "We've still got a lot of gear there but for now the Bunker's shut down. Everyone has been dispersed except for the core team. Once Saneh and Bishop have dealt with Larkin we'll cease ops."

"For how long?"

"At least six months, maybe more. We need to lay low until Chua and Flash give us the all-clear." He sipped from the coconut with a straw. "Anyway, I could get used to this."

Ice shook his head. "I've been lying on my back pretending to be an idiot for four years, bro. I can't sit around on my claw all day." He held up his makeshift limb and activated the aluminum pincer.

Vance almost choked on his drink. "Good to see you haven't lost your sense of humor."

"Only thing that kept me going. But seriously, is there a role for me in the new PRIMAL?"

"Of course there is. There will always be a place for you on the team."

"You know what I'm asking, Vance."

He studied his friend's face. "Let's play it by ear, brother. There's plenty to do while we're here. I'll book a fishing charter tomorrow and when Chua gets here he's going to give us some surfing lessons. I'm keen to get some diving down-range as well."

"I need to get back on the tools."

"All in good time." Vance finished his coconut, dropped it in the sand, and kicked back in the chair. He tipped his hat low and closed his eyes. "Let's just enjoy a bit of down time."

"I've had enough down time."

Vance opened one eye and watched as Ice climbed out of the deckchair and strode across the sand toward the bungalows that housed the restaurant and accommodation. He shook his head and followed him past the weatherboard huts. Ice didn't seem to have any problem walking on the carbon-fiber leg. The big man easily traversed the steps into an open-sided hut filled with gym equipment. He loaded up the bench-press with steel plates. "You up for a session?"

"Sure, why not."

Ice lay on the bench, grabbed one side of the bar with his hand, hooked his claw under the other, and lifted it off the supports. He grunted as he pushed out a dozen reps.

"You're getting the hang of that claw."

"I need one that will hold a weapon." Ice racked the bar.

"Mitch is working on it." Vance swapped places with him under the bar and began his own set.

"Did you have any problems finding Larkin?"

"Yep, but Ivan came good."

"Ivan's still around?"

"Yeah, Chua's best operative."

"When are they going to prosecute?"

"The last thing I heard was that Bishop and Sanch were in position. Should be wrapped up any time now."

Ice nodded. "Good!"

***

GUYANA, SOUTH AMERICA

The two olive-drab four-wheel drives struggled along the muddy track that had been carved through the jungle. Heavy trucks and other construction traffic had turned the single lane into a quagmire of mud. It had taken the convoy well over an hour to wallow along the ten miles from the sealed highway to this point; ten miles of dense unrelenting jungle.

As the vehicles emerged into a clearing they were confronted by a newly constructed detention camp surrounded by a chain fence topped with razor wire. Tall guard towers manned by machine gun wielding soldiers capped each corner of the three hundred square meter facility.

The four-wheel drives parked in the muddy clearing outside the entrance. The doors of the lead vehicle opened and a squad of soldiers dressed in jungle camouflage and black berets alighted, taking up security positions. They scanned the surrounding hills through dark sunglasses, their AK assault rifles held ready. Once they were in place additional men from the second vehicle formed a tighter inner perimeter. Only then did the occupants of the second four-wheel drive appear.

Thomas Larkin frowned as his leather brogues sank in the mud. He surveyed the new facility with a critical eye and turned to the uniformed man who accompanied him. The Guyana Army Colonel wore a proud smile. "See, we have built it exactly as you wanted."

Larkin nodded. "And the construction workers?"

"My men took care of them."

"Excellent." He turned his back on the facility and wiped sweat from his brow as he gazed back up the lush green valley to the distant hillside.

"Do you want to see inside?" the General asked.

He snapped his attention back to the facility. "Yes, of course."

As they made their way through the gate and into the facility they were being watched. A tiny camouflaged camera lodged in the fork of a tree captured stills and broadcast them to an observation post three miles away.

In the OP, Bishop lay beside Saneh beneath a camouflage net draped over the dense undergrowth. Clad in jungle fatigues, faces painted green and black, and wearing lightweight belt rigs, they had rucked heavy packs for two days to reach the location. After setting up they had waited another three days for the convoy to appear.

Once the high-resolution imagery from the remote camera uploaded to Bishop's iPRIMAL he ran it through a facial-recognition app. It was a positive match. He turned to Saneh and gave a nod.

She lay behind two pieces of equipment. On a compact tripod she looked through a digital targeting scope. Beside it was the control module for a drone. She'd already positioned her pizza-box sized quadcopter in a nearby clearing. With the press of a button the little aircraft soared into the air. She watched the video feed on a screen mounted to the controls as she piloted the drone down the valley.

Bishop pulled the cover from his modified Windrunner rifle. Equipped with a smoothbore .50 caliber barrel, Mitch had only recently perfected the ultra-long-range laser-guided sniper system. Lifting the rifle into his shoulder Bishop activated the digital scope. The integrated ballistic computer was linked to the iPRIMAL network and pulled wind and atmospheric data from the drone as it flew down the valley.

"I've got eyes on the target," reported Saneh after a minute.

Bishop glanced at the iPRIMAL strapped to his wrist where he could see the video feed from the quadcopter. Larkin was being escorted out through the security gates toward his vehicle.

"Laser is on," she said.

Bishop placed his eye back on the scope. At three miles Larkin was a tiny figure. A red crosshair appeared over him. He lined his own green crosshair up with the marker from Saneh's drone. When he squeezed the trigger the bullet would travel down range, the tiny sensor in the nose sniffing out the laser that the drone painted on the target.

Before Bishop could take the shot a loud crack rolled up the valley.

"Target is down! There's another shooter."

"What?" Bishop checked the screen of his iPRIMAL. The security detail returned fire into the jungle. The shattered body of Larkin lay on the ground. The image grew in size as Saneh flew the drone closer revealing a growing pool of blood. "Laze the body." Bishop lined the scope up.

"On target."

The rifle barked as it spat another high velocity guided bullet.

"One thousand, two thousand, three thousand," Bishop counted as he chambered another round.

"Impact," reported Saneh. "Larkin confirmed KIA."

"Switch to the guards."

He turned his attention to the drone feed. The camera swiveled to the gunmen who were blazing through ammunition. Saneh centered the feed on one of them. The man was yelling into a radio as he pointed at the hills.

"On target."

Bishop aligned the crosshairs and fired. The Windrunner bucked against his shoulder and he worked the bolt. The rate of fire up the valley increased as the machine gunners in the guard towers added their firepower to the mix.

"Target down." Saneh switched to another of the guards. "On target."

Bishop fired again.

"Drone's hit. Switching to direct targeting." Saneh shifted from the control station to her targeting scope. The field of view was much narrower than the video feed but she had a clear line-of-sight to the machine gun towers. "East tower, on target," she said as she activated the scope's laser designator.

Bishop focused on the machine gunner and fired another round. They repeated the process until all four towers were eliminated. The jungle went silent. Whoever had killed Larkin was in the clear.

"OK, let's get the hell out of here." He stripped the warm barrel from the sniper rifle, stowed it in his rucksack, and grabbed his suppressed Tavor carbine. "Leave the cam net."

It took them mere seconds to finishing packing their gear, message Mirza for extract, and head off for the ridgeline behind them. Less than five minutes later, when they crested the ridge, a dull thud of rotor blades reverberated up the valley. Bishop spun and spotted a helicopter thundering toward them. "That's not ours," he said as they dove for cover.

"A reaction force." Saneh pulled out her targeting scope.

The helicopter swooped over the detention facility. It was a green Bell 412 utility helicopter equipped with door-mounted miniguns. They watched as it circled above the jungle like a hawk searching for its prey.

"They've spotted something," said Bishop as a door gunner on the helicopter blasted the jungle. The minigun sounded like a buzz saw as it lashed the canopy with lead.

Saneh had extended the tripod on her scope and was focusing on the terrain below. A muzzle flashed in response to the helicopter. "Someone's returning fire."

He shrugged off his rucksack and assembled the sniper rifle, loading a fresh magazine. "That poor bastard isn't going to last long. Can you laze the chopper?"

"I'll try."

Standing and balancing the rifle in the fork of a tree, Bishop could see Saneh's laser designator flickering on the helicopter. As he aimed, the door gunner continued blazing at the jungle. He exhaled and fired.

The chopper lurched. He worked the bolt, loaded another round, and fired again.

"Hit," Saneh reported as one of the helicopter's engines flashed. "On target."

Bishop fired one more shot as the chopper banked away streaming black smoke. Stripping down the rifle he stuffed it back into his rucksack.

Saneh packed up her own gear. "Good shooting, Tex."

"All in the laze, babe." Bishop slung his pack over his shoulder, grabbed his Tavor, and led them along a spurline. Moments later they reached the track they had used to infiltrate. He checked his iPRIMAL. "Do we want to eyeball the shooter? We've got time."

Saneh scanned ahead. Their designated helicopter landing zone was a clearing only a few minutes further along the track. "Why not? I'll cover you."

They stashed their packs in the undergrowth. Bishop waited beside the track while Saneh crouched in a firing position further up the hill.

They didn't have to wait long. Within ten minutes Bishop heard someone breathing heavily as they climbed the hill. He lifted his Tavor and aimed into the jungle. The figure that emerged was dressed in a similar fashion to him; jungle fatigues with a belt rig. He wore a floppy bush hat and was carrying an AK assault rifle, with a sniper rifle slung across his back. His shirt was drenched in sweat.

"Hold it there," growled Bishop, his finger poised on the trigger.

The man stopped, dropped the AK on the ground, and raised his hands with the palms facing out. "I'm guessing I can thank you for dealing with that chopper."

"You on your own?"

"Yeah, wish I wasn't."

The voice sounded familiar. "Take the hat off."

The assassin removed the hat revealing a freshly shaved head smeared in camouflage cream. It was Charles King.

"I wasn't expecting to run into you again, Mr. King."

The former GES boss's eyes narrowed.

Bishop saw the moment of recognition.

"Aden."

He nodded.

"You came here to kill Larkin, didn't you?"

"Yeah, but you beat me to it."

King stared down the muzzle of the Tavor's suppressor. "I guess you could shoot me now and you've tidied up all your loose ends."

He cradled the weapon and glanced back at Saneh whose Tavor was aimed at King. She lowered her weapon and gave him a nod.

"No, the slate is clean," Bishop said.

King shook his head. "Not the way I see it. This is the second time you've saved my life. I owe you."

"There won't be a third." Bishop turned and walked back to where he'd left his pack. Saneh shadowed him, and the pair continued down the footpad toward the landing zone. He glanced over his shoulder and wondered if their paths would cross again.

EPILOGUE

DENKENDORF, GERMANY

Kurtz stared out the window of the Lascar Logistics tilt rotor as it winged its way over the green patchwork fields. It had been five years since he had been home to Germany. A lot had changed since he'd lost his job in the police force and left without saying goodbye. He finally felt like he was a part of something again, that he had a purpose in the world.

What the future held for PRIMAL remained to be seen. What was certain was that he wanted to be a part of it; he owed it to Aleks to continue. He swallowed; it seemed like only days had passed since the crazy Russian had given his life to rescue him. The whine of hydraulics interrupted his thoughts and he watched in fascination as the engines rotated skyward slowing the aircraft as they approached their destination. Wiping his hands on the leg of his jeans he breathed deeply and considered what he would say to his parents.

The tilt rotor shuddered as it entered ground effect and a moment later it touched down with a gentle thud. The engines powered down and the Lascar Logistics copilot appeared from the cockpit. The man gave him a nod and opened the cabin's side door. Kurtz grabbed his bag and stepped onto his father's manicured lawn.

The back door to his childhood home swung open and his mother strode out on the patio with her hands on her hips and a scowl on her face. Her fierce expression softened as she recognized the lanky blonde-haired man walking slowly toward her.

The tilt rotor's engines spun up behind him, the blast from the rotors pushing him forward. It lurched into the sky with a roar as his mother fought her way through the wind and wrapped him in a hug. The air settled as the aircraft disappeared leaving them alone.

"I thought I'd never see you again," she sobbed.

He'd never seen his mother cry. She had always been stoic, a woman that he had never wanted to let down. After he was dismissed from the police force he had been unable to face her. His shame had driven him to the world of contracting. The one thing he was thankful for was that it had led him to PRIMAL.

"I'm sorry I left, mother," he said choking back his own tears.

She broke away and stared up with bright blue eyes. "I drove you away."

He placed his arm around her shoulders and they walked toward the house. "It wasn't your fault."

She wiped the tears from her face. "Your father is going to be so happy to see you. How long are you going to stay?"

He shrugged. "I'm not sure when I need to go back, a few months, maybe more."

"Oh, wonderful." She opened the door and he stepped inside the old house. Nothing had changed.

"I kept your room the way you left it," she said. "Your father popped out to the supermarket, he should be back in a few minutes."

Kurtz stood in the kitchen and smiled. It was good to be home.

***

SPAIN

The tiny single-bedroom cottage had a thatched roof with stone walls and an open fireplace. It perched on a hillside overlooking a vineyard on the outskirts of Requena, a small town close to Valencia.

Bishop's parents had bought the property years ago, a retreat in the town of his mother's birth where the two journalists came to unwind. He hadn't returned since their funeral. Killed in a terrorist attack, they were buried in the town's cemetery. That was the first place he had taken Saneh when they arrived earlier in the week. She had laid flowers on their grave before they drove to the cottage.

It had taken two long days for them to clean and return it to a livable condition. But, when they did it immediately felt like home.

"So what exactly are we going to do for a shower?" asked Saneh as she lay naked on a duvet in front of a crackling fire.

"You've been doing just fine with the outside. I thought you liked the romance of a wood-fire heated bath amongst the vines," replied Bishop from where he was standing at the kitchen bench in his shorts.

"Oh how civilized. You do realize that a woman needs running hot water and electricity?" She tossed her head back and shot him a seductive smile as he finished arranging dried fruits and cheeses on a tray.

"But that's not as romantic." He placed the tray on the floor and slid in behind her kissing her neck and shoulders.

"You also need to shave." She leant away to avoid the stubble on his chin.

"In that case we definitely need running water. I'll get a builder up first thing tomorrow morning."

"A proper outdoor bathroom might be nice."

"We don't really have a choice. This place is pretty small."

"About that. We will probably need some more space in the future." She selected a fig and slipped it into her mouth, savoring its sweetness.

"All in good time. Damn, I forgot the wine." He got up and reached for the bottle that he had left to air on the bench.

"Not for me."

"Really, it's very good. From a local winery."

"I'm sure it's wonderful. But, I can't."

Bishop poured his own glass. "What do you mean, you can't?" His voice trailed off as he realized exactly what she was saying. More space needed in the cottage and no wine. He locked eyes with her and a broad grin split his features. "Are you telling me what I think you're telling me?"

She nodded.

JACK SILKSTONE

Bishop drank in her beauty as she lay on the duvet dappled in the soft glow of the fireplace. From her long elegant legs to her full breasts, plump lips, almond-shaped eyes, and flowing hair. "How long?"

"I found out before we left for Guyana."

He frowned. "You mean you put our child in danger?"

"The way I look at it, I kept my child's father out of danger."

He couldn't wipe the smile from his face. "I'm going to be a dad."

She laughed. "Yes you are, Aden. Are you OK with that?"

"Are you kidding me?" He returned to the duvet and wrapped his arms around her. "I couldn't be happier."

She wriggled free of his grasp and turned to face him. "You know this means things are going to have to change." She wore a stern face that let him know she was deadly serious. "There's not going to be any more running around getting shot at. My child is not going to grow up fatherless."

He nodded.

"I'm not saying you're done with PRIMAL. I'm just saying the others can take more of the risks from now on."

"OK."

She tilted her head. "OK? You're OK with that?"

He leant forward and kissed her. "I'm going to have a child with the most beautiful woman in the world. How could I not be OK with that?"

"You're happy with taking a desk job and hanging up your rifle?" Her eyebrows were raised.

He kissed her neck. "If it means starting a family with you, then yes."

She turned her head and pressed her lips against his. "You have to promise me that when Vance reactivates PRIMAL you're not going to run off."

He traced his fingers down her side. "I promise. Although, there is one thing I need us to do before the baby arrives."

"Oh yeah, what's that?"

"Go back to Africa and see those rhinos."

Saneh turned, pushed him onto his back, and straddled him. "I like that idea."

"We're going to need somewhere to stay while the builders turn this place into a real home."

She smiled and leant forward to kiss him again. "You're going to make an excellent father, Aden Bishop."

"I've already decided on a name."

"Oh, really."

He smiled. "I think we should call him or her, Aleks."

A tear ran down Saneh's cheek. "That's a beautiful idea."

***

Keep reading for a preview of PRIMAL Renegade.

AUTHOR'S FINAL WORDS

Well, that concludes the Redemption trilogy. I hope you've enjoyed reading it because I have really enjoyed writing it. It's been an epic journey for the PRIMAL team but it is by no means the end.

As some of you already know I've begun work on a new series that takes place in the year 2055. No, it's not going to be aliens and spaceships, it's going to take the concepts and ideology of the PRIMAL team into the near future. It will bring with it challenges but also opportunities to introduce a new world, new tech, and new characters. You never know, some of the original team might still be around. I'll let you know when the first in the series is ready.

Before you start emailing me hate letters for ending the contemporary PRIMAL series, check yourself. Because I haven't. In fact I've already nearly finished the next in the series. There are going to be plenty more PRIMAL books as Bishop and the team face the challenges of the organization's new model.

Thanks again for all the awesome reviews and keep spreading the word.

JS, out.

P.S. I've slipped in the first chapter of my latest book PRIMAL Renegade so keep reading.

EXCERPT FROM PRIMAL RENEGADE

PROLOGUE

NORTH LUANGWA NATIONAL PARK, ZAMBIA

The black rhino stood calmly with her calf in the shade cast by a camel thorn tree. The film crew that watched from less than a hundred yards away didn't in the least bit bother the majestic grey beast. She was familiar with the humans and their vehicles. As long as they kept their distance they caused her no concern.

Two cut-down safari trucks were parked to take advantage of the soft morning light. A cameraman and a sound technician stood in the back of one with a BBC journalist in the other. Uniformed park rangers sat behind the wheel of each vehicle, ready to beat a hasty retreat if the rhino decided they had overstayed their welcome. The black rhino, unlike their cousins the white, were renowned for having a short temper, especially the mothers.

It was an instinct Afsaneh Ebadi could relate to. Four months pregnant, Saneh was already fiercely protective of the tiny life growing inside her. Not as protective as her partner Bishop though. It had taken all of her charms to convince him that she would be perfectly safe with the film crew and their ranger escort.

The striking former Iranian intelligence operative had joined the group that morning, not willing to miss an opportunity to see the rhino calf. She sat in the front passenger seat of the truck that carried the journalist, dressed in the same khaki dungarees and work shirt as the rangers.

In the opposite vehicle, Christina Munoz, a photographer and her close friend, shot stills of the rhino and film crew. Saneh caught the eye of the petite brunette and flashed her a grin. Christina smiled back and turned the camera on her.

Tossing her long hair she pouted, pretending it was a fashion shoot. With her Persian features, full lips, and mane of dark glossy hair, Saneh was a natural in front of the camera. The photographer giggled and Saneh pressed a finger to her lips reminding her that they were still filming.

Christina poked out her tongue and directed her attention back to the job at hand.

Saneh smiled contently. North Luangwa National Park was a paradise for her. Almost completely untouched by tourism and protected from poaching it was one of Africa's few pristine wildlife reserves. She tipped her head to one side as she watched the rhino and her calf, listening to the words of the journalist.

"Behind me is Kitana, the black rhino, and her calf. This particular animal is important because she is one of only a handful of breeding females left in Zambia." The journalist had a crisp British accent that reminded her of David Attenborough. "Reintroduced to the Luangwa National Park in 2003, the black rhinos are making a slow comeback. This young calf is the third to be born in as many years. She lives here under the watchful eye of the Luangwa Rangers, a local force trained by volunteers. But, while this is a good-news story for the future of black rhinos here in Luangwa, the same cannot be said across Africa. With less than four thousand animals remaining and a ferocious appetite on the black market for their horns, the rangers are fighting a losing battle. They simply do not have the resources to protect them all. So far this year, Kruger National Park in South Africa, only a thousand miles away, has lost a dozen rhinos to poachers. At this rate we can expect the black rhino to be extinct in less than ten years."

Saneh watched the noble beast and her calf with a heavy heart. The mother had two horns; the one at the end of her snout was long and curved, a potent weapon with which to defend her offspring against lions and hyenas. Unfortunately it could not protect her from poachers. The British journalist was on the money; her partner, Aden Bishop, and the other volunteers were fighting a rearguard action. Every day animals across Africa were killed for their horns or tusks. Why? So ignorant rich assholes in China and Vietnam could adorn their desks with carvings and pop pills containing the same chemical compound as their fingernails. It made her so angry. She took a deep breath and tried to relax as the journalist wrapped up the filming of his piece.

A faint noise caught her attention and she looked up. She spotted the electric drone circling above them and gave it a wave. Bishop was keeping an eye on her.

The PRIMAL operatives had been in Zambia for a little over a week. They'd flown in from Spain where builders were turning their tiny cottage into a family home. With PRIMAL shut down they had decided to spend a few months working with Christina and her boyfriend Dominic Marks at the recently established Luangwa Anti-Poaching Academy.

Saneh and Bishop had met Dom, a former New Zealand soldier, only a few weeks earlier. They had been visiting Christina at Kruger National Park and saved her from an attempted kidnapping. It was there that the Africa bug had bitten them both. Now they couldn't get enough of the exotic wildlife roaming the rolling savannah and lush flood plains.

"That's a wrap, people," announced the journalist. "Let's get back to camp for breakfast and tea."

Saneh gave the rhinos one last glance as the drivers started the vehicles. When the BBC team was ready they drove back to the track that led through the bush to base camp.

"So when will you broadcast your piece?" Saneh asked the journalist a mile into the trip.

"My crew will edit it and send it back to London tonight. Should be hitting the airwaves tomorrow morning."

"That soon?"

"The joys of technology. So how do you fit in here? Your partner works with Dom doesn't he?"

"Yes, we're friends of Christina. Taking the opportunity to see a bit of Africa while we can."

"I understand that. I can't get enough of the place."

Saneh smiled. "Yes, it has that effect." She turned and took in the surroundings as they covered the last few miles through the bush.

As they pulled into the camp she spotted Bishop standing in front of the low-slung building that served as the schoolhouse and headquarters. He was an unremarkable looking man. Medium height with an athletic build, he wore camouflaged pants cut off at the knee, battered hiking boots, a short-sleeved khaki shirt, and a faded blue Yankees cap. The hat covered a mop of shaggy hair that matched the stubble on his face. Intelligent brown eyes and a lopsided grin greeted her as she jumped out of the truck, walked across to him, and flung her arms around his lean waist. "How are your little spy planes going?"

"Not great, we're getting some kind of interference on the signal. How was the trip out to see Kitana?"

"It was lovely. But, now I'm hungry."

Bishop touched her growing belly and kissed her. "You never stop eating. Come on then, let's find you something."

"Steak, I want a steak," she said as they made their way toward the camp kitchen.

"That kid's got to be a boy with the amount of red meat you've been craving. Oh, by the way, Kruger is heading up in the next few days. He's going to help us out for a week with some training." He referred to a South African PRIMAL operative who was one of their most capable warriors.

"How's he doing?" asked Saneh as she opened the fridge.

"He sounds a little bored."

She found a steak on a plate and pulled it out. "That's the biggest issue facing Vance and Chua. When they shut down operations they released an army of adrenaline junkies on the world."

Bishop took the plate from her and turned on the grill. "Hey, some of us are doing just fine."

"Sure you are." She kissed him on the cheek.

***

SHANGHAI, CHINA

Wang Hejun's apartment was perched on the top floor of one of the tallest residential towers overlooking Shanghai's business district. The beverage baron was one of the wealthiest men in China. With a net worth estimated at close to twelve billion dollars there were only a few internet entrepreneurs who sat higher on the Forbes China Rich List.

The apartment encompassed the entire penthouse level. Originally three separate residences, he had combined them into a single high-rise mansion. His study, formerly one of the master bedrooms, was where he spent most of his time now he was retired. Decorated in a garish interpretation of Italian baroque that included gilded mirrors and intricately carved furniture, it was where he kept his most prized possessions. Jade carvings, fine porcelain, and other works of art were displayed on either side of the room. In the far corner stood an illuminated glass cabinet with his prized collection of ivory, bone, and horn carvings. They represented trophies of exotic animals, with thousands of hours of work by master carvers to craft them into precious artifacts of the highest order.

Hejun sat at his desk in a silk robe nursing a glass of Maotai as he stared intently at the gilded television on the wall of his study. On screen a black rhino and her calf were standing in the shade of a tree. He didn't understand the journalist; he had never learned the language of the *gweilo*. No doubt wailing about the animals' dwindling numbers or some such rhetoric. That was the weakness of the West, he thought. They did not seem to comprehend that nature was a resource to be exploited for the betterment of man.

His eyes never left the magnificent curved horn that adorned the beast's snout. The black rhino was one species missing from his extensive collection. The Chinese government's ban on rhino horn had made it increasingly difficult and expensive to procure them. Black rhino horn had become impossible to find. But here, on his television, was one of the finest examples he had ever seen. He hit a buzzer on his desk and a moment later the door opened and his assistant appeared.

"Yes, Mr. Hejun." Sung Je was in her mid-thirties with an attractive round face. A tailored skirt and suit jacket emphasized her slender build.

Wang pointed to the screen where the journalist was still talking. "I want you to get me that horn," he croaked.

"Of course." Fluent in English, Sung had no problem reading the tag line across the bottom of the screen. She committed the location of the animal to memory.

"Do you want it sent to a carver?"

Wang shook his head. "No, I want to see it complete. Then I will decide what I want to do with it."

She bowed. "Very good, sir. Will that be all?"

"I want the horn as soon as possible. I will happily pay a premium."

"I will contact our supplier immediately." Sung turned and left the room.

Hejun continued watching the television until the segment about the rhino had finished. Then he turned it off, left his desk, and walked across to the ornate glass cabinet in the corner of the room. The interior was lit showcasing the intricately carved rhino horns and ivory inside. Delicately opening it, he took out one of the horns. The artwork was finely detailed; it would have taken a skilled artisan thousands of hours to work the delicate scrolls into the horn. The carvings represented power, longevity, and health, things he craved more than all else. This collection, along with his business empire, would be handed down for generations to come. It would be his legacy.

***

Sung had been to the Shanghai Greater Exports office on a number of occasions to collect packages for her master. Located in the sprawling Shanghai docks, the office gave the impression of a legitimate company. Run by gangsters, it was a one-stop shop for anyone looking for access to the Chinese underground trafficking market. Illicit goods including endangered animals, military weapons, or even human slaves, were all available for the right price.

She parked Hejun's Mercedes into a parking space outside the office and introduced herself to the middle-aged woman behind the front desk. She was ushered through to see the man who controlled the gateway to illicit goods, Zhou. She didn't know the gangster's last name nor did she feel it necessary to enquire. She cared only that he could deliver the black rhino horn her master desired.

"Ah the pretty Sung Je back again to do the bidding of her wrinkled master." Zhou sat behind a large desk on which laid no less than a dozen cell phones, the tools of his trade.

Sung fought the urge to vomit as the gangster's eyes lingered on her. The man had a habit of licking his lips every few seconds. He reminded her of a bloated lizard she had seen at the Shanghai zoo. "Hejun would like you to procure something for him, something of great rarity."

"Of course, he desires only the finest ivory."

"He wants a black rhino horn."

Zhou sneered, "Of course he does but there are none to be had."

"There is one in Zambia, Luangwa National Park."

He locked eyes with her. "How much is he willing to pay?"

"Whatever it costs."

Zhou's tongue circled his lips. "I'll see what can be done."

"He wants it as soon as possible."

"Then I will have an answer for you today."

"I will wait."

"That is not necessary. I will call you and confirm the price. Unless you wanted to stay for a different reason?" He licked his lips again and watched her stride out of the office. Maybe he would offer Mr. Hejun a discount for a night with her, he thought. He smirked; the old dog had probably already had his way with her. He reached for one of his cell phones and dialed a number. As it rang he imagined what Sung Je would look like naked, bouncing on his lap.

***

PORT OF MOMBASA, KENYA

Six thousand miles away in a rusted warehouse a battered phone on a greasy workbench rang. David Mboya scowled from the stack of crates he sat on. The leader of the poaching gang let the phone ring a half-dozen more times before it finally got the better of him. He threw his beer bottle against the sheet iron wall where it shattered. "Kogo, answer the damn phone!"

A moment later another man appeared; shorter, skinnier, and with a shaved head. Julius Kogo was Mboya's right hand man and errand boy. "Yes, Mamba." He used the former Ugandan paratrooper's nickname, a reference to the African snake renowned for its ferocity and speed. Grabbing the phone off the cradle he pressed it to his ear and listened before turning to his boss. "It's Zhou, says he has another job for you."

Mboya climbed off the crates, uncoiling his wiry frame to its full six foot five. Without a hint of fat, the ebony-skinned African was an imposing sight. His hair was clipped short, a testament to his time in the military. He wore a faded check shirt that was unbuttoned, revealing a lean torso covered in scars. "I don't want to talk to that piece of shit. He ripped me off on the last shipment of tusks. Tell him I'm going to find a new buyer for this batch."

Kogo relayed the response to the Chinese gangster on the other end of the line. "He says he has something big this time."

"He always does." Mboya opened the refrigerator next to the bench and pulled out another bottle of beer. He twisted the lid off using the crook of his bicep and downed half of it. "Give me the phone, you idiot." He grabbed the handset and raised it to his ear. "Zhou, you crooked Chinese hyena, do you have the money you owe me?"

"I paid you the agreed amount."

"Yes, but then you doubled the price you sold it for."

"That's not true."

"I saw it on the internet, Zhou. You might think we're all monkeys you yellow bastard but we're smarter than that."

The gangster paused. "Fine, I will make it up to you on this next consignment."

"Tell me more."

"I have a buyer for a black rhino horn."

"That's great, Zhou, but I don't have a fucking death wish."

"You can name the price."

He took a swig from the beer.

"I'm talking big numbers, Mboya, two, three hundred thousand."

He smacked his lips. "Make it five." He could hear Zhou hissing through his teeth. "Most black rhinos are protected by armed rangers. Not the usual dead beats, I'm talking ex-military and police. I'm going to need more men who are willing to take the risk and I'm going to have to find a rhino with a big enough horn."

"Do you know North Luangwa National Park?"

"I do. It's in Zambia."

"There is one there."

"There are also rangers. Your number just became six hundred."

"Fine, but I am not paying you extra money for the elephant horns."

"They're called tusks and I've just spent three hours packing the latest shipment you ordered. I will include the black rhino horn for a total of eight hundred thousand, American dollars."

He could hear Zhou typing on the other end. "I have a ship due in at Mombasa on Friday. Can you have the entire shipment ready by then?"

Mboya drained the last of his beer. "Transfer a hundred grand into my account now and we will get to work."

"You've never needed money up front before."

Mboya lobbed the bottle at the back of the warehouse where it shattered. "You haven't asked for a black rhino horn before, Zhou. Make it happen." He passed the phone back to Kogo who returned it to the cradle. "We're going to need at least five men."

"Any preference?" asked his second-in-command.

"For this job, only the best, and I want one who knows Luangwa."

"OK, boss."

Mboya pulled another beer from the fridge. "And Kogo, make sure they're killers."

***

Check out PRIMAL Renegade at www.amazon.com

BOOKS BY JACK SILKSTONE

PRIMAL Inception
PRIMAL Mirza
PRIMAL Origin
PRIMAL Unleashed
PRIMAL Vengeance
PRIMAL Fury
PRIMAL Reckoning
PRIMAL Nemesis
PRIMAL Redemption
PRIMAL Compendium
PRIMAL Renegade
SEAL of Approval

ABOUT THE AUTHOR

Jack Silkstone grew up on a steady diet of Tom Clancy, James Bond, Jason Bourne, Commando comics, and the original first-person shooters, Wolfenstein and Doom. His background includes a career in military intelligence and special operations, working alongside some of the world's most elite units. His love of action-adventure stories, his military background, and his real-world experiences combined to inspire the no-holds-barred PRIMAL series.

jacksilkstone@primalunleashed.com
www.primalunleashed.com
www.twitter.com/jsilkstone
www.facebook.com/primalunleashed

CPSIA information can be obtained
at www.ICGtesting.com
Printed in the USA
BVHW050728201218
536072BV00014B/472/P

9 781533 617637